In my darkness.
You are the only light.

unawakened
fate

Vegas Wolf Pack Series,
Book One

AMANDA NICHOLE

Unawakened Fate

Cover Design by: OkayCreations

Edited by: Amanda Nichole

Contents

CONTENT WARNING

Unawakened Fate is a paranormal romance between an awakened wolf shifter and an unawakened wolf shifter. While this book is rooted in the supernatural it includes real-life elements which may not be suitable for all readers. Some of these include references to alcohol consumption, violence, and mental health struggles with panic attacks. Additionally, it explores themes around generational trauma, domestic abuse, addiction, and implied sexual violence. This book ends on a cliffhanger as it is book one in a three-book trilogy. Please note that due to these elements, this book is intended for adult audiences and is not recommended for anyone under 18 years old.

If you have chemistry, you only need one other thing.

Timing.

But timing's a bitch.

~Robin Scherbatsky

Dedication Page
To my students in the graduating class of 2026,
who reminded me that dreaming big doesn't stop just because you grow
up.

Prologue

Cain

My muscles twitch imperceptibly as I shift the claws on my dominant hand. The thin patience I had when arriving today has long since evaporated. The room stinks of all forms of bodily fluids and will require a good hosing down. The constant screaming, sobbing, and crying coming from the huddled, tied-up lump on the floor causes a dull ache between my temples as I pace the room, trying to let some pent-up aggression out.

This interrogation is taking too long.

A threatening growl escapes my throat.

We haven't gotten any information on the location of our missing tech, and time is running short for us to get it back before it can be used against us.

Someone leaked information that we have some bleeding-edge technology we were about to release. Before going to market, a single encryption key was transported out of the city to get the data certified. That key was stolen in transit, and our courier was slaughtered. After hours of backtracking, we traced the leak to a wolf from Deacon Marlo's pack in Reno, his nephew Kole.

We granted Kole access to our territory to study at UNLV at the special request of his Alpha and Uncle. He is a guest here, but he isn't one of us. And now, after fourteen hours of interrogation, he is playing dumb and not spilling the information we need. Dante, Alpha for our Vegas Pack, believes Kole is holding back on us.

None of us will be safe if this shit gets into the wrong hands. It could out us as a species, which would tear down not only our pack but all of them.

The sniveling and whining continue, "Please... I don't know anyth...." The loud crunch of bones breaking under a strong foot abruptly stops the calculated groveling and opens the door to more outright screaming.

"We know you leaked the information on our route. What we need is who gave you the information and who you told?!" Jake shouts over the cries, turning the heel of his steel-toed boot on the mangled hand and throwing another solid punch to the nose for good measure.

Jake likes to do the dirty work, sometimes too much. By giving him the ability to be our top interrogator behind the scenes, he gets to quench his need for doling out pain in a controlled way. This arrangement benefits us because rather than having to clean up after an outburst, Jake works out his aggression here, where we need the answers anyway. Jake has demons, but he is good at what he does, so we sometimes overlook the means when he gets us the ends.

Today's session, however, is dragging on longer than anticipated, and the fluorescent lights overhead begin to turn on automatically with the sun setting. The addition of the bright light shows off the work Jake did over the past few hours. Blood splatter covers every surface from the early hours of breaking Kole in. The stench of sweat, urine, and vomit hang in the air as Kole wheezes trying to pull in air through what must be at least one punctured lung that accompanies several broken ribs.

Jake rarely allows Awakened to shift during his interrogations due to our species' rapid healing when we transition. In this session, he graciously allowed Kole to shift, only once, to heal his injuries, which might have killed him by now. I doubt Jake will be giving second chances at this stage, but killing the Reno Pack Alpha's nephew will be a declaration of war. A war we aren't ready for, especially considering we just lost our competitive edge in transit.

Jake lifts his boot, yanking a handful of blood-matted hair, and crouches lower to whisper, "If you're so set on lying to us, I will be sure to send each and every piece of you to that sister of yours up in Reno. Don't make your family pay for your incompetence."

The gasp that escapes his mouth would have been inaudible if it weren't for our heightened sense of hearing. Kole slumps, exhausted, all the fight leaving him at that moment. Jake's moss-green eyes meet mine, and he gives me a sharp nod which tells me he finally has him. Now it is just a matter of time until we know everything. I return his nod and exit the metal door at my back.

Maybe the day is looking up after all.

Chapter 1
Bri

T en minutes. That is all I have to survive, and I'll finally be able to clock out. At this point in the night, my eyes are blurring, and it is all I can do to keep moving from customer to customer without falling asleep. The clicking of the clock's hands echoes as my heartbeat pulses through my temples. A headache has been brewing behind my eyes for the last hour, and the glow of the service screen is doing nothing to help with the pain.

Why did I choose to work at a call center? I hate people.

"Mr. Flerson, that promotion will be good for eighteen months at a zero percent interest rate. That gives you until May 2nd to pay it off without incurring any interest charges." I rattle off before finishing the last dregs of my warm two-hours-ago coffee.

"No, sir, you won't pay a dollar of interest if you pay it off by that date," I clarify as calmly as I can while rolling my eyes for the third time this call. I adjust in my seat. My back is still aching from my morning workout, and my legs are stiff from sitting for so long. If I didn't know better, I would think my roommate was trying to torture me with this new weight-training routine. Who gets up early and wants to work out?

My name certainly isn't on that list, and yet the ache in my quads continues to distract me as I stretch, rolling my ankles under my cubicle in search of some relief.

"Was there anything else I can assist you with today, Mr. Flerson?" I pause. "No, thank you so much for calling, and you have a great night." I finish as sweetly as I can muster under the circumstances. I've been on this call with him for over twenty minutes; this one call will bump my average for the entire day. I'm sure of it.

"Did you finally get rid of him?" my coworker Cynthia asks, leaning back around her cubicle, salt and pepper hair falling into her tired brown eyes.

"Yeah, thank goodness we aren't slammed. The last thing I need is Steven breathing down my neck about call times tonight. Especially after I did him a favor by taking the extra shift last minute." I complain, rubbing my eyes, so I can focus on the notes I have to enter into the account. On days like today, I wish I had a strong backbone. I wanted to say no. Hell, I needed to say no after the week I've had, but here I am, covering anyway.

"Thankfully, I'm finally done." I sigh while disconnecting from the servers and hanging up my headset for the night. I roll back my chair, looking over my area to be sure I have everything to head out. My cubicle doesn't contain much. A few bright photos of me out with my closest friends after graduation on our "we did it" road trip before college. A small oscillating fan, post-it notes with reminders for updates to our products, and of course, a small candy dish now looking pitifully lacking. I make a mental note to pick up a new bag before Monday.

Keith, the late-night IT manager and one of my closest friends, saunters over, appearing unaffected by the late hour.

"You ladies headed out for tonight?" he asks, his voice deep and smooth as he runs his fingers through the tuft of his disheveled dirty-blonde hair.

"Oh yes!" Cynthia chirps a little extra enthusiastically, lighting up at his attention. "It's time to get back to the house, so I can sleep a bit before the kids are up for school tomorrow." She smiles and shifts her attention to me. "Want me to wait for you, Bri?" she asks, already shuffling herself toward the exit. Deep down, Cynthia still believes Keith and I'll end up together, contrary to my constant rebuke and denial.

"No, thank you, though. I'll see you on Monday." I answer as she heads for the door, winking as she glances back over her shoulder with a mischievous sparkle in her eye. I love working with Cynthia. At forty-eight, she has a big laugh and a wilder imagination. She is always spilling gossip about the associates on the floor and making stories out of rumors she hears. There is never a dull moment, and it is nice to have a mom's perspective every once in a while, especially since that particular role is vacant in my life.

"You and Liv going out tonight?" Keith asks, pulling my attention to him as he tilts his head to the side. I sit there, analyzing him as he leans lazily over the cubicle divider.

Keith is twenty-four and good-looking with his wild sunshine hair, deep almond eyes, and dark-rimmed glasses, but his height attracts most girls. Well, that and his infinite charm. Keith has an ease about him that makes you feel comfortable despite him towering over most of those around him. Coming in at just over six-foot-four, he is a complete waste of height due to his lack of coordination and nonexistent competitive drive.

In high school, all the coaches threw themselves at him, always explaining they could coach him up to his height. They always ended up disappointed when Keith refused to be their puppet. Keith wasn't a team sports kind of guy. He was a loner until he befriended me and later Liv. Keith likes technology more than people, and he is always messing around on the computer. He has saved me and my laptop on more than one occasion from some virus or cookie threatening to lock my system out.

I wasn't surprised when he took an IT position here and was able to quickly move his way up to a manager within the department. He was the one who got me this job two years ago as a way to earn some income over minimum wage while I finished my Bachelor's degree at UNLV. Unfortunately, I couldn't work with him because I lacked technical skills and was moved to customer service instead.

When I met Keith for the first time, I was ten. He was thirteen and was the nerdy new kid who moved into the apartment across from my foster family. He was the first person I spoke to after my brother died, and even then, it had taken him weeks to get anything out of me. He would pester me with questions I would never answer until we finally bonded over which ice cream truck treat was the best.

Bomb Pops, of course. No contest.

Not that I could afford them, but those were Sammy's favorite, so now they are mine.

Keith is a tech wizard with an incredibly sophisticated brain and a witty, dry sense of humor. You can never play Jeopardy or Trivial Pursuit against him because he knows more useless facts than I ever thought possible, but he isn't cocky about it.

Keith became the big brother I never got to have. He is the reason I had a home-cooked meal most nights in my preteens. I never said anything, but somehow he always knew when things got bad for me at the foster home and would force me over to his house for dinner under the guise of schoolwork or some elaborate scheme he was working up. He is the human equivalent of a golden retriever. All jolly and affable. Even his head tilt right now reminds me of those dog videos.

"You and I both know I'm off to bed. Liv had me up at seven this morning with some new butt-defining HIIT workout. I'm too old to be up this late," I pout, knowing full well that at only twenty-one, I should be living the Vegas life, going to clubs and bars and hanging out with my friends. Unfortunately, finishing school, so I can choose my future and carve my path, is too important to me.

"Old?!? No. No. No. These are your party years. You'll look back in twenty years and wish you slept less," he replies only half-serious in his dismay. He is one to talk. He never partied while he was in school. He only ever hung out with Liv and me and did side jobs for his school friends as a way to earn some extra money around his class schedule.

That said, he did take home his fair share of one-night stands that wished they could be more, but he hadn't found his match or anyone who could hold his attention for long.

"I'll be happy to get right on that as soon as I hibernate for twelve hours. This is my second double this week, and I have two papers due before my class on Monday," I retort while stifling a yawn and grabbing my oversized bag full of schoolwork, textbooks, notes, and my purse before heading toward the parking lot.

"You coming to Liv's birthday party tomorrow night?" I shout over my shoulder, slowing down a step to hear his response. "She swears it won't be a big thing, but knowing her, half of the school will show up." I continue rolling my eyes dramatically.

Liv has been my friend since the first day of middle school. We couldn't have been more different, but the duality of our friendship makes us work. She makes me more outgoing and spontaneous, and I make her more responsible and focused. At least, that's what I tell myself. She is the rich to my poor, the light to my dark, the sparkle to my snark, and the only reason I stuck around this crazy city after high school when everything in me wanted to take off and get as far away as I could.

College was never a possibility in my world. As far as I knew, no one in my family had ever gone to college. Liv opened my eyes to how the other half lived. A whole group of middle and upper-class people believed that college was the only way to be successful, and at a time when all I wanted was to not end up an addict like Elaine, my mother, I bought right in.

"Yeah, I'll be there," he replies, turning to head back to his office on the far side of the room. "But if she tries to set me up with another one of her sorority friends, I'll leave and take the good liquor with me, and maybe the sorority friend too." He sends me off with a wink and a wave over his shoulder.

I laugh out loud as I push through the employee entrance doors heading out to the nearly pitch-black evening, smiling a little to myself, because I know Liv already has someone in mind. She is always trying to set him up. Liv fails to realize that Keith needs someone bright who can battle him intellectually, and, no offense to Liv, her sorority friends aren't even close. At least he is a good sport about it. Plus it gets him laid from time to time, which keeps him from being a cranky asshole. Win-Win.

The wind whistles between the buildings, sending loose trash swirling at their bases within the industrial complex. My hair blows around erratically, tangling and crossing my face. I try tucking the strands behind my ears while juggling my now empty "Death before Decaf" coffee cup, large Harry Potter school bag, and wrap-around purse without any success. The sound of my footsteps is lost in the gusts as clouds blanket the sky, holding in the city light and causing a soft ambient glow. A few struggling parking lamps flicker in the distance, illuminating a handful of beat-up cars parked in the lot.

Headlights wash over me, blinding me for a moment, and I lift my arm to wave at Cynthia's dusty white minivan as she passes, heading home for the night. I turn back toward the lot. My blue, twelve-year-old Kia sits parked near the corner.

I can't wait to finish school.

I tug my jacket closed with no available hands and eye my deteriorating transportation. Once I do that, I can finally upgrade this old POS. Honestly, it is surprising the thing still runs. Save for a few chips in the royal blue paint and a barely noticeable dent in the front bumper which honestly wasn't entirely my fault, but try telling a police officer that your fries fell over and you were reaching for them. See how far that gets you; She is perfect. She isn't sleek or modern, but she is mine. She gets me where I need to go.

I juggle my coffee cup into my teeth while reaching for the door handle, and I climb in, hefting my oversized school bag onto the passenger seat, littered with various detritus. Old mail. A rogue hair tie. A long-since-emptied coffee cup. Notes from my marketing class. A hammer with a pink handle from an old tool set. I have a little bit of everything because you never know what you might need. At least, that is my retort if anyone makes a snide comment about me needing to clean the thing out.

I dig through my purse for my phone, hoping to throw it on the charger. It is constantly dying, and I need some charge to call Liv on my way home.

The wind blows everything around, causing my long brown hair to tangle and block my face. I close my door to cut off airflow and grab the rogue hair tie from my passenger seat floor

—*Point for organized chaos.*

And tie a messy bun on my head.

A resounding metal-on-metal bang pulls my attention to the left, to the far end of the lot that backs up to an abandoned-looking warehouse, one building over from the call center. I turn to see what the commotion is all about. I can just make out a handful of oversized men dressed in dark clothing engaging in what appears to be a heated discussion near the back corner of the warehouse.

Two men stand with their backs to the warehouse, just outside its delivery door, facing me. The shadows from lights on the building nearby obscure their features. On the other side, two additional men stand with their backs to me, slightly shrouded by a dark SUV. One holds an aluminum bat at arm's length and has apparently just struck the dumpster to his left.

That answers my first question regarding the loud bang.

A third guy, who might be the driver of the SUV, stands with the largest security dog I've ever seen. Both appear to be scanning the area on high alert and are ready to cut ties at any moment. It makes me wonder what they could be arguing about in a back alley warehouse district this late on a Friday night.

I reach for my phone, finally locating it in the deep fathoms and folds. I open my camera app, flip to the video setting, and turn off the flash before pressing record and holding onto the hope that it has enough battery to get this fight.

Imagine the YouTube gold, a bunch of beefed-up gangsters getting into a street fight.

Through my cracked window, over the wind, I can faintly hear the argument growing heated, and then suddenly, one of the two guys opposite the big slugger pulls out a gun—the flash of silver startling me. I feel like I'm watching a crime documentary in real-time, and thanks to the copious amounts of *Dateline* Liv binged over the summer, I know this won't end well for anyone.

I find myself holding my breath, absentmindedly digging in my bag for my keys with my non-filming hand. The need to get out of this area is tugging at me, but my eyes and the iPhone camera are locked intently on the scene unfolding before me.

My heart races, thumping loudly in my ears as Batman and his Viking friend bravely, or maybe stupidly, puff their chests while simultaneously backing away from the new threat. The security dog, *God, that thing is gigantic,* snarls, padding closer to the danger.

Batman walks to the trunk, reaches in, and tosses a gym bag at the gunman's feet, leaving the bat half sticking out. The gunman drops his gaze to the offering before flicking his eyes back to his opponents, his lips in a curling up vicious sneer. A deep sense of hatred emanates from him before he lifts his weapon.

Bang. Bang. Bang.

Gunshots ring out and echo off of the walls surrounding the lot. A scream escapes my mouth. My hand, dropping my keys in my lap, covers it a moment too late. Time stands still for a fraction of a second while the Viking starts to fall. Then, all at once, the giant wolf-dog leaps at the gunman. All the other men dive for cover and weapons.

Then all hell breaks loose.

Chapter 2
Bri

I drop down in my seat as low as possible, hoping my scream gets lost in the chaos that follows as a bead of sweat forms at my brow. I keep the video recording while my eyes peek over the dash, scanning the parking lot for an alternate exit. Hopefully, one that doesn't involve driving right past these guys.

The only other exit is blocked by a run-down purple semi-truck that I will never be able to get around. I refocus my attention toward the alley, my only way out.

By now, the driver has pulled the giant blonde man behind the SUV and rips off his shirt, revealing broad shoulders and a chiseled set of abs.

Way to go, Bri. So not the time to be checking out the murder-y gang members.

He tears up the shirt quickly, making it into a tie designed to go around the downed man's thigh while holding the rest of the shirt on his shoulder, applying pressure. I shift my gaze to the fight and gasp, my mouth agape. One man lays flat on the ground, clearly in pieces, the dog still ripping at his throat, while Batman is in a wrestling match with the original shooter's buddy.

Now is my chance. I'm shaking, and my heart is in my throat. Adrenaline courses through me as I use my one available hand to search more urgently for the keys I dropped a moment ago. Finally, gripping the cold steel in my fingers, I slam them into the ignition and bring my car to life.

As soon as my car starts, my headlights illuminate the shirtless driver, with the stunning display of abdominal muscles, causing him to whip his head around and look at me, surprise evident on his face. He shouts something I can't quite hear over my heartbeat, echoing in my ears, and the radio which sings in the background. His shout pulls the attention of both the dog and his bat-wielding compatriot.

Shit!

I immediately drop my phone into the recesses between the seat and the door, and I reach for the wheel with both hands.

As I refocus my attention on my exit, the original shooter and his buddy are solidly dead, lying on the ground, no longer moving, just to the left of the alley at the warehouse's double doors. The Tahoe is still idling to the right, next to my exit lane, and it appears that the two uninjured guys are now loading the injured, or maybe dead, Viking into the back seat. Blood pools on the ground and drips from him in an amount I can only assume is lethal. The duffle bag is nowhere to be seen.

"Oh no," I whisper, noticing the dog prowling straight toward my car. It locks eyes with me, and I can't move. The gun-metal glow transfixes me. For a brief but intense moment, I'm drawn into their beauty. Gone is the fear, worry, and anxiety as I gaze deeply into their electric pull. Something familiar tugs at me deep within the recesses of my memories, and just as quickly, it is snatched out of my reach.

I study the animal striding confidently toward me. Though it is only a few hundred feet away, it moves swiftly, blood dripping from its beautiful black-brown coat. Its predatory, silver eyes are brighter than any animal I have ever seen before, and they wear an expression of such pained frustration that I start to wonder if I'm losing my mind. The dog's focus stays on me as it closes the distance between my car and the alley.

I snap back to reality and drop my car into gear, finally willing myself out of the frozen shock I feel.

I just witnessed a double murder! Fuck. I just filmed a double murder. What the hell am I thinking?

Despite her age, I hope my old Kia can get me out of here. I slam my foot on the gas pedal, peeling out of the parking spot. My tires scream from the acceleration and send a cloud of burnt rubber into the air. Then they grip the asphalt, and I'm off. I jerk the wheel to the left to avoid hitting the oncoming four-legged threat. As I pass the dog, I can hear its frustrated growl. It leaps toward the car, bouncing its paws off the driver's side door as it narrowly misses landing on my hood by a fraction of a second.

My Kia passes the black SUV and flies to the end of the alley, reaching the side street which leads me into the city, and I throw the wheel to the right. With no destination in mind, I drive on instinct alone, knowing I have to get far away if I want to survive this. After several erratic turns down backstreets, I find my way onto the freeway but never stop checking for the Tahoe in my rearview.

After what feels like hours of aimless misdirection, I find my way back to my apartment complex, feeling my muscles tight and sore from the tension of holding the wheel. Stress coils through me as I complete a few last-minute random turns, so I'm not followed. My pulse has barely regained its regular beat. My hands are still shaking, and my breathing is short and chopped as I reach for my phone, only to find it dead.

Perfect.

I catch my reflection in the rearview as I turn the car off, chucking my keys back into the pit of my bag. My pale, freckled skin is flush, my fire-flecked-brown eyes overly dilated, and way too big on my face. My rich, chestnut brown hair falls out of the messy bun on my head and onto a sheen of sweat that lines my forehead.

I'm still me, though I feel as if that all could have gone differently had the dangerous men stopped me from escaping.

Hands slam onto my window, and I jump out of my seat, looking for something to defend myself, and grab the rogue pink hammer brandishing it threateningly.

More points for my messy car.

"AGGGGHHHHHHH," I scream as I panic, wondering how they could have possibly located me or my car.

"BRRRRRIIIIIIII" my roommate shouts while opening my door. "What the hell happened to you? Keith just called and said there were shots fired downtown when you left. Why didn't you answer your phone? I called you a million times! I thought you were dead!" she demands as I slowly climb out of the driver's seat on my unsteady legs. She stops rambling and really looks at me for the first time. Concern marring her face.

"You heard them." It is a statement, not a question, and then she wraps her arms around me and squeezes.

"You are OK. Keith said the police thought maybe someone was hurt because they found blood in your work parking lot, but no one has been to the ER with bullet-related injuries." She explains, rambling to calm herself down as much as to calm me down.

I guess the Viking didn't make it if they never got him to the hospital. Make that a triple murder.

I feel... numb. I know that, logically, I should be feeling something. Fear, anger, distress, anything, but I just feel numb. Like I watched it play out in someone else's body. Maybe the long hours were keeping me from processing everything. I'm drained.

I pull away from Liv, avoiding her questioning eyes, and lumber up the stairs to our second-floor apartment. She follows behind me, silently giving me room but never removing her steady eyes.

"I'm fine, Liv, just a little shaken up." It is all the relief I can give her. I'm still not sure I know what happened.

Did that guy die? What happened to the other two bodies? Should I report it? And what was with that dog? I've never seen eyes that looked like the moon peeked out of them. Why can't I get the image of them out of my head?

All the questions bounce around aimlessly in my head while I go through the motions of undressing, showering, and brushing my teeth and hair.

Before climbing into bed, I take my phone and connect it to my laptop, pulling up the six-minute video and saving it to my hard drive, the cloud, and the USB flash drive I used for class notes. Lastly, I email it to myself on an old account before deleting my send history and shoving the file into a Gmail folder, just in case.

I shut down my laptop, place it back in my oversized bag, and take the flash drive, hiding it beneath the loose floorboard next to the wall by my bed, where I also keep a small amount of emergency cash and a picture of Sammy and me. When I'm sure the floor is secure, I slide my Ikea nightstand over to thoroughly cover the plank.

Once my head hits the pillow and my eyes finally close, my brain courteously replays the entire gang fight beginning to end, in painstakingly slow detail. Eventually, I drift off to sleep. The last things I remember are the two metallic-silver eyes staring right into my soul.

Chapter 3
Cain

I really fucked up this time. We had been seen. It is bad enough that they didn't return our shipment, but we left a witness, and not only a witness, but Jay saw her phone in her hand, so she probably has the whole damn thing on video.

I can't believe how much this is spinning out of control.

I turn the corner, heading down the elegant hallway within the VP Tech & Securities home offices. The Vegas Pack runs one of the most exclusive and high-end security firms on the West Coast. We handle everything; business security, cybersecurity, building security, personal security, and surveillance.

Our Awakened wolves are available onsite and virtually as technicians, bodyguards, video operators, perimeter security, driver transport, and bouncers. Keeping our paws on the pulse of this city is how we stay ahead, by being everywhere. Vegas Pack may not have the numbers of some older packs, but what we lack in quantity is overwhelmingly made up for by the quality of our contributing members, who are experts in their fields.

Because of this, the loss of our cutting-edge facial recognition data software is an embarrassment and an intentional blow to our credibility. I have ideas about who would set such a thing up, but Dante wants proof before moving in.

VP Securities will lose millions in contracts along with the rights to future patents if another firm buys it and can bring it to market first. Not to mention Presley will be pissed if the technology she created is credited to anyone else.

Because of this and our rogue witness, my mood is worse than it has been in days. My wolf is restless. His hunting instincts are on full alert, compelling me to search for our prey.

Not today.

A growl escapes my throat as I fight to control the urge to shift in this hallway. That would only lead to shredding a perfectly good pair of jeans and keeping me from breaking this news to my Alpha, delaying the inevitable. Instead of choosing the coward's way out, I place one foot in front of the other until my breathing evens out.

As I approach the end of the corridor, nearing his nearly-closed door, I hear both sides of a phone conversation. I walk in without knocking and slide into the seat across the main desk while instantly recognizing the voice on the call.

"... our allegiance holds only because I have allowed it. It would be best if you remembered to respect your elder, boy. I would hate to put you or your tiny pack in your place." The voice on the phone threatens, a lilt of an Italian accent hanging.

Dante sits across the desk from me in a high-back leather chair facing his over-the-top command station desk. He has fourteen computer monitors adorned with security camera feeds, data, stocks, and various emails. The tension he carries is evident in the rigidity of his broad shoulders.

He wears his hair shaved close to his head. A thick red-brown beard covers his strong chin, which he strokes idly when lost in thought or trying to solve a problem. His face holds sharp features with gray-blue eyes, and his lips are thin and currently pursed in a hard line. While he appears to be considering his next words rather carefully, a pull at the corner of his mouth gives way to amusement in his eyes as he responds to Deacon's blatant threats with flippant humor.

"But Deacon, how could you possibly think you could handle me or my... what did you call it? A 'tiny pack'? I can't say I have ever heard that description before. As I hear it, you have enough trouble keeping your family members in line to try and overstep your territory. How **is** your nephew doing these days? Still attending University?" Dante asks with a smirk in his voice. The information hangs in the air between them. Not an admission. Just enough nuance to confirm he has Kole in his possession.

Dante isn't ruffled by the threat laid at his feet by the only other Alpha in the state. Deacon Marlo, the Alpha of the Marlo Pack in Reno, has been a leader in the state ever since we were just young pups learning to shift.

While Deacon was once rather foreboding, his aging body and dark desires have slowly been breaking him down. He won't be able to hold his pack for much longer, let alone have the ability to challenge Dante, the youngest Alpha in the country and arguably the strongest.

Dante finally turns and raises his steel-blue eyes to meet mine as he lifts an eyebrow in silent question. I grimace and shake my head in response. The shipment has yet to be located. He alters his posture, leaning away from the desk, the phone in his ear, his fingers returning to pull idly at his bearded chin.

"Oh, and Deacon, I hope nothing comes out about you meddling in our Pack affairs. It would be a shame to have to start selling body parts. I hear kidneys are going for a pretty penny these days." Dante ends the call while the threat is still ringing in the air. He turns his entire focus on me, and I see the mix of anger and pain behind his eyes for the first time.

"What the hell happened last night?" he asks before continuing. "Erik is still recovering. Pres said we barely saved him. He had to have three silver bullets dug out of him before he could shift and begin healing. It took seven more times before the bleeding stopped, and Erik's wounds were healed enough to allow him to rest. I trusted you to handle this." His disappointment, rage, and concern are all laced in the quick words.

"It's my fault," I state as calmly as I can muster. "They got greedy, thought they could take the money and keep the tech. Jake used his particular skill set to let them know we weren't playing games, and then one guy pulled a nine. He had Erik down before I could clear him. They were trying to make a name and move up the ranks. That won't be an issue now. I have Jake heading the clean-up since his hot head sent this out of control, which brings me to our other problem." I explain, pausing to let the information settle. "There was a witness."

His head tilts, and he presses his shoulders back in his chair, and he processes this new obstacle, fingers again pulling at his beard. "Who?" It is only one word, but the weight it carries is more than evident.

"A human girl. Shift worker getting off late." I reply, squaring my shoulders to take the blame.

"What did she see?" he asks, his words clipped.

"We believe she saw... everything, and worse, she may have video or pictures." My response is laced with anger at our inability to secure the scene.

You let her get away!

"And where is the girl?" He asks, his eyebrows pull together, forming lines at their center, and his lips purse as he waits for a reply.

After a long pause and the release of a deep breath, I drop my gaze to the floor. "We lost her. I lost her." The words tumble out, carrying the weight of my shame. I shake my head, trying to forget how her eyes dilated like saucers as her mouth gaped, not only in fear but in surprise.

I couldn't hear her heartbeat over the God-awful country music she was playing, but her pulse vibrated frantically at her throat. Never will I forget the expression etched on her pale, freckled face. The image is eternally burned into my brain, patiently waiting to appear every time I close my eyes just to remind me of my failure.

My inability to protect my team, retrieve the tech, or keep this entire shit show from snowballing has my teeth grinding. I pull myself out of the memory, looking my Alpha in the eyes with resilience.

"But I have Erik's team pulling footage from the parking area and the SUV surveillance to see if we can get facial recognition. It was dark, and the parking lot is older with limited coverage, which is part of why we picked it to begin with, so we may get nothing. If we can get the car plate, we may have her that way, assuming she owns that vehicle."

I rise from the chair and begin to pace, not liking the disappointment radiating off my best friend at the huge liability walking around Vegas, able to tear our world apart at any moment.

"Put Presley on the precincts. If this girl gets it in her head to file a report, we will need to intervene immediately. Also, have her actively scan gossip and news outlets. That way, we get this story before they do. Stay on the license plate and identity. I need this girl in our custody ASAP. I'm not too fond of loose ends, Cain. Clean this shit up." He orders and turns back to his monitors, expanding the video screen that shows Erik in the infirmary, still out cold.

My fault.

Guilt assaults me. My stomach clenches, and I turn to leave. My mind is going through every scenario, so this won't happen again.

"Pres found where they are keeping our stolen tech. We will meet when Erik is conscious and set up details for its retrieval," he relays as I walk out of his office without being dismissed, the door slamming in my wake, anger rolling off me in waves.

Dante may be my Alpha, but he is also my best friend and the only one to whom I would kneel. I'm an Alpha by blood, but Dante's second in command by choice. My best friend is more corporate. He is logical, decisive, and even-tempered. In contrast, I'm made for the front lines;

responsive, tactical, and lethal. While we would butt heads occasionally, we find a way to make each of our roles work.

It is all about balance. I trust his judgment, and he trusts my follow-through. Usually, being the second means I have my days to myself, but with all the political turmoil lately, Dante needs me present. If I ever get Deacon Marlo alone, I will end his line and force Dante to combine the two territories to form the only unified pack in the state.

I storm down to my office, my thoughts wandering back to the girl's face. Her pale white skin shadowed in a dusting of freckles as it flushed in panic, her honey eyes wide.

Where are you, little witness?

This constant pull I have to her is strong, incessant in its need. My wolf paces under my skin in anticipation, urging me to follow the tug. To throw myself into the hunt as I wait, primed and ready. My hand fists at my side as I fight to bring him to heel, refusing to allow him to take over and resuming the vice grip of control that usually comes so easily to me.

Find her.

He demands, tempting my resolve.

She will not escape again.

I vow. My wolf settles within me, satisfied with my intention, knowing that the chase is on and, soon enough, we will uncover the truth.

Chapter 4
Bri

*M*y paws pound solidly on the packed earth. The blinding sun creeps behind the ridge-filled mountains, no longer warming the desert floor. I narrowly avoid a sharp cactus to my flank as I cut around the corner of the Red Rock trail. The birds cease their chirping songs as I near the nearly dried-up stream bed, pausing to get a drink and slow my heart rate.

As the wind crosses the stream, I catch the scent of a ground squirrel to my left and take off in pursuit. Twigs snap under my massive paws as I glimpse their movement under a large sagebrush bush. I alter my course and push my hind legs gaining on the fleeing creature that continues to dart left and right to avoid capture.

Knock. Knock.

The noise is faint, but it distracts me, slowing my stride. Where did that come from? I turn my head from side to side to ensure I haven't been followed or spotted by humans. Nothing. I'm alone. I turn back, realizing I have lost the trail, and give up my chase. It's time to head back anyway. Dante will want an update, and I sure hope Presley has the answers I need by now.

I turn west and head back through the underbrush down the trail that had been closed for the last several weeks due to a rock slide.

Knock. Knock. Knock.

I freeze. Now I'm sure I hear something, and I spin around, hackles up, searching for a threat.

"Bri..? Are you getting up?"

Who the hell is Bri? Where are these voices coming from?

Knock...

***

I wake with a gasp to a knocking on my door, with sunlight barely emanating from behind my thick black-out curtains. My body protests at the thought of moving. Every muscle aches because of the evil workout Liv forced upon me yesterday, coupled with the stress of the night before. I murmur, pressing my face into my pillow, and let out a strangled groan.

What the hell kind of dream was that? Who is Dante? Presley? I must have been deep in it.

I shake my head slightly to clear the fog.

"Come on, Bri, you have to get ready," Liv whines through the locked door. She pauses before adding, "I have coffee." This declaration makes my mind up for me. Sighing deeply, I roll over and grab my phone off its charger. I swipe off a flurry of notifications without bothering to actually read them and check the time. 5:46 pm!

I snap up, instantly regretting the move, as blood rushes to my head, causing a slow but steady pulse. Another whimper squeaks out, and I swing my legs off the bed. My feet land on the soft gray carpet.

"I'm up....up" I yawn at her through the door as I gingerly trod across the cold wood planks, crack it open, and grab the "Coffee goes well with Coffee" mug in Liv's outstretched hand, grumbling an unintelligible thanks.

"Only two hours to turn into your hot self," she chirps over her shoulder in a sing-songy voice as she dances away, already sporting rollers in her chestnut brown hair and a half-completed face of makeup. I hadn't noticed the music blasting out of her room. Her rhythm matches the beat of her swaying hips, covered only in a thin teal robe, even though her vocals are far from in tune.

Closing the door, I fall back against its hard surface, resting my head back as my eyes close, wishing this night could be avoided altogether by crawling back into my warm cocoon of a bed. Instead of more hibernation, I drag myself to the bathroom, briefly catching my reflection while searching for a pain reliever and a shower.

My skin seems paler. Dark circles line my eyes which also appear muted against my washed-out skin. Exhaustion evident after a night of tossing and turning while dreaming about shoot-outs and wolves. My temples pound and I pick up my coffee mug, blowing a long breath onto the top before taking an extended pull. The hazelnut-caramel richness hits my taste buds and warms me to my core. I release a long sigh, beginning to feel human again, and then turn on my Spotify to give myself some music motivation while starting the shower.

An hour and a half later, wrapped in a towel, I emerge feeling significantly better, singing along to a Morgan Wallen song. My hair has a part down the middle and dual French braids leading to a high ponytail. My makeup is done with a natural glow using some extra concealer and attention to a smokier eye to combat the dark circles.

On my bed, two outfits lay flat, courtesy of Liv's overbearing control freak tendencies. The first is a skin-tight, one-shoulder little black dress that will fall mid-thigh with a peek-a-boo cutout on the right side. The second is a lacy red bralette with a form-fitting black pencil skirt containing a small slit at the back. Neither is my style, which leans more toward leggings and oversized hoodies lately, but tonight isn't about me.

I choose the second option and pair it with my black combat boots because there is no way my legs can handle heels for an entire evening while recovering from the endless jump squats Satan made me complete yesterday. I spray myself with my Red Delicious DKNY perfume, enjoying the rich fall scent before grabbing my phone and a small clutch on my way out into the living room.

Liv is standing in the kitchen, digging a bottle of water out of the fridge. She is dressed in a thick emerald green corset which accentuates her already large breasts and tiny waist. She pairs it with a black silky wrap skirt and six-inch stiletto heels. I'll never understand how her muscular, tan legs aren't sore, but I'm always jealous of them all the same.

Banshee, Liv's cat, is lounging lazily on top of one of the cabinets, his striped tail dangling in front of its hinges. He glares at me as he casually cleans one of his paws.

What are you looking at, fleabag?

"We're out of energy drinks. I set the last one on the table for you. Figured you would need it. How are you feeling?" She asks, giving me a once-over, unasked questions swirl in her sea-green eyes. She is worried about me.

"I'm fine. Just tired. I want to forget last night," I answer honestly with a sigh.

I see Liv visibly relax as I continue, "but I can't drink too much tonight," I stare into her eyes. "I repeat: Cannot. Get. Drunk. Tonight." I state pointedly. "I have two papers to write tomorrow, or I'll lose my A in Global Business Strategies."

"I make no promises," she responds with a twinkle in her eyes and then rolls them as she continues, "We both know you'll get it done. Relax, I only get one birthday a year. Let's just have a good time and worry about tomorrow, tomorrow. How do I look?" She asks, giving me a twirl, a seductive smile, and a hip shake.

"Old.... I mean, what are you doing with yourself? Look at these wrinkles. Just letting yourself go..." I announce sarcastically in response while walking over to hug her. We stand holding each other for a long time. Liv is one of the only people who I can depend on. She may be impulsive, spontaneous, and incapable of following any schedule or outline, but when I need her, she always steps up.

"Happy Birthday Liv. Twenty-two looks good on you," I whisper, giving her an extra hard squeeze before pulling back, reaching into my clutch, and sliding out a small wrapped box.

"I told you not to get me anything!" Liv exclaims, setting down her water before snatching the box excitedly. She tears the ribbon and slides the top off. Her jaw-dropping as she realizes the contents of the box. "Coachella?!?" She gasps. "Bri, these are VIP tickets. These cost a fortune!" Her shocked eyes flip up to me. "How?"

"Magic," I respond with wiggling jazz hands and a giggle. She doesn't need to know I spent months saving so that I could afford them. I took a nice chunk out of my savings, but the pure gratitude in her eyes makes it all worth it.

"Come on. We need to get to your parent's house before we are just late instead of fashionably so." I add dramatically.

She hurries over to put Banshee into her room for the night, yelling at him to behave before heading back into our living room. I link my arm into hers and steer her toward the door. She squeezes my arm tightly for a moment, a smile lighting her entire face. With a laugh, I push Liv into the slowly cooling evening before setting the alarm and hurrying outside behind her.

While inserting my key into the lock, the hairs on my neck stand up. The feel of someone's eyes on me has me glancing back toward Liv, but she and the Uber driver are engaged in conversation, saying their hellos as she opens the door to the backseat.

For a moment, my eyes scan the parking lot cautiously while turning the lock to ensure our belongings are safe for the evening. I don't see anyone who stands out, but even nearing the Uber, I can't shake the uneasy feeling rippling through me.

Get it together, Brielle! You are overtired.

I shake my head and take a deep breath before climbing into the Uber behind Liv, adding a brief hello to our driver. The car's harsh chemical smell indicates the owner recently cleaned it with strong-smelling products. I try to focus on the scent while buckling in, working through my nerves. It's not only feeling this overwhelming paranoia that I'm constantly being watched or followed, but I also have some PTSD when riding in cars.

Driving myself had once been an enormous hurdle to overcome, and it had taken almost three years before I could get into my own car without thinking about the accident. However, being a passenger in someone else's car gives me a bit of anxiety due to my life being out of my control, especially in smaller cars, where I tend to feel claustrophobic or trapped.

I try to find a way to distract myself and decide to pull my phone from my clutch and finally look through the notifications from the previous day. I take a deep breath and focus on each app to clear away my nerves.

Four missed phone calls and eleven unread text messages sit on the screen. Two of the calls and ten of the messages are from Keith, from last night, trying to see if I'm ok. One of the calls is from an unknown number with no voicemail. Another is from Cynthia, though she left a hurried voicemail, completely overreacting.

It doesn't surprise me that she has already heard about the gunshots. Drama and gossip are her favorite topics of conversation. Especially since it was such a close call for her. I'll have to call her back tomorrow and let her know I'm all good. I send off a quick text just to ease her mind.

> Hey Cyn, I'm ok. I left before anything happened. Thanks for reaching out. I'll call you tomorrow :).

The lie comes easily enough. If I pretend nothing happened, maybe I can convince myself it hadn't. A similar text goes out to Keith while also letting him know we are on our way to Liv's parent's house. He'll meet us there after his shift which ends at ten.

When I finish making sure everyone is up to date, I open a Google tab to search for any information from the news on what happened last night. I'm sure to see something about the bodies from outside the warehouse or some gang-related story, but after scrolling through several pages, the realization hits that there is nothing but a report of a few gunshots heard in the area.

What happened to the two guys I knew didn't make it out of there? Or the guy they hauled into the back of the SUV? Or all the blood from any of the aforementioned suspects?

It unnerves me that everything is so hush-hush. I know what I saw. At least two guys died last night, and no one is talking about it.

What if I hadn't gotten away?

I shake my head abruptly. No what-if scenarios, or I'll drive myself crazy. I got away. That is what matters. Now it is time for me to try to move past it. Keep my head down. Finish school. Get out of here.

Next to me, Liv hums along to the radio as she shoots off texts to people about the party. I throw a fake smile and force myself to relax, rolling my shoulders. It is her big day and possibly the last birthday we will spend together before heading out into the world to pursue our careers, hers in broadcast journalism, mine in business marketing. I have an interview coming up for a job in Boston that I'm desperately hoping to land. So tonight is all about my best friend. Everything else will just have to wait.

Our Uber pulls up to our destination, a two-story 4,000 square-foot house on the south side of town in a gated community. When I say Liv comes from money, I don't mean it modestly. Her folks are loaded and network with all of the elite in town.

Her dad, Edward McCoy, has been an advisor on more boards than I can keep track of, in addition to his political affiliations and running his law firm. Her mom, Lila McCoy, is the ultimate trophy wife, always throwing functions, completing charity work, and volunteering with PTA or HOA functions. From the outside, their family is a perfect postcard of what a family should be.

A glimpse behind the veil shows nothing different. They are two of the nicest, most caring people I have ever known. Edward has a quirky sort of humor and loves old westerns. Lila loves rescuing small yippy dogs and can feed an army at a moment's notice. The two of them are obnoxiously in love. They are the fairytale, but their lives haven't always been easy.

They always wanted a big family, but it took them years to finally conceive. After many failed attempts, they got Liv. She is their pride and joy. They shower her with all of their love and affection. That love later flowed onto me as they took me in as a second daughter. Keith's family weren't the only ones who stepped up when my mom disappeared for chunks of time or when I lived with another absent foster family.

Our driver let us out, saluting a goodbye as he drives off. Music is playing and can be heard all the way out on the street. The house is already teeming with college students, almost all of them I don't know despite attending the same school. Liv waves and shouts hellos as we march up the stamped concrete driveway to the front door like celebrities on the red carpet.

Liv grabs the door handle without knocking and walks into her old home. The bass inside reverberates off the walls as the DJ mixes popular radio hits. Cater waiters bustle through the crowd with trays covered in varying alcoholic drinks while people dance with drinks in hand.

Liv grabs two shots off a passing tray and extends one to me. I take it from her and inhale a long sniff, catching a hint of watermelon.

Please don't be tequila.

"Bottoms up, Bitch!" Liv shouts over the music while holding hers out. I tap my shot to hers in cheers while forcing a smile and tipping it down my throat, feeling the burn as it slides;

Watermelon Rum.

Liv cries out a whoop of excitement as she sees a group of her sorority sisters and pulls me deep into the dancing crowd.

I shove my phone into my clutch and wave as she reintroduces me to the bubbly bleach-blonde trio of Mila, Seneca, and Aria. I've met them all before, but we aren't friends, more acquaintances who all know Liv. A friend of a friend.

I begin dancing with them, reaching behind them to set my clutch on the edge of the DJ's stage, freeing my hands, so I won't have to hold it. Liv takes the center of our circle, and we dance on and around her. One of the blondes, maybe Seneca, I can never keep them straight, leans over to me and compliments my outfit. I thank her, laughing about it being Liv's choice, before falling into the rhythm.

Dancing has always been my thing. Liv and I were on the dance team in middle school, and our love for dance started there. We danced at clubs and even went line dancing to scratch the itch. We were also constantly dancing around the apartment. Dancing makes me feel free. It is the one time in the world when everything melts away, and the music takes over.

Liv flags down a server, and we all do another shot. This one is a lemony vodka concoction. At this rate, I know I should have eaten before coming here, and I mentally make a note to grab something when we take a break. A few times while we dance, guys wander up to try and dance with one of us.

The trio loves attention, and any that comes my way, I quickly shift to them. It's not that I'm not single, but I don't have the time to invest in another person. Who knows where I'll be in six months? I don't want to be like my mom, stuck somewhere because of a man.

We dance for almost an hour, taking shots of varying flavored liqueurs before I spot Lila and Edward standing by the entrance to the kitchen. I nudge Liv, nodding in their direction. She lights up with a bright smile and takes off through the dancers toward them.

I reach around the girls, grabbing my purse before turning to catch up with Liv. We leave the dance floor, weaving through the now overwhelming number of people. Liv brought in quite the crowd. She runs the last few steps leaping into her dad's hug, while I gently hug Lila.

"It is so good to see you, Bri," she softly whispers while squeezing me. "How are your classes coming? Almost done now, right?" She asks, pulling back to look at me. Lila appears so youthful she could be Liv's older sister. While Liv has her dad's sea-green eyes, everything else comes from her mother. Lila has the same heart-shaped face, olive skin, and deep chestnut locks.

"Yep, just finishing up my classes for the fall semester, and then I have one more semester with my capstone course in the spring," I reply proudly. The McCoys had offered to pay for my schooling when Liv and I graduated, but I refused. I'm not a charity case. I worked hard to get a scholarship with grants and other financial aid.

I got through with minimal student debt, mainly because Liv paid the rent on our apartment. Additionally, I worked to pay for food, my phone, car insurance, and gas. I have also been saving for the last two years, so I can afford to move wherever my career takes me.

"I can't wait to get the invite to your graduation ceremony," she replies with a bright smile that reaches her chocolate brown eyes.

"Hey now! It's my day!" Liv interrupts, slurring her words a bit, squeezing between us and surrounding her mom in a hug.

"Happy birthday, my Livinia," Lila laughs, kissing her daughter's forehead, "When did you grow up? You look absolutely breathtaking, my dear." Her eyes sparkle as she tries not to cry. She scrunches her nose and pulls Liv into the living room, talking her through the menu for the night.

I turn and hug Edward in greeting while smiling up at his bespectacled face. Mr. McCoy's hair is dark but graying at his temples, and he has wrinkles around his eyes which time has carved deeply into his skin from years of smiling.

"How are you tonight, kiddo?" he asks playfully, trying and failing to sound younger than he is.

"Oh, you know, barely holding onto my sanity. Two papers are due tomorrow, and I'm working more hours than I should." I respond cheerfully, the alcohol buzzing in me. Liv's dad worked through college too, and he understands the strain the last few weeks can provide. He places a hand on my shoulder, patting it lightly as he gives me his two cents.

"If anyone can get it completed, it's you. Just remember to take some time to enjoy it. You are almost to the finish line, but you want to have some good memories to look back on that don't involve you going to that job of yours or locking yourself in the library for all of your free time." He gives me a grin, knowing I won't listen, but I'll try to take it to heart anyway, and then he leaves to handle issues with the catering bill.

I walk off, grab a bubbly fruit-infused drink from a floating tray, and cozy up against a wall in the living room, using it for balance as the room sways slightly. I take a moment to survey the room and begin to notice many people I had classes with from campus, most of them I have never spoken to before. Liv has always been the life of the party. I tend to stick to the sidelines.

I didn't make any new friends in college. Instead, I just stuck to the two I already had and focused on completing my classes with no issues. I lift my drink in a wave at some people I remember Liv introducing me to at a sorority function last year, but I don't go over to them. Instead, I pull out my phone, hoping to see a text from Keith stating that he is on his way despite it only being a little after ten. No new notifications.

I take a long drink from my glass as the hairs on the back of my neck stand up. The feeling from earlier is back. Like someone is looking at me. I can almost feel their gaze. I glance up casually, forcing a fake calm, but wondering in the back of my mind if I should try to find Liv.

Everyone seems to be enjoying themselves while dancing, drinking, and chatting with friends.

I'm losing it. I need food to clear my head.

That's when I see him. My eyes are yanked across the room like a magnet drawn to its pull. Tall, Dark, and Dangerous. He is leaning against the far wall on my right, talking casually with another guy who has his back facing me. He is maintaining his conversation, but his eyes slide over toward me, sweeping up my body in a way that I can only describe as ravenous. When his eyes reach mine, they lock for a long moment before he glances back to the conversation in front of him.

Yummy.

I adjust my phone in my hand and snap a discrete photo.

I stare at him, unable to look away. He appears to be in his mid-twenties with dark brown hair that falls just over his thick brows. His eyes are dark and deep-set, but I can't decipher their exact shade. He's tall, over six feet easy, and has a lean, athletic build. His black T-shirt is stretched across a broad chest and cuts off the tattoos that line his arms. There is an intensity in how he is casually standing, which makes him appear relaxed but does nothing to take away from the threatening confidence he exudes.

Damn, he's delicious.

The corner of his mouth tips up in a grin as he brings his beer to his lips for a slow drink, his eyes flicking my way again.

Shit!

I force myself to look away as I realize I have been staring, and a blush creeps up my neck and cheeks. I turn away from him and focus on centering my breathing while pretending to play some game on my phone.

Calm yourself! He's just a hot guy. It's not like it's been eight months since anyone has touched you. Damn it, had it been eight months since Brenden?

I curse at myself while my eyes close to clear my thoughts, alcohol fully buzzing, causing me to imagine McSteamy peeling my clothes off and finding better uses for those lips. I let out a small whimper and bite my lower lip to bring me back to the here and now.

"Hey you," a masculine voice interrupts my thoughts while a hand brushes lightly on my bicep. I jump, pulling away with an audible gasp, my drink sloshing over the side of my cup. I cringe, hoping my inner monologue isn't written all over my face. A face that, I'm sure, is tomato red at this point. "Sorry to scare you." He continues sounding more familiar now. I look up to see Keith staring down at me. Concern etched between his brows. "You ok, Elle?"

I exhale audibly, "Sorry, just a little jumpy since last night. When did you get here?" I ask, reaching up to hug him. He smells like minty gum mixed with mountain fabric softener and is wearing a dark green long-sleeve button-down with gray slacks.

"Just a minute ago; I saw you before the birthday girl," he replies, and I notice the gift bag in his other hand.

"She ran off with Lila a little bit ago. I haven't seen her since. Let's see if we can track her down." I offer brightly, stepping away from the wall and looping my arm in his. My eyes glance back across the room, hoping to get one last look at my mystery man, only to find him gone.

I look around as I walk off with Keith, but I don't see him anywhere. I shake my head, hoping to erase his sexy image from my brain, only to lose my balance and stumble a bit, clinging to Keith's arm so I don't fall.

Thank you, too many shots on an empty stomach.

"Sorry!" I shout a little too loud over the music to Keith, "Can we also locate some food? I may have skipped that step." I ask, looking up to see him trying not to laugh at me.

"Sure, Little Ellie, we can get you some food." He responds while laughing and leads us in the direction of the kitchen. I hate that nickname. He knows it too. It was the one he always used to push me over the edge when I was too chicken to try something. Luckily for him, I'm just this side of too drunk to fight him on it, especially as we enter the kitchen, and the smell of Mexican cuisine assaults my nostrils.

Nachos and Tacos. Yes Please!

Chapter 5

Cain

Earlier that day.

    I drive back to the VP Tech & Securities complex downtown feeling better after my run despite my curiosity over the weird voices. Pres texts that she can get the license plate and will have the owner's information shortly.

    My wolf is still restless, but at least I can focus on finding and silencing our witness. My mind brings up her haunting image at the thought of her. She has pale, freckled skin, large honey eyes with dark full lashes, and a pouty bottom lip that looks ready to be chewed on. Her face had been appearing in my thoughts all day.

    I park in the back of the building and head for the comm floor. Presley, Dante's baby sister, has been our technical genius since she returned from her time at UC Berkeley. She had been accepted there on an academic scholarship and studied Cybersecurity earning her bachelor's degree last spring. I scan my keycard and pull open the door to her office.

I find Pres hunched over her keyboard, noise-canceling hot pink audio headphones over her ears. She has an office similar to Dante's, with sixteen monitors and TVs displaying varying information and code. Additionally, she has several servers against the walls and cabling running all over the room. On the screen, directly in front of her, is my witness.

The witness.

I correct myself silently. She isn't mine. In this picture, contrary to the snapshot I hold in my mind, she's laughing and looking into the camera with a fiery glint in her eyes like she has a secret. Gone is the heaviness I saw in them last night. Her brown hair falls in loose curls well past her shoulders and flutters around her. I wonder for a moment how long ago this picture was taken. Presley clears her throat, catching my attention and making me realize I have been staring too long.

She turns around, chewing her bubble gum, and slides a dark blue folder across the table toward me. I grab it, opening the folder to see the information she gathered. The same photo from her screen stares back at me, and it takes more effort than it should to look over the words on the other side.

Witness Dossier

Accessed: 11/2/2022

Name: Brielle DelaCourt

Known Aliases: Bri

Birthdate: November 29, 2001.

Age: 21

Residence: 1479 N Heritage Oaks Blvd Apt 216, Las Vegas, NV 89119

Phone Number: 702-321-4321

Description: 5'6. 155lbs. Brown Hair. Brown Eyes. Vision corrected with contact lenses.

Medical History:

2011: Broken wrist and head contusions reported at 10yo due to an automobile accident.

2017: Orbital fracture with swelling, two broken ribs with multiple torso contusions, and a large laceration at sixteen. No reason is listed.

The patient checked out AMA once the bleeding was controlled and the lacerations were stitched.

Allergies: Silver

Occupation: Customer Service Representative at Citi Corp. and a Senior attending the Business school at UNLV majoring in a Bachelor of Science in Business Administration and Marketing with a 4.0 GPA.

Mother: Elaine DelaCourt - 41 yo female

Born: Las Vegas, NV.

Education: High school dropout.

Current profession: Unknown.

Last known profession: Exotic Dancer at the Spirited Rhino.

Legal: Three misdemeanor drug possession charges, two counts of prostitution, two DUI's including one tied to reckless driving and endangering a minor, which led to two years in federal prison, and one eighteen-month stint in a county jail for the robbery of a corner store while under the influence.

Current location: Unknown

Father: Unknown, Not listed

Siblings: One half-brother deceased, Samuel Brinkley, died in an automobile accident at the age of 12.

There is that name again.

"Bri...Are you getting up?"

The memory of the words that had broken through my mind during my run. This wasn't a coincidence. I haven't been able to get her off my mind all day, and now as she stares up at me from the dossier that Presley compiled, I only want to know more.

I look up to find Presley watching me intently with her eyebrows lowered. She pulls down her headphones, placing them behind her neck.

"Our witness is basically a Girl Scout with a shitty family history that had her bounced into some not-so-great foster situations." She announces. "No criminal record, no gang affiliations; she even has a good credit score. This is not our normal case." She spouts off, indicating each point with a finger, and then blows a bubble of her bright pink Double Bubble gum, popping it with a loud snap before continuing.

"She hasn't made any moves to go to the police. It appears once she made it home, she hasn't left, and according to her phone records, she hasn't made any outbound calls or answered any incoming ones. I won't be able to see her texts, view her emails, or listen to her calls until we can mirror the device. I have someone sitting at her house to see if she leaves, and I've got a tracker on her car. If she makes a play, we'll know."

"Do we have any information on her living situation? Boyfriend? Roommates?" I ask partially because it is relevant to me being able to have the access to her that I need, but also because I need to know if she is taken. Everything inside of me clenches, waiting for the reply.

Why do you care?

I don't know why I need to know, but I do.

"She's not very active on socials. I don't see anything about a boyfriend in the last six months or so," the tension in my stomach relaxes some, "but she occasionally appears in pictures with another girl with hashtags that say roomie. After pulling her university records, her emergency contact is one Livinia Rae McCoy of the Vegas McCoys. Her daddy is the law firm McCoy & Gamble. The address listed matches. We'll need to tread carefully. She may not be important, but she is connected, and that could cause some real issues." Pres finishes, impressing me with how thorough she has been. It's astounding to me some days that the little ten-year-old redhead, who followed Dante and me around as teens, is now such a force. In my mind, she'll always be Dante's baby sister, but she is also kind of scary. I turn, closing the folder as I head back out the door, waving thanks for her information.

"You busy tonight?" She yells at my back, causing me to pause and turn around. The mischievous look on her face while she smiles too brightly tells me the wheels are turning in her mind; she is up to no good.

"Why?" I ask her, drawing out the question.

"Our girl will be attending a party tonight at the McCoy residence. Her roommate is turning twenty-two. I need someone at that party to ensure she isn't talking, and while I would normally send Erik since he is friendly and charming, you'll have to do," she replies with a smirk spinning back around in her chair.

I can be charming.

I think absently while my heart lifts at the thought of seeing her again. The reaction my body is having to this girl confuses me. I can't remember the last time I had this type of response to any woman. In fact, I can't remember ever calling one for a second night or wanting more than sex. It never crossed my mind to want to see a female again, let alone spend time with them.

Finding women comes naturally when you are over six feet tall and built like I am. I'm not even on a dry spell.

Maybe I need to head back to the club tonight?

A growl escapes my lips, causing Pres to look back surprised. My wolf doesn't seem to like that idea.

"Send me access to her school calendar and work schedule when you get them," I demand, not giving her an answer about tonight, and head back out the door, grumbling under my breath. "And for the record, I'm very friendly." I hear a muffled laugh behind me as she replaces her headphones, and I stroll into the hallway toward the elevator headed to Dante's office.

He has his back toward me as I enter, soft electronic trance music emanating from his speakers as he works. I pause for a moment, looking out over the city through his floor-to-ceiling wall of windows. The look of Las Vegas as it falls into night is almost magical. Lights twinkling and shining on every building give the city energy, which feels alive. There is no other place like it.

I clear my throat, gaining Dante's attention, and lift the navy folder in my hand, "I have the information on our witness." I state simply. "I'm headed out tonight with Jake to tail her, ghost copy her phone, and get a feel for the threat."

"Keep me updated. The last thing we need is a leak right now," he replies without bothering to try and take the folder and turns his attention back to his screens. "Erik is up. We'll have a meeting when you two return tonight. Let's say midnight. We need to get this contained."

I walk out, texting Jake on my way, telling him to meet me at the party address at nine-thirty that night. I have somewhere I need to check out first.

***

After swinging by my apartment to shower and change. I head to the address listed in the information file for Brielle. I park across from her building, blending in with the other vehicles so there is a straight shot to her stone-washed, second-floor front door. I spot the wolf Pres has on watch duty almost immediately and am pleased to see it is Jay, one of our best. He acknowledges me with a dip of his chin, and I return the gesture.

As I wait for her to leave for the party, I reopen the file from my passenger seat.

Who are you Brielle DelaCourt?

On the outside, she is your typical college senior, working her way through the rest of school, but something told me there was something so much deeper than that to this girl.

The haunting nature of those eyes, which are now burned into my brain, told me she has seen horrors before, that she has the spirit of a fighter, and just the thought of her having to face those battles alone has my wolf aching to defend her.

Movement in front of the building catches my eye as a small white Toyota pulls up with a neon pink Lyft sign on one side of the windshield and a black Uber sign on the other. I sink back into my seat to ensure I can't be seen as the apartment door opens, and a bouncing tan-skinned brunette emerges.

From the folder, I know this is the birthday girl, Livinia McCoy. She impresses me as she navigates the stairs with a speed and grace I wouldn't have pegged from looking at those heels, and she beams at the driver, exchanging hellos.

A pop of red catches my eye, and I redirect my stare to the apartment door, only to lose my breath. Brielle is standing there in a lacy red bra top paired with a tight black skirt. Her midsection peeks out between them, showing off her pale, freckled skin and a small gem dangling in front of her belly button. Her dark hair is tied back from her face showing her sharp jawline. She wears a little makeup around her eyes, bringing out their lightness and accentuating their expressions.

She's mesmerizing. I can pinpoint the moment she feels my stare. Her back straightens, and her shoulders tighten. She scans the area as if looking for a threat.

Good girl, you can never be too careful.

Her awareness gives me a sense of pride that it shouldn't. She shakes her head slightly, rolls back her shoulders, and proceeds to the Uber; a smile pasted on her face that doesn't meet her eyes.

And then they are gone. I send off a text to Pres telling her to send Jay in to stage the apartment with eyes and ears now that the coast is clear, and then I slowly pull out after their Uber, sending a wave at Jay.

Getting into the party isn't an issue. It appears as though over a hundred people are in attendance. I wave at the gate guard after stating where I'm headed and park a street over from the event to ensure I won't be boxed in if I have to get out of there. I send Jake a pin of my location, and then I study the file again while I wait to ensure there is nothing I'm overlooking.

My eyes venture back to the photograph and the smile she wears in it. It's genuine and reaches her eyes easily, causing them to crinkle at the sides.

Why haven't you gone to the cops, Brielle? You seem like an intelligent girl... what are you hiding from?

Her silence after seeing our confrontation with Marlo's goons last night puzzles me.

I don't have long to think about it before Jake arrives, dressed nearly identically to me in all black, accentuating his deep mocha skin several shades darker than my olive one. Jake is all hard lines and intensity. I don't know if I have ever heard him laugh or seen him relax outside of his wolf form.

He was a late addition to our pack after not being discovered until he was eighteen. His dad, a Moonshire wolf from one of the most prevalent packs in Texas, had a one-night stand with a stripper on a trip to Vegas. He'd never gotten her number, and she'd had no way to contact him. Worse, she died in childbirth, leaving Jake an orphan in and out of foster care his whole life. Foster families never really knew how to control him, and he spent years running away only to be forced into worse and worse homes.

Our pack found him camping in Mount Charleston while we were on a run and smelled his wolf locked within him. Most people believe crazy theories on how shifters are created—everything from being bitten on a full moon to rituals and sacrifices.

The truth—you need shifter DNA and an Alpha's bite to activate the genes. We all carry venom in our bite for unifying our mating bonds, but Alphas have the additional element which also Awakens the locked DNA allowing for the wolf to be released. If an Alpha bites someone with shifter DNA, they Awaken. Most shifters are Awakened on their tenth birthday as a right of passage once they are old enough to understand the importance of our secrecy in this world.

It was relatively rare to have a shifter become Awakened as late as Jake because most shifter children came from mated couplings, and the children grew up knowing what they were.

Jake had no idea what lived inside him until our pack took him in, and while he started late, he took no time falling into the life we lived. Dante made him lead enforcer less than a year later. If I want a job done, any job, he is always my first call.

"Did Pres give you the info on our witness?" I ask while stepping out of my vehicle as he approaches. His moss-green eyes meet mine, and he nods.

"What's the plan for tonight?" he questions, his tone all business.

"We are eyes and ears while Pres has someone setting up the apartment. Also, we need to get her phone so that it can be mirrored." I respond and roll out my shoulders to give off a more casual demeanor before we head toward the music.

The party is in full swing when we walk in. The DJ is blasting electronic pop hits, and people are everywhere. We walk through the front room and off toward a larger living room area that opens up for a dance floor.

I scan the room, looking for my girl in the sea of gyrating bodies while simultaneously eyeing it for any threats. Everything in this house screams money. Everything is precisely coordinated, from the crown molding to the hand-woven rugs to ooze the feeling of wealth

—*what a waste.*

I'll never understand throwing money around just because you have some, and I have acquired a rather significant sum over my years as Dante's second in the pack. In fact, I have more money than I know what to do with, but I know I would never waste it on gold-plated mirrors and Austrian crystal chandeliers.

The crowd parts, and I see her moving her body in a seductive rhythm. I freeze midstep, my gaze locking in on her ass as it sways back and forth to the beat while she sings loudly, off-key, along to the song. She is with several other college girls, but none of them pull my focus as I watch her grind playfully onto the birthday girl.

Distracted by a passing blonde, Jake doesn't notice I have stopped, and he slams into my back, bringing me back to the moment and the task at hand.

I lean over to his ear, so we aren't overheard. "I'm going for the phone. Cover me. I'll need a distraction if this goes south." Jake nods, throwing his eyes around the room with practiced precision. I move through the crowd, trying to blend into the background as much as possible by bouncing to the beat.

My eyes never leave Brielle, and I fight to appear non-threatening. About halfway to her, I spot a drunk frat boy coming up behind her. He grabs her by her hips and presses her back into his body. I inhale sharply, my instincts threatening to take over as I pause to see this play out.

Get your hands off her!

A growl rattles in the back of my throat as I focus on trying to hear what he is saying in her ear over the blasting music, but it is drowned out.

My eyes flick to Jake, who has circled behind them, warning him not to cause a scene. I motion with my chin to the small clutch purse that Brielle placed on the stage's corner while she is dancing.

Jake nods, adjusting his path, and swipes the bag before heading down a hallway on the back side of the room.

I turn my attention to the dancing crowd to see Brielle has managed to steer Mr. Wonderful off to one of the blondes dancing alongside her.

Good girl.

I continue my path towards them, wanting to get a closer look rather than pivot and circle all the way around to meet up with Jake. As I close in, the urge to cart her away from all the male gazes is strong.

What is it about this girl?

I slide between their group and the DJ table, reaching my arm slightly, drawn to the skin peeking out on her back. A moment before I touch her, I pull back.

Get your head in this. Jake is waiting. You can't risk her turning around!

It takes all of my willpower to pull my hand away. I take a deep breath, catch a hint of apples and vanilla, and drop my nose to inhale her scent more thoroughly. I nearly trip over my feet as I realize two things simultaneously.

One—she is a wolf, not strong enough to have been Awakened, but it is in her scent.

Two— she is my Mate.

Chapter 6

Cain

*F*uck!

This just got a whole lot more complicated. A growl settles in my throat as I take off toward the hallway, my mind spinning.

I turn the corner and slam into Jake, who already has the phone hooked to the burner, which would be its ghost mirror.

"I need another minute to get it synced. Pres hit a snag with the passcode." Jake recites, but the words float over me as I stare at the ceiling. No one in our pack has found their mate. It is extremely rare to find them outside pack gatherings and retreats.

Go back to her.

"What's wrong?" Jake asks; his tone of voice changes, and his back straightens as he notices my changed demeanor.

"She's one of us. Unawakened." I respond, leaving out the fact that she is my Mate. That is a conversation I'm not ready to have. Jake's face drops. He, of all people, knows how rare Unawakened wolves are in today's world. The ghost phone lights up, showing an exact copy of the wallpaper on Brielle's phone, a candid photo of her and Liv on a beach running from a wave.

"Get her bag back before she notices it's gone, and meet me by the door. We have what we need, and we'll need to bring Dante in on this one, and Jake?" I pause, waiting for his attention. "This new information stays between us, Pres, and Dante. That's it. Got it?"

Jake nods, his face still shocked as he turns his back and walks out to the party.

Bring her home.

My inner wolf wants to claim her, and honestly, at this point, I'm having a hard time telling him no. I wipe my hand down my face, exasperated, and exit the back of the hallway cutting through the kitchen to get back to the front room.

I lean against the far wall for almost ten minutes and grab a beer from a passing tray to keep my hands busy. I easily spot Brielle as she moves into my line of sight off the kitchen, talking to the McCoys, Livinia at her side. I have seen Mr. McCoy in enough commercials to be able to identify him without anything being in the dossier.

Watching her light up as she speaks with him warms my insides in a way that feels foreign to me. She is comfortable with them in a way she hasn't shown around the other partygoers. She laughs. The sound reaches my ears now that I'm further from the music. It isn't boisterous or loud, but it is full and instantly becomes my favorite sound.

She touches his arm. A smirk falls into place as a cater waiter interrupts apologetically, pulling him away. She looks uneasy for a moment as she realizes she is alone in a room full of people. She begins looking around for someone, anyone she knows. I quickly turn to grab another beer from a passing server just as Jake returns to my side.

He tilts his chin toward the door as a sign we should leave, but my eyes are glued to Brielle, leaning against the far wall and tapping through her phone. Jake's gaze follows mine.

"Cain, we've got to go." His words have an urgency laced through them, but I need to see her, to memorize her. Her shoulders tense slightly as if she can feel my eyes on her, and she carefully pulls her eyes up to seek the source of that touch. Her eyes search left and right and then fall on mine. She stares at me with a level of heat that makes my cock jump in response, hardening immediately.

Mine.

My wolf is panting and snarling inside me on instinct. I hold her honey eyes a moment longer, memorizing the flecks of orange, gold, and brown. I grin, bringing my beer up to my lips to appear casual as a red sheen creeps up her neck,

And oh, isn't it a beautiful color on her.

She drops her eyes and turns away, bringing another smile to my lips as I imagine making her skin pink everywhere.

Out of the corner of my eye, I see a tall blonde guy with dark glasses heading straight for her, and my hackles go up. Jake turns to grab my shoulder and force me out of the house before I do something stupid like attack some random guy. As Jake leads me away, I hear a soft moan.

Make that my new favorite sound.

I look back for one final glimpse of her, only to see her arms swing up into a hug with him, one he returns for far too long.

Fuck me. I thought she didn't have a boyfriend. Great job, Pres. Way to miss that one.

I stumble out the front door, remaining upright only through the strength of Jake's hold. Every fiber within me screams to go back inside. To shift. To claim what is rightfully mine. Strong hands guide me out the front entrance and down the landscaped front yard.

Mine!

My wolf repeats over and over like some cell-bound psych patient. I storm off down the street, Jake hot on my heels but no longer forcing my progression. We don't say a word to each other. I can see the questions in his eyes as his mind spins.

I howl. Full and loud with no thought to the neighborhood in which we stand. Then, I bend forward, wondering if I should give in to the shift so I can run off this emotion. I'm panting, my heart racing as if I have just run a great distance.

"What the fuck, man? Are you good? I have never seen you so much as lose your cool on a mission. What the hell happened in there?" Jake questions, his voice furious, his body full of tension.

"Nothing. I'm good." I respond tersely, running my hands through my thick dark hair before pulling out my phone.

I'm so NOT good.

Pres answers on the first ring and begins talking before I can get a word out.

"Hey, eyes and ears are up and running in our girl's apartment. I would set the video to motion, so we don't have to comb through so much, but the bad news is they have a cat. I have access to all her cameras and microphones on the network and her cell phone here on the main system, and it should be sending info to the mirror phone. Every picture taken, text sent, email read. We have access to it all...." Pres rattles off before I interrupt her speech.

"We have a problem," I blurt out, no longer waiting for a pause. "Is Dante still in his office?"

"No, he left about an hour ago to meet with a new supplier downtown. He should be back by midnight for the meeting. Why? What's going on?" Pres quickly replies with a lift in her voice that is somewhere between excited and concerned.

"Well, you certainly missed a few critical points on our witness. For one, she's one of us, Unawakened." Presley audibly gasps, stopping her constant gum-smacking for a moment while I pace in front of the SUV, Jake observing me closely. I continue, "Two, she definitely has McCoy's support. I saw them with her tonight. They could be a problem if we need her to disappear. And three," and perhaps what pisses my wolf and me off the most, "she has a boyfriend." I snarl the last word as if it disgusted me to have to utter it. Not at all liking the taste of it in my mouth.

"How is that even possible? Dante finding Jake six years ago was an anomaly. I'll dig deeper into the mom and see if I can trace her movements. It's possible neither of them even knows they have the genes, or it could have come from mystery dad." I can hear Presley typing furiously on the keys as she speaks, working through every angle.

"Get what you can before midnight. I'll be monitoring the phone," I reach my hand out, and Jake drops the mirrored device into my hand, "Jake and I will be back for the meeting, and Pres..." I pause while I wait for the clicking of the keys and the smacking of the gum to silence before I continue in the voice I only use in my role as Dante's second, "This information stays within the advisory council. I expect there will be no more surprises." The threat I lace in my tone hangs in the air as I end the call and turn to Jake, who stands waiting for his orders.

"What happened just now stays between you and me. I want you outside the party ready to ensure they make it home. Alone." I emphasize the last word, ensuring he knows it isn't a suggestion. "I'll text you if she orders an Uber," I add as I jump into my SUV, slamming the door without waiting for a response.

Jake will follow through.

I think as I drop the car into gear and take off. As I pass him, he raises his arm in a wave and turns back up the street, heading for his SUV, which needs to be moved into the line of sight of the door.

I drive back to our headquarters building and march into my office, slamming the door behind me. I throw myself onto the oversized leather couch and close my eyes to try and calm down. I have a little over an hour until our meeting, and I have to find a way to settle my wolf without letting him out to run.

Just go get her. She would be safe with us.

My wolf pleads as I try to use logic on the beast living within me. I grab the mirror phone, opening it to see the wallpaper photo of Brielle hugging Livinia, both girls frozen in a fit of laughter. Her smile helps to calm my racing heart. She can both relax and excite me in the same moment. I guess that's how it is when you find your fated mate.

I click on the photo icon, hoping to see more. She has thousands of photos on her device and uploaded them to the cloud, which I can scroll through. I know the tech is working because new photos are still being added from the party, including her most recent shot with her boyfriend.

Mine.

My grip tightens on the phone, and the sound of it starting to splinter is the only thing that keeps me from crushing it all together. The selfie shows Brielle making an exaggerated surprise face while the fuck face next to her appears to be fake, attacking her like some kind of deranged vampire.

Wonder if he knows those fuckers are real. Maybe we could introduce him, two birds and all that.

I keep scrolling back. There are more with them laughing between takes, blurred shots with too many people moving, and a boomerang shot of her friend Livinia jumping between them. She is clearly very intoxicated, but I can see from some overly seductive images with a taco that at least she is eating, which makes me feel better. I close my eyes, pinching the bridge of my nose to alleviate some of the stress I have growing there.

She has a boyfriend. She doesn't know I exist. She has a whole life.

I think to myself, hoping to convince some part of me, so I can distance myself from the ache that started growing in my chest.

She doesn't belong to me.

The last one hurts the most because I instinctively know how much of a lie I'm telling myself. My wolf growls back.

Mine.

I am so fucked.

I glance back at the phone, seeing all the small thumbnail images. One of them suddenly catches my eye. It is also from tonight but earlier in the evening. I click it open to see a distant, shaded image of myself while leaning by the door and talking to Jake. I hold a beer in my hand and, by all accounts, look relaxed, though I know that it is a facade I have engineered over the years to ensure no one knows if they have gotten under my skin.

She took my picture. Sneaky girl. Now, what are you going to do with this?

My dick hardens at the possibilities. A devilish grin spreads across my face as I wonder if fuck face knows she was taking pictures of me. My reverie is interrupted by the vibration of an incoming text. Not on the phone I have in my hand but on my device. I pull it out of my pocket to see a text message from Jake.

> **Lucas is watching the party house. I'm headed back for the meeting. Your girl is still inside. I haven't seen her since we left.**

> **She isn't my girl. Did the boyfriend leave?**

I ask, inadvertently holding my breath and hoping I can stop worrying about that for the time being.

> **I haven't seen him.**

Fuck.

I put both phones into my pocket and grab the files I have and water from my office mini-fridge before heading down to the conference room on the medical floor. This is shaping up to be a really fucking terrible weekend all around.

Chapter 7
Bri

The one thing I can always count on at one of Liv's parties is a good time. Distraction is Liv's specialty. After getting some insanely delicious Mexican food in me, Keith, Liv, and I dance, drink, take photos in the prop booth, and start a conga line. The McCoys excused themselves hours earlier, and the catering staff is now beginning to pack up.

Keith left around one o'clock with one of the blondes from the trinity, Mila maybe, and Liv is letting one of the seniors from her Theories of Communication class take her back to his place. I'm pretty sure this isn't the first time, but with Liv, I can never keep track of the revolving door of men she always has flocking around her. Meanwhile, I spent the entire night looking for the dark McSteamy around every corner.

I open my phone to order an Uber while walking out to wait in the front yard. My eyes wander up into the cloudless sky, which allows just a tiny twinkling of stars to peek through the Vegas ambiance. I imagine you can see stars in every other city in the world, but most of the ones here are down on the Vegas strip performing, not up in the night sky. I think that is one of the things I looked forward to most in getting away—quiet, dark, and stars.

As a kid, one of the best memories I have is of my brother, Sam, and me when I was six or seven. My mother, Elaine, brought home another dealer to try and work off her debts and score more Oxy. She was constantly working to afford her drug of choice, which was a damned expensive habit.

Sammy snuck us out of our budget suite. He did it in part to protect me from the man but also to protect my innocence, which I held onto until he died. Until she killed him. That night we rode our bikes, gifted to us by a radio toy drive the previous Christmas, until we were out in the desert on the North East side of town. We sat out in the dirt staring at the stars for what felt like hours, though thinking back, it was probably less than one.

I remember my brother promising me that one day we would live somewhere we could look at the stars whenever we wanted. Where they weren't covered up by the bright lights of some flashy city, somewhere with a porch we could sit on and lightning bugs we could catch.

He joked that the stars were just a bunch of lightning bugs up there, reminding us to keep trying to grab them. We'd never seen lightning bugs, but his teacher read a book that had them in it, so he was sure we would be able to find them.

I remember looking at him. His curly brown hair was too long and fell onto his forehead. He had Elaine's pale skin and freckles but carried his dad's ocean-blue eyes. Though he was only two years older than me, he always seemed older and wiser somehow.

I've almost made it out of here, Sammy. Just six more months, and I will see some lightning bugs.

The stars, sometimes even the lack of them, remind me of Sam. They make me wonder where he would be today. Would he have gone to college? Would we have left here already? I'm hit with the sad reality, not for the first time, that I'll never know. That because of my waste-of-space mother, I'll never find out. I reach for the scar on my left wrist, the only physical reminder I have left of my brother, and run my fingers down it idly.

A teardrop falls onto the knuckle of my right hand, pulling me from the past. I wipe the stream of tears from my cheeks that I didn't realize were falling.

Thanks, alcohol, for the sentimentality.

I can't remember the last time I cried while sober. Alcohol is the only thing that brings me to this place emotionally. I have always wished I became the chatty or flirty drunk, but no, I'm the sappy drunk. Woe is me.

My phone lights up with a message that my driver is two minutes away, and I spend that time going through the photos on my phone from the night, choosing the best ones to send to Liv to post tomorrow.

She is big on her social media and makes sure everyone in her life is aware of everything she does, everything she eats, and every person she spends time with. It's become a living time capsule of her life. I'm just happy I make the highlight reel most days.

As I swipe, I come to the photo I took of McSteamy and stop. Heat fills me as I remember how his eyes slid over my body approvingly. The way they confidently held my gaze, challenging me to look away, begging for my submission.

I wonder what he would look like from between my legs... his five o'clock shadow of a beard teasing my inner thigh, his tongue tracing its way up to...

At that moment, my Uber arrives, and a notification flashes over the photo. I blush pink to the tips of my ears, cursing the moisture between my thighs. I shove the phone into my clutch and head for the Prius, taking deep breaths to calm my now-racing heart. I can't ever remember reacting to any man this intensely. I'm not Liv in the boyfriend department, but of the three relationships I've had, I've done my fair share of exploring my sexual side. None of them have gotten my panties wet just thinking of them.

It looks like it's time to dust off my vibrator and maybe redownload my dating apps. Clearly, it's been too long, and my body is simply reminding me that it has needs. It is time to pay them some attention.

It isn't until I'm getting into the Uber that I notice the black Tahoe parked a few houses down, and while it doesn't seem out of place in a neighborhood like this, it is one of the only vehicles left on the street, and there is someone in it.

I mentally go back through who is still inside. Caterers, sure, but they have the two vans in the back. Everyone else left before Liv, and it wasn't like most college kids could afford a shiny new Tahoe. I continue to act normal and greet my Uber driver but keep checking to see if my gut feeling is right. The SUV is too familiar, and maybe I'm paranoid, but I'm not so sure after the shit I saw last night.

Don't be ridiculous, Bri. How would they have found you, even if they knew who you were? You aren't at home or work. You didn't even bring your car.

I let out a breath trying to reign in my imagination, but as we pull out, the Tahoe's headlights turn on, slowly pulling out of its space.

It could be a coincidence...

The Uber driver navigates out of the complex and heads south toward the freeway. Moments later, so does the black SUV.

Shit. Shit. Shit.

We jumped on the I15 and head north. So do they.

I pull out my phone and quickly send Liv a text.

> **I think I'm being followed.**

No response.

> **There is a black Tahoe behind my Uber that left the party when I did.**

No response.

What happened to hoes before bros!? Sisters before misters!? Besties before the resties!?

Apparently, getting laid is worth more than my life. Think, Brielle, what could they want?

I haven't gone to the police. I haven't told anyone about the incident or the video.

Shit, I have the video! Could they have seen my phone?

It had been twenty-four hours, and I have been silent.

There is no way I could have been followed or tracked down. Right? Think!

As we get off the freeway, I keep my eyes on the back window, my palms sweating and my pulse hammering in my ears. The Tahoe falls a few cars back due to my Uber driver's rather erratic driving habits.

Remember to give this guy a decent tip.

I panic as I see the lane change happen, and the Tahoe is back on our tail. I turn my phone around and snap a picture, quickly sending it to Liv in case this becomes some true-crime documentary playing out in my real life. I can't see much of the driver other than their broad shoulders, and the SUV doesn't have a front plate, so I can't get any data that way.

I'm going to be kidnapped and murdered, and no one is going to have any leads.

I think frantically, trying to remember anything useful from all of the serial killer shows Liv is always watching on the couch while I study while silently cursing myself for leaving my pepper spray in my larger purse.

As we approach the left turn off of Flamingo onto my street, my driver pulls off into the assigned left lane and slows down for the blinking yellow arrow. I tense, wondering if I can get a better picture of the driver as the cars between us continue straight, but strangely, the Tahoe never moves left, and instead, accelerates past us, continuing on Flamingo.

I am an idiot.

I sigh, turning back in my seat to face forward, bringing a questioning look from the driver.

I must look batshit crazy.

I give him a small smile and then send another text to Liv.

> **False alarm, I must be drunker than I thought**

> **Text me tomorrow to let me know you're good**

The driver finally pulls up to my building, and I mumble a polite farewell before hobbling up the stairs to the second floor, pulling out my keys to unlock the door. I throw my keys into the bowl by the door and enter the alarm code into the system. It flashes green and alerts me that it has been turned off, only to have me immediately reset it to "Armed Home," so the door is still alarmed, but the motion detectors aren't.

I head for the fridge to grab water, realizing the Monster Liv pulled out earlier for me still sits untouched on the table, getting warm. Placing it back into the fridge for the morning, I remember we are out, and make a mental note reminding myself to add energy drinks to my grocery list along with the candy for my work stash. I pull a can of the wretched cat's food out and dump it in his bowl before discarding the can to the trash.

Why does it have to smell so bad?

I lumber down the hall, opening Liv's door to let Banshee out.

You're welcome, you ungrateful shit.

I don't know why Liv insisted we keep him earlier this year when he showed up crying for food in the neighborhood. He hates me, and the feeling is mutual. Liv didn't have the heart to turn him away, and after several long-winded debates, he took up residence in her room, and he has had a cocky swagger like he owns the place ever since.

I continue down the hall toward my room, water in hand. I know I need to get some Ibuprofen into my system as soon as possible if I want to get through my two papers later today. I throw my clutch on the bed and kick off my shoes as I walk into the bathroom. I take a few painkillers and drain the rest of the water bottle in an attempt to fight off the hangover that'll inevitably follow this night of drinking. I turn on the shower to let it heat up while I walk to the vanity to take off my makeup and brush through my hair.

Once I finish, I shed Liv's outfit and step under the burning stream. The heat of the water feels fantastic on my skin, and I melt into it even as my skin flares to lobster red. My eyes close, letting the water beat down my shoulders, rolling them under the strong jets as the heat massages the stress away. I lather my loofa with my vanilla sugar exfoliating soap and scrub the sweat away.

As I clean my body, my thoughts drift to a tall, dark-haired mystery man. His full lips, the way his eyes caress every inch of my body. I imagine how his hands would feel on my skin; wonder if they would be insistent and rough in their grip or if, instead, they would tease me, slow and seductive, as they graze lightly across my hips.

I shudder, heat pooling in my core while a picture forms in my mind. I watch my hands slide across the planes of my stomach, only now I see his larger, stronger ones in their place, leaving a trail of suds that slide over me, lighting up every nerve. His hands grab my breasts, covering them in soapy vanilla-scented bubbles, and their agile fingers tease my already hard nipples. My body responds immediately, sending electricity to my skin's surface, raising goosebumps on my arms and causing tingles up my overly sensitive neck.

My breathing quickens, and my pulse speeds up as they delicately circle and pinch each taut mound. I imagine his tongue caressing them, sucking and nibbling with greedy intent. It is like he is here, stepping into my shower, fully dressed in tonight's black shirt and jeans. He is unfazed by the jet streams of water as he closes the distance between us, forcing his body against mine. His hands replace mine with a possessive grip as his eyes devour all my exposed skin hungrily. I moan, biting down on my lip, enjoying the almost painful grip as I take in his exquisitely crafted chest, now more visible with his soaked shirt clinging to every muscle.

His dark eyes lock on mine, and my mind focuses on how they never look away as his hand descends at a painstakingly slow pace. The anticipation I feel as his hand inches closer has my heartbeat drumming in my ears. My mouth falls open, and I pull myself into him, hoping to get his hand there faster. A whimper escapes my lips as the need pulsating from my clit has me trembling. He smirks down at me, fully understanding how lost I am in his touch.

I gasp when he finally relents, reaching his destination and placing his thumb firmly over the throbbing nerve. My head falls back, and my eyes close as I focus solely on the feel of his rough hands on my body. He starts slowly and then increases his rhythm and pressure in equal measure.

My breathing is heavy now, panting out of me as I fill with need, driving myself closer to the edge. Every sensation is magnified; each drop of water sends a ripple of electricity that intensifies the feeling of his touch. My quivering legs start to give out, and he guides my body back onto the shower wall, using his to prop me against its colder tile, a pleasant contrast to the boiling happening inside and outside of me.

His pace increases, and two fingers slide inside me, causing my walls to clench greedily around them. My back arches forcing my chest harder into his as he begins pumping firmly while his thumb continues to circle my clit with an agonizing tenderness that has me bucking my hips into him.

He moves his other hand from the wall, seizing my breast forcefully, and then rolling my nipple in a way that gives me just a touch of pain with my pleasure, causing me to call out in ecstasy.

"Oh, mmm God...."

A growl rumbles out of him as he bites at the other nipple, licking it with his tongue before sliding all the way up my neck and across my jaw. Sensation overwhelms my senses as I fight to feel everything at once. His teasing tongue, his tantalizing thumb, and his relentless fingers; all have me losing the ability to think anything coherent.

Need courses through me as I float closer to my peak. His hand slides up to my throat, applying enough strength to force my eyes to his in a lust-filled surprise. His eyes darken to a cold silver, making him more intense and sexier.

"Cum for me, Bri."

He demands in a voice threaded with desire before squeezing his grip sharply as my brain explodes with pleasure. No longer able to hold back, I let my full orgasm go, riding the avalanche as all the pressure built up crashes out of me in pulsating waves. I cry out, clenching as the sensations roll through me, stealing my breath before leaving me in a sated haze. He waits until my throbbing ceases and my breathing settles before guiding me to the floor, my legs no longer capable of holding me up.

"Good Girl."

Lust flashes in his eyes as I take in his praise. Warmth settles within me as I watch him lift his hand to his lips to lick my taste off. He stares into my eyes with his gray gaze as each finger is sucked clean. I spend a moment admiring the sharp lines of his jaw, the dusting of facial hair making him appear slightly disheveled as water drips from the ends of his dark brown hair. He leans down, his lips headed for mine as I tilt my chin up, longing for him to be connected to me again, needing his touch more than air. My brain can't cognitively puzzle together the pull I feel to him, the way I crave him like an addict would a drug.

My eyes fly open with a start.

What the fuck?

The steam in the bathroom is as thick as a cloud, and I'm panting on the shower floor, completely sated. My orgasm is still slowly pulsing between my thighs. I don't think I've ever cum so quickly. I didn't know I had such a vivid imagination.

God, imagine that body of his in my bed.

Chastising myself even as it crosses my mind.

I don't even know this man and probably will never see him again.

I collect myself off the floor, turn off the shower, and grab my fluffy black towel. It's wrapped around me quickly before a second towel is thrown on my hair. I'm dizzy, partly from the drinking, partly from the heat in the bathroom, and, if I'm being honest, partly because of the intense orgasm. My body still tingles with every touch of the fabric as every nerve feels heightened.

I throw on an old beat-up pair of pajamas and crawl into bed, setting my alarm for later that morning, so I can get to the library with enough time to finish my papers, and then turn my ringer on in case Liv needs me for anything before then.

As I drift off to sleep, the last thing that crosses my mind is that somehow I know this man, he is familiar to me in a way I can't quite place, and a part of me hopes I'll see him again.

Chapter 8

Cain

I arrive first in the conference room. My head is still at war with my instincts to get out of there and run to my mate. Before I can let myself do that, I take my place to the left of the head of the table and wait for the rest of the team to arrive. I flip open the mirror phone and look through it, checking her texts and call log for clues about what we are dealing with.

I see a few texts from a contact she had named Keith, who I assume is the boyfriend based on their context. They came in shortly after the incident last night. Things like:

> **Where are you?**

Did you make it home safe?

Answer your phone!

Elle, I'm worried. Text me back.

He calls her Elle?

My heart clenches, not wanting to see the pet name or feel its familiarity. She didn't respond to him for hours. In fact, she didn't message him until she left for the party tonight, based on the time stamps. I look over the texts she sent him tonight and curiosity peaks within me.

She lied to him. She told him she only heard the shots while leaving. Nothing about Marlo's guys. Nothing about me chasing her down. Nothing about murderers, dead bodies, or large bags of cash. Nothing. Why keep our secret?

Jake clears his throat as he walks in, pulling my attention to him as he sits next to me.

"Are you going to tell me what happened earlier, or am I supposed to pretend I didn't have to pull you from that house? I know you want it kept low, but I gotta know if your head is in this before we take another shot." Jake asks, his eyes searching mine for unspoken answers, pleading with me to give him something. I can tell his confidence in me is shaken. He needs something.

"I just wasn't ready to run into another Unawakened. It rocked me, and my wolf wanted to protect her. He feels like she is already pack," I tell him, lacing enough truth into the lie to give it life. "I'm good. We need to tie up these loose ends, so we can focus on what we are going to do about her." I finish as Pres strolls in, headphones still in place, folders stacked in her arms, and bright pink gum popping on her lips. She drops the stack in the middle of the table before sliding one to Jake and me. She then sets one in front of each of the five other open chairs in the room and picks up the projector remote to begin setting up her presentation on the main screen.

The Vegas Pack's advisory council has six seated members. Seven if you included Dante. The pack chose this setup so he would be the deciding vote if anything on the board came to a tie. Dante Stone is our Alpha, and his word is law, but he understands the need for advisors and a team to help guide his decisions.

I sit as his number two. Officially his COO or Chief Operations Officer for the company. Presley has maneuvered her way into the third spot just behind me on pure talent and ingenuity and is titled our CTO, Chief Technical Officer. We need her mind to keep this company running.

Next come Erik and Jake, our head enforcers, both sharing the title of Vice President of Security Operations. They split the city in half downtown, covering the north and south sides, respectively.

Last up are our pack ambassadors or Chief Communications Officers, James and Elijah. Both are a few years older than the rest of us, and their primary role is keeping the peace with the neighboring packs on the West Coast so we can keep lines of communication available.

Since Dante took over, they've been an invaluable asset claiming us allies across seven states. The only pack we've never been able to sway is the Reno Pack. Deacon Marlo's pack. Years ago, he tried to set up a bad-faith deal with Dante's father, which would've effectively joined the two territories.

In the original negotiations, they would rule together under one umbrella of a Nevada Pack, but Deacon got greedy wanting more and more domain to fall under his purview. Marcus, Dante's father, never agreed to Deacon's terms before he died, so the leadership turned over to Dante as the next Alpha in line even though he was only twenty-one.

Deacon still believes he should own the Las Vegas territory and does everything he can to push at our borders and make us appear unfit to the other packs. James and Elijah spent their time traveling from area to area on damage control. Only Elijah will be at the meeting tonight as James remains in northern Washington on a pack retreat with five of our security guys. We'll have to loop him in when he returns.

Once everything is set up and ready, Presley sits opposite me on the right of Dante's seat. I can tell she is tense from her posture and the slight pinch in her brow. She also avoids my gaze, which I feel like a kick in the nuts. I don't think I've ever yelled at Presley before or pulled rank the way I did today. It was a dick move over some information she probably couldn't have been able to find with the notice she had.

I should apologize.

I move forward, leaning across the table to catch Presley's gaze when Erik comes limping through the entrance with a brace holding up his right shoulder and a thick bandage still wrapped around his left thigh. My gut clenches at the sight of him, guilt reeling inside me.

Shit. It'll have to be later.

"What is this, a funeral? Who died?" Erik laughs. "Come on, guys. Stop looking at me like that. I'm fine. I'll be out running you before the week is out." He continues, his cocky smile firmly in place. His color looks good, and he'll be alright in a matter of days, thanks largely to our rapid healing. We haven't had a close call like that since we lost Marcus, so we are all a little on edge.

He flops down into the seat next to Jake, throwing his feet onto the table as he leans back. He has a glint in his eye as if waiting for someone to chastise him, but no one does, and he uses his boot to slide his folder closer to his hand.

"So, is this meeting about the tech we still don't have or the bitch you guys let get away?" Erik asks casually, flipping through the pages in front of him. I'm on my feet and lunging before realizing I've moved. My hands squeeze in fists as Jake jumps up and places both hands on my chest to stop my momentum.

"Whoa there, Cain," He says in a low whisper while bobbing his head around, trying to get me to look at him instead of Erik, who drops his feet to the carpet and pushes back in his chair, ready to defend himself. I snarl, grinding my teeth with effort, and slide my eyes to Jake's moss-green ones. "Do you need to take a walk?" He quietly asks, trying to reign in my unexpected outburst like I'm a child incapable of controlling myself.

Defend your Mate!

My instincts are raging under my skin, and my hands shift into paws before I can stop them.

"Sit down." The command is simple and should be easily followed, as the words come from my Alpha, who has just entered with Elijah at his heels. His face is unamused by the minor tussle happening in his boardroom.

"We've got shit to sort out." Dante finishes as he finds his seat at the head of the table, and Elijah rounds to sit next to Pres. My eyes return to Erik's, and a threatening growl creeps from my throat. He drops his gaze immediately, submitting with a tentative whine before I can force myself back into my seat. Jake slowly sits back down but never takes his wary eyes off me.

"Alright, now that we've completed the theatrics. Here is where we are at," Presley begins standing up to control the projector throughout her presentation.

"Thanks largely to Jake's interrogation work, we were able to locate and identify the Marlo cell downtown. The two guys we met last night were bottom feeders, new to the organization. We couldn't get any information out of them due largely to the fact that someone ripped them to shreds." Everyone's eyes flash over to me, and I cross my arms over my chest defensively, shrugging as she continues, "The information provided by Kole has been beneficial. He let us know that Deacon sent him here, with several Reno pack members, to recruit behind our backs while also trying to gain any intel they could on our operations. The problem with that plan was that the six people in this room were the only ones with the clearance necessary to get Deacon the leverage he wants to make a full push for the state." She pauses for effect.

"Since I know each person here is a trusted advisor, we know that the leak came from one of our direct subordinates and that they were only given the information shortly before we shipped. This tells us two things. First, that one of our own is tainted. We are fairly certain Marlo's goons had no idea what they were stealing, just that it was a high-value item for us. Second, Deacon has moved a larger contingent of his loyal wolves into our territory. He has been keeping them under the radar, so he can infiltrate from within the city when he moves to take out Dante and remove him from his position as Alpha."

She flips to the next screen while we each take a moment to think over who we contacted about the shipment, newcomers to our pack who could've allegiances elsewhere, and also what this might mean for the timeline of taking on the Marlo pack.

"Jake, Erik, I need a list of everyone who had access to shipment information within twenty-four hours of leaving this facility, as well as your ideas of possible suspects within the hour," Dante orders as he slides the tracking paperwork down the table to them.

"We have seven recruits from the surrounding areas that have come to us within the last six to eight months. I can send those personnel files to Pres and have Elijah and James reach out to their previous packs for verifications. They should've been fully vetted, but some came before Pres returned from school in June and may have fallen through the cracks of the older system." Erik explains as Jake takes the paperwork and looks through the checkpoints listed to compare them to the on-duty guards. Elijah looks to the list of recruits, splitting them between his and James's coverage area as Dante nods and then returns his attention to Presley.

"Our next issue is that this afternoon, I was notified that someone was trying to find a backdoor into my facial recognition software. I placed silent alarms within the code, alerting me to any changes made or anyone trying to gain access without granting them entry. So, as of right now, they don't know what they have; however, whoever they are using to get in, is pretty good and is using the encryption key to gain access. I've had to block them at several different access points to ensure they aren't able to read what they can now access. The benefit is that I know where the network they are using is located, and the building is pretty low security. We could be in and out tonight without much resistance from the company;

however, I imagine Deacon has some added security on site which may throw a kink into retrieval." She finishes this point by showing a slide with the building schematics in a more run-down area of central Vegas, off the strip, west of downtown.

Dante looks over the blueprints on the screen, calculating our chances. "Cain? How soon could you have a team ready?"

"I could have a squad of five ready to be in and out in under an hour. If we wanted bigger perimeter protection, it would take closer to two hours, and I need Pres on my inside team to ensure we get everything they have." I voice, my eyes going to Presley to gauge her response. Her eyes light up, and a smile tugs at her mouth as she braves a glance at Dante.

"Absolutely not," he responds without so much as a second thought. "Take Mason. He held the job while Pres was away at school. She can let him know what we are looking for," he offers, not even looking over at his younger sister.

"I'm going. Mason may be a capable stand-in for me, but he isn't me, and if he misses something, it's all for nothing." Presley states, rising out of her chair defiantly.

"I won't risk you out on a field assignment. You can be in Mason's ear, and he can wear a camera so you can see what he sees," Dante responds, turning his eyes to face her.

"Not to overstep," I interrupt their stare down, pulling Dante's attention my way, "but we need Pres for this job. They could've put the code anywhere, and she is the only one I would trust to get it all," I explain, trying to cut the tension between them. I look Dante in the eye.

"No offense to Mason, but I need her." Dante's eyes go from me to Presley, standing with her arms crossed and shoulders squared, determination evident on her face. He leans back, his fingers going to his beard as he glances back at the blueprints again.

"Take a team of ten. Use the extra bodies in teams of two on the perimeter. I don't want anyone else hurt. You'll stay with Pres for every step, or she doesn't go. If anything happens to her, you die. Erik, you'll be our wheels for this one since you aren't a hundred percent yet. Pick a second driver from your team. You are in at two-thirty, and this wraps up before three. Understood?" His last question is for me, and I nod.

"Nothing will happen to her." I vow with every bit of strength I can throw into my words and move to get the team ready, but Presley's voice stops me.

"We aren't done." She announces, flipping the screen from the blueprints to a picture of my Mate. A rumble rolls out of me.

Mine.

"This is our witness, Brielle DelaCourt, goes by Bri, from the Marlo confrontation last night, and this is the video she filmed." Presley pulls up the video and lets it play out. All of us suck in a sharp breath when the gunshots happen. From this video, I can hear Brielle's scream, heavy breathing, and panicked self-talk. Erik attempts a joke that doesn't land, and I grip the arms of my chair as the footage shifts to me in my wolf form coming towards her before she drops the phone into blackness.

The film doesn't end there, though, as we can still hear tires squealing, my paws hitting her door, and her erratic profanity as she makes it farther away. I don't think I've ever heard the f-word that many different ways before, and I grin a little at her foul mouth.

When the video ends, Pres continues, "Jay got our eyes and ears up in the witness's apartment, and Jake and Cain were able to mirror her phone, so we have access to all incoming and outgoing messages via text, call, or email. So far, our girl has been pretty quiet and has even blatantly lied about what she saw; however, she did make several copies of this video and has even sent an email to an address I can't trace. So at least one copy of this thing is in the wind, but otherwise, it looks like everything she copied was local, and we could easily pick it up or have her hand it over." Presley takes a moment to flip to a different screen before continuing.

"Some new information we've ascertained over the last few hours includes the fact that she is Unawakened. Presumably, the DNA came from her dad's side since we have no information on him. But her mom, Elaine, has been in and out of the system and around others of our kind with no flags. We are ruling her out for now. We believe that Bri has no idea about what she is, so we must tread carefully. Additionally, she is protected by the McCoy family. Records I was able to dig up even show that they were in the process of trying to adopt her while in high school, but it looks like it fell through because Elaine wouldn't give up her rights."

"On paper, our witness is completely clean. She has a small contingent of friends, never joined any clubs or societies at UNLV, and can be found at work or in the on-campus library in her off time. Phone records show she has been in contact with a few marketing firms, all on the east coast, and she has a calendar date set for an interview later this week with a Boston firm. Her finances are strong, considering she is a college student with no family backing. It appears she doesn't spend her money on much. Lastly, I can see that she has no contact with her mother and hasn't in several years. She never even visited her when she was in prison." My head is spinning with all this information.

"So basically, we can't make her disappear because she has too many people, but we might be able to keep her quiet?" Dante asks, his brows scrunched in concern. "What are we thinking? Threats? Bribery? Show of force?" He continues.

Jake is the first to speak up.

"Coming from a life in the foster system, she isn't going to trust us without reason, especially after she saw us kill two guys."

"We are friendly with the Boston territory. We sent them the Ostler twins last summer, and their Alpha's niece, Jess, is in our pack on our covert team." Elijah adds.

"We have access to her phone, right? Why can't we end her and send messages to everyone that she's run off? She's planning on moving away soon anyway. We move up her timeline." Erik offers as a solution. I snarl.

End him.

"Because we aren't a bunch of senseless murderers," Dante interjects, rolling his eyes before I can completely lose my cool. "I think we need to get to know her, see where her head is, see if we should be discussing awakening her. Some people can't handle this life, and we need to be sure before we try to bring her into it." He turns to Presley. "Who do we have available to attend her classes, maybe take her on a few dates, get inside her head?"

"I mean, she's hot, so I would totally be down," Erik announces, a lopsided grin appearing on his face.

"That won't work. She has a boyfriend." I interject, hating to use the word but loving that I have a reason to keep him as far away from her as possible.

"Actually, I looked into that." Presley pipes up. "The guy from the party is Keith Anderson. He appears in many photos with her over the years, but when I looked deeper, his socials show him taking out a bunch of different girls with no real consistency. The guy is a bit of a manwhore, but it doesn't appear he is with her or that he ever has been," she continues with a bit of an *I told you so* smirk, "and I believe that Cain would be our best fit here. He is in our inner circle, so we know we can trust him while we work on this leak. He was in his wolf form for the video, so she won't recognize him like she could Erik or Jake, and from her photos tonight, it appears she already has a bit of interest." Presley bites down on her lip to contain her laughter as she flips the slide to the discrete photo Brielle had taken of me at the party. All of the eyes in the room look up at the screen and then shift to me with varying smirks.

Damnit Pres.

"Can I trust you with this?" Dante asks, not beating around the bush. "We only get one shot at this."

I consider the task.

I get to be close to her. I can keep everyone else away from her. I can keep her safe. She will be mine.

"I can do it," I state firmly, convincing myself as much as everyone else in the room.

"If you need any tips, big guy, I would be happy to give you some pointers," Erik jokes with a growing smile that only makes me want to punch him right in the face.

"You wish. Maybe try healing, so I can kick your ass without feeling guilty," I snap back, relaxing a little.

"Let's focus on tonight. We are in and out. No surprises," Dante orders, effectively ending the meeting. He stands and walks out, pulling Elijah with him. Erik hobbles out, complaining about a lack of food. I sit there a moment longer, and I feel Jake's stare.

"Say what you need to say," I ask, looking over at him.

"This girl has you some type of way. I think you need to be careful. I can tell how invested you are. Don't forget the point of this is to ensure she doesn't talk." He declares unease in his gaze as he stands and walks out of the conference room.

I sit alone for a few minutes contemplating how this whole thing will work. I don't want to manipulate her or lie to her. Even the thought of betrayal makes my heart ache, but I must put the pack before myself. She is a threat to us; I should think of her that way. She may be my Mate, but she isn't even a wolf, and there is no guarantee she ever will be. I need to get my head right.

I stand and send off a few texts to the team with meeting times and locations. For tonight, I'll focus all my energy on getting back what Marlo stole from us. Brielle is a problem for tomorrow. Tonight is about revenge.

Chapter 9
Cain

Our teams arrive at the south entrance to the building at 2:20 am. It is still pitch black outside, save for the ambient lighting provided by the city. We decided to roll in two teams of four, leaving Erik and Jay behind in the vehicles, ready to get us out at a moment's notice. My squad consists of Presley, Wyatt, and Hudson, and we'll be the breach team headed for the second floor.

Hudson is only twenty-one and still in college, but he has been in our pack his whole life and trained in all forms of combat, so Dante believes this is a good shot for the kid to prove himself.

Wyatt came to our pack from one of the Washington packs a couple of years ago. His older brother was next in line for their pack Alpha position, and Wyatt didn't want to have to fight it out when that time came, so he left his pack and joined us. He has Alpha DNA, but his strength is no rival to mine or Dante's, so he's not a risk of overthrowing us.

Jake's team consists of Mason, Jess, and Carter, who'll hold the perimeter and the first floor once we are inside. Mason is the oldest on the team at thirty-one, and he used to be our head of all things tech before Presley graduated and came back with more knowledge and ability than we could have hoped. Rather than fighting for the position, he graciously stepped into a more active role within the company's front-line security. He is quickly becoming our best sleuth, able to break into any number of doors and disable alarms at neck-breaking speeds.

Jess is our best undercover agent; she is unassuming, petite, and can speak several languages. She doesn't come across as threatening due to her sunny disposition and bright smile, but years of training in the Boston pack make her devastatingly lethal with small weapons. She is both great at distraction and capable of excellent off-the-top-of-her-head bullshit explanations, which has worked a few times to get us out of some less-than-desirable scenarios.

Last is Carter, Erik's best friend and about the most laid-back guy I have ever seen. He can keep his cool in every situation and follows orders without question or delay. Carter is twenty-four and originally came from Los Angeles, just wanting a change of scenery. My guess is he'll move on again in the next few years; that is just the type he is. Even now, he won't live in the pack apartments and chooses to sleep in his renovated van instead.

The teams line up outside the building across the street and await my instructions.

"We'll be using the rear entrance. Once inside, we'll follow the hallway to the stairs. Jake and Mason will clear the first floor on the right when we reach them, and Wyatt and Hudson will clear the left. It should be vacant. Once the sweep is complete, Jake and Mason will remain on that floor and post on the two entrances. Jess and Carter, you will patrol the surrounding area on foot while Erik and Jay stay in the loading bay, be ready to get us out of here. My team will then head upstairs, split and sweep into the office. Pres and I'll go in. Wyatt and Hudson will monitor the stairs and the emergency exit door. Set radios to channel four. Test them now." I order and wait as each member clears their radio checks, ensuring their earpieces and mics work.

"We should be in and out in about eight minutes. We'll let you know if it takes longer to find and process the material from their servers. I want radio silence unless there is an issue. As a reminder, our rendezvous spot is Zeek's. If shit hits the fan and you can't get out with us to the vans, we'll meet at 3:30 am there. Questions?" I conclude, looking each member in the eyes to be sure they are ready. "Let's move."

The six of us cross the street as a unit, hugging the shadows as we move in near silence. Jess and Carter immediately fall into character and begin flirting with each other as they walk in the opposite direction on the battered sidewalk, looking like a young couple getting to know each other while out for a late-night stroll.

My team stacks up on the door, and Mason moves to the front to remove the alarm trigger and pick the lock. After about a minute, the door opens, and we file into and down the long hallway.

The offices are dark and musty with an undertone of pumpkiny chemical air freshener. The ceiling tiles are moldy as if they have recently survived a significant leak and are moments away from breaking loose. The search teams split off to their designated sides while Pres and I wait for Wyatt and Hudson at the base of the stairs. My radio chirps the all-clear moments before they retrace their steps back to us. Jake moves to the backdoor while Mason posts up near the front.

"In position, front doors clear," Mason sends into the radio, and we wait a moment longer for the all-clear.

"In position, back door clear," Jake mimics.

"We are quiet on the perimeter," Jess whispers, not wanting to draw any unnecessary attention to the strolling pair.

"Bays are clear," Erik chirps finally.

We proceed up the steps as quietly as we can. Our intel informs us that there is a guard on this floor, but if I know Deacon, he'll protect his stolen goods with more than a single patrol. A grunt of annoyance sounds as I push Presley farther behind me and allow Wyatt to lead us through the door at the top of the metal staircase, Hudson following at the rear.

The door squeaks as it opens, causing us to pause as we let the sound simmer and die off. One by one, we emerge from the staircase and split off in the two directions of the floor. This floor appears to contain several businesses separated into four areas. We pass a pediatrician's office door with brightly-colored lettering and a cartoon dog as we continue looking for suite 314. Pres hangs behind me. My radio comes to life as we pass a public restroom.

"We have action out front. One male headed inside the front door. Parked in employee parking, I assume this guy works in one of the offices here." Carter's voice rings out.

"There are twelve companies in this building; he could belong to any of them. Let's hold and see where he goes. Mason, pull back and let him get where he is going."

"Copy pulling back from the main door," Mason echoes. The silence lingers as we all freeze, and the waiting seconds drag as the mystery guy approaches the building.

"He has scanned in and is heading for the stairs. I couldn't see his ID, but this dude is tall," Mason relays.

"Wyatt, Hudson find a spot to hide," I order quietly while ushering Presley into the restroom we just passed. Our new arrival pops out of the staircase door a moment later and turns our way. He is tall, well over six feet, maybe six-foot-five. He has a black baseball cap covering half of his face, a pair of loose gray joggers, and a t-shirt that says, "There's no place like 127.0.0.1". He walks past the restrooms at a leisurely pace, and I notice the AirPods in his ears. Leaning closer, I can make out a strong bass and what sounds like a heavy metal guitar.

He continues down the hall and into a door at the end on the right. Dread hits me as I look over at the number on the pediatrician's door and do the math... two doors down, and he just walked into 314.

Shit.

"We have a problem. The guy just walked into the workplace we need," I whisper into my mic, wondering where we go from here. "Erik, pull up the blueprints for me and tell me how many exits we have once we get inside." I wait, assuming he is following my order, but Wyatt comes on the radio before he can respond.

"Hudson and I just dropped two wolves coming out the 300's wing of offices. They were on patrol on this back side, young, poorly trained. We were able to knock them both out. They are gagged and zip tied in the closet, but that means we are on the clock." He recites, sounding a bit out of breath.

"Any injuries?" I ask quickly, assessing our new reality.

"Hudson may have a shiner for a few hours, but otherwise, we are all good," Wyatt responds with a smile in his voice.

"Alright, boss, once you enter, there are two additional exits. One is a fire escape straight ahead and to your right before you hit the target office. The other is the door I assume Wyatt and Hudson are at, which is the left-most corner from where you are entering, next to a break room and a corner office. This wing only has three official offices, a conference room, some storage closets, a breakroom, and a restroom with entrances from the inner hall and the breakroom. The rest of the space is cubicles in the center." He lists off as I decide where we go from here. I look at my watch. It is only 2:37 am.

What is this guy doing here?

"Ok, here's the plan. Pres and I will go in the front. Wyatt and Hud enter through the rear door, we have swept this floor, so unless we hear from Jake or Mason, we shouldn't have any surprises behind us. Remember, we aren't here to kill anyone. We are here for our tech and any information we can grab quickly. I want quiet take-downs. Stay together. We enter at 2:39 am," I end, turning to Presley, whose face is broadcasting her concern.

"Your only role here is data retrieval. I don't want you getting into a fight. If I go down, you leave. Do you hear me?" I end my statement with command in my voice, and Presley clenches her jaw. I know it isn't in her nature to run, but I won't let anything happen to her.

A minute later, we enter the offices, which are brightly lit, despite the hour. As I slide through the doorway, a guy is strolling away. He hears the door open and turns to look over his shoulder as I launch at him, his heightened hearing giving him away as more than human.

Launching at him, we roll to the floor, my arm wrapping around his throat in a choke hold to cut off his air and prevent him from yelling out in alarm. Pres jumps in behind me when he finally passes out, grabbing the zip ties off my belt, fastening them around his ankles, and moving his wrists to add a second tie. I secure a gag around his mouth to prevent screaming when he wakes up and sigh, grateful that I haven't had to pull my knife.

Awkwardly shifting his weight to move him behind the vacant cubicle to my left, I report that we have one patrol down over the radio quickly before sweeping the menial offices heading toward the executive suite at the end of the hall. It isn't the office the tech should be in, but I want to be sure no one will be coming behind us. All the cubicles are cleared except the now-napping and gagged Awakened by the front door.

Moving further along, I crack open the large office door and scan as we enter. It appears empty, the lights are off, and the computer shut down. I quickly sweep the wardrobe and behind the desk to ensure we haven't missed anything before heading back toward where we just came from. When I reach the cubical with our unconscious friend, I turn left and head down the hall, past the emergency exit, before hearing Hudson on the radio.

"Two down in the break room. Wyatt got stabbed in the ribs and is now shifting. We can see one more in the hallway headed toward you." He rattles off the information, and I can hear Wyatt's wolf panting in the background as he shifts to heal. I push our pace, moving us to hug the corridor wall at the corner, ready to pounce on the patrol headed our way.

He smells me a moment before he turns the corner, a sound of alarm escaping his lips before I'm in motion, knocking the now out-stretched gun from his grasp before he can fire.

Wyatt is right; these guys are young and poorly trained.

The weapon flies from his hand as my arms chop his wrist, and my boot catches him under the jaw. A loud oomph sounds as the guy hits the floor, not completely knocked out. Presley throws herself on top of him, rolling his solid weight as she restrains his arms behind him as I make a makeshift gag.

Once the restraints are in place and he can't sound the alarm, we move him back into the cubicle with his buddy, who is starting to wake up. I take a moment to search them both, removing their IDs and weapons, saving both for more inspection later.

So far, I'm impressed with Presley's ability to follow my lead while stepping in and being hands-on when necessary. She might make an excellent field agent one day. Not that Dante would ever allow that. The risk is too significant, especially if anyone discovers that the pack princess is out in the open. We would have packs from every direction wanting to steal her for her breeding capabilities and Alpha lineage.

I turn to look at her, seeing only determination and focus in her eyes. I signal for her to grab the gun down the hall, and we move toward the office we need.

I pause to update Wyatt and Hudson before setting up at the office door.

"Ready?" I whisper to Presley taking a moment before we breach to be sure she can handle this. We haven't run into the guy who showed up yet, and I wonder if maybe he is one of the two in the breakroom with the rest of my team.

"Absolutely. I can do this," she says, but I'm unsure if she is saying it for herself or me. I nod, look back at the door, notice the light emanating from under it, and prepare myself for what may be inside.

I swing the door open as quickly and quietly as possible while moving inside to get us out of the exposed hallway. As I enter, I notice our tall mystery man posted up at the desk, his back to us, headphones over his ears as he concentrates on the code flowing up on the screen in front of him. Presley shuts the door silently, and I approach the back of his chair while pulling a syringe out of my vest, ready to subdue him.

"Jax, I told you I needed time. I've never seen code this clean before. It's like every possible scenario has been thought through and protected. Whoever wrote this," He turns his head, and his eyes grow large as he realizes I'm not who he is expecting. I pause for a fraction of a second, recognition flooding me before I plunge the needle into his neck and duck slightly to cover my face.

It's the boyfriend? Well, I guess just the friend. What are the fucking odds?

He slumps forward, his eyes closing as the medicine puts him to sleep for thirty minutes or so. I turn toward Presley as she stares, mouth agape, at the guy I'm now moving to the floor. "Hurry up, you have six minutes to get all your code back and find any copies," I order while moving Keith further out of the way, so she has room to sit down.

"That's the guy. The witness's friend. He's using the stolen encryption key to hack my software?" she asks, temporarily frozen in her spot by the door. I can't read her expression as she stares at the man lying on the floor. She seems unable to comprehend the coincidence of this man being here.

"Ya, small world. Come on, Pres. We have to move." I say before getting back on my radio. "We took out our mystery guest in the office and the patrol in the hall. Hudson, how is Wyatt?" I ask, searching Keith's pockets for his phone while planning to dig into this guy's life.

"He is no longer bleeding and will be able to exit when we get out of here. We don't think anyone got an alarm for backup, so we are clear and awaiting your orders to head back to the vehicles." Hudson answers with a loud, crunching noise, which sounds suspiciously like he is eating.

Fucking kid.

Presley moves to the seat and begins typing a mile a minute, screens opening and changing faster than I can keep up. I click to open the phone and use our knocked-out boy's face to unlock it.

I scroll through his apps and notifications, seeing the messages to Brielle, who he had saved in his phone as "Little Ellie," with a rather obnoxious picture of her in a teal onesie. I also see text messages from tonight under a number he hasn't saved, thanking him for the orgasms and telling him all the things they would like to do to him the next time.

Well, I guess he is seeing someone else.

My wolf relaxes a bit within me. I click through a few more messages and don't see anything relevant.

I slide through the settings to see his most used apps and look up abruptly as Presley curses under her breath before her fingers go furiously back to work. I realize she is talking to herself, a bit of back and forth with the unconscious guy about him thinking he is so bright before a small compliment about something he has implemented. I return my focus to the phone and notice a strange app with several hours logged daily, but it isn't one I recognize.

I quickly search the downloaded apps, find the overused black tile, and click on it before getting blocked by a password.

Well shit.

I guess we are taking his phone now too. I quickly search his body, but he has no weapons, and his wallet has only a few cards, his ID, which verified the information we already know, and an old photograph of a young woman that appears to be a few decades old. I snap a photo of the picture and place the wallet back into his pocket.

"Where are we at, Pres? We are running out of time!" I ask before switching to the radio for a status report from outside and downstairs. All posts return as clear, and my eyes return to Presley pulling a couple of USB drives out of the desk drawers.

"He has a part of the security code moved to an external device. I need to find where it is so everything is clear," she responds, shoving the drives into their ports and loading the windows. "Give me another minute, and we should be all good."

I look around the office more closely now to ensure there aren't any security cameras. Aside from the large desk and computer equipment, an oversized couch sits next to the adjacent wall with a small coffee table at its front. The other side of the desk has no additional chair, and the only window has blinds and curtains, both of which are closed. There is nothing personal in this office to show me any more information about this guy, which leads me to believe this is more of a temporary situation.

"Got you!" Presley exclaims loudly before covering her mouth and turning toward me, her eyes wide with guilt. "Sorry!" she whispers aggressively. "I found it. We can go." She grabs her things before changing her mind. "Actually, give me a second. I'm going to leave him a little surprise in his system." She smirks mischievously as I move toward the door, careful not to disturb anything else. Pres is behind me a moment later, and we are ready to leave. I look over my shoulder at the guy I thought was dating our witness knowing this coincidence will be a problem.

"Wyatt and Hudson. Head back. Jake and Mason, we'll meet you at the back door. Moving now." I rattle off before quickly moving out and down the hall toward the stairs.

I hear the two wolves struggling with their binds as we pass them and head for the exit. We are down the stairs and back with the team in under a minute. The six of us exit the first floor through the same door we originally entered and hustle across the street to the parked SUVs in the loading bay. A moment after we reach the vehicles, Jess and Carter casually stroll up and climb in.

I sigh, reveling in a moment's relief. We got the encryption key and haven't lost anyone in the process. Erik and Jay pull out of the parking lot one after the other and head in two different directions when they reach the main road. A safety precaution we started months ago to ensure no one follows. I sigh, letting some anxiety go about our current predicament.

One problem down, one to go.

I pull out my cell phone and text Dante a short message.

> **Job's done. We are clear.**

Chapter 10
Bri

The annoying ringing of my alarm on my phone wakes me. My body is stiff and feels a bit like it was hit by a truck.

Thanks, alcohol.

I sigh, reaching to shut off the resounding noise rolling my ankles and stretching my legs under my covers, pointing my toes and lifting my arms over my head as I yawn. Today is going to suck.

Damn you, Liv, for making me drink so much.

At the thought of her, I pull my attention back to my phone to see if she has texted. Opening my phone with my face ID, I click on my messages.

Safe and completely satisfied

She sent her message with a winking emoji and an eggplant.

Gross.

The phone drops onto my chest, and I pinch my fingers between my eyes, squeezing the bridge of my nose in an effort to combat the headache nestled there. I roll over and grab the water from my nightstand, pulling open the drawer to get some ibuprofen out. I'm going to need a lot of help today.

It takes me about twenty minutes to get my body up and going for the day. I shower quickly, trying and failing not to think about what I had done in this shower last night.

It may be time to start looking for someone new in Boston.

I smirk, thinking about getting out of this city and being able to make a new life for myself far away, finding someone to spend my life with, and settling down in a house with a porch where I could look at the stars and maybe even see some lightning bugs.

It isn't that I don't love Liv and Keith, but I need to find a home that doesn't constantly remind me of Sam, Elaine, or all of the houses I have moved through over the years. I'm tired of feeling the pain of my past and want to find a future that allows me to stand on my own two feet.

I dress quickly and grab my bag containing my books and laptop. I also throw on my purse before I head to the kitchen. The sun streams through the windows as I enter our living and kitchen area. Banshee lays sprawled out, basking in the rays on the living room carpet. He chooses not to acknowledge my presence which is completely fine, and I carefully step toward the fridge pulling out my last energy drink and throwing an extra water bottle in my bag for later.

Opening the cupboard, I grab a Quest protein bar for breakfast and decide to pick up some coffee on campus. Glancing at the cat's water bowl, I roll my eyes while adding some to it before gathering my keys and purse and saluting the sunning cat on my way out the door.

Campus isn't as crowded as it usually is on the weekdays. Most students are out enjoying the temperate weather before it gets especially frigid. Well, for Vegas, anyway. I have on a pair of soft black leggings and an oversized blue hoodie that I borrowed from Keith several years ago.

Borrowed...Stole...

It is mine now and is my favorite to wear when I study because the library is always so over-air-conditioned. His extra-large frame is probably better suited for it than my medium one, but I love its oversized feel and its ability to carry all my snacks.

As I cross the campus, my gaze slides over the few students hanging around outside, throwing a football back and forth, while others are laughing under one of the trees on the edge of the grassy area. I take the final bite of my protein bar and stroll up to the coffee cart, one of my only splurges since attending UNLV.

I step into the line while wiping my hand on my leggings and pulling out my phone. I send a quick text to Keith, checking in to make sure he is all good since I haven't heard from him since he left Liv's party last night. It is only a moment waiting before I feel eyes on me again. Hairs stand up at the base of my neck, and my heart rate accelerates while I try to appear nonchalant. I pull on my laptop bag, slightly turning my head to locate the source of the attention. It is then I see him.

My heart skips at the sight. He is no longer in his all-black bad boy attire and is wearing a pair of low-slung, tight blue joggers with a white tank top that shows off all the tattoos covering his chest, arms, and shoulders. He has a backpack over both of his shoulders and is wearing sunglasses, but I would recognize him anywhere. His focus doesn't appear to be on me as he slowly strolls through the quad.

Where did you come from? How come I have never noticed you before?

A throat clearing behind me pulls me out of the trance that seeing him had placed me in. The line had moved up while I zoned out, and it was almost my turn to order.

"Sorry," I mumble, stepping to the front to wait. I casually glance over my shoulder to realize I have lost him again. Spinning quickly to see if I can locate which way he went, only to find him two people behind me in the coffee line staring at his phone. Panic sets in, and I finish my spin, cursing myself for being so obvious and hoping he hadn't noticed I had been both gawking at him earlier and looking for him now.

Imagine if he knew what he did to me in the shower last night.

A blush rises up my neck as I fixate on the memory until it is my turn to order, and I step up to the barista, Cheryl, who I know far too well.

"Hey Bri, you want your usual today?" She asks while wiping down one of the frothing stems.

"Yes, please! And can I have an extra shot? The party last night went a little wilder than I expected," I say, remembering the conga line Liv started sometime after midnight. Behind me, I faintly hear what sounds like an animal growling, and it takes everything in me to not turn around to see what it is, knowing McSteamy is somewhere behind me too.

"I heard it was wild, Jill didn't get home until late, and Mila did her walk of shame early this morning. I'll get that right out for you." She ends with a knowing smile and turns to yell to Mark, "I need a venti, triple-shot, caramel macchiato, no foam, stirred," she recites it flawlessly, giving me a wink as I throw a five into the tip jar and tap my card on the reader to pay for my drink.

I slide to the other end of the cart to wait for them to make my drink and text Liv.

> McSteamy is HERE! In the coffee line!

> NO WAY! So he does go here. I told you! Did you get his number? What did you say? Tell me every-thing.

> Of course not! I panicked and pretended he wasn't there.

> What?!? Why?

> Because he is ridiculously hot, and I'm me.

I sigh, cringing internally as I wait for her reply and wishing I had her brazen confidence from time to time. I mentioned him to her last night after being unable to find him. I even showed her the photo I had taken to see if she had seen him before. She hadn't, but it was a big university with many different majors he could have been a part of.

The three dots indicate Liv is texting me back as a hand touches my shoulder to get my attention. I jump, turning.

"They called you," McSteamy utters, his deep voice rumbling as he speaks, and he throws his chin toward the cart before slowly removing his hand from my shoulder. I feel its absence immediately and turn to look at the spot it has just been.

"Oh, thank you," I respond breathily and immediately blush with embarrassment, quickly tucking my phone into the hoodie pocket, hoping he hadn't seen the screen. I had been so distracted texting Liv that I didn't notice his approach or apparently hear my name. My eyes look up into his for a moment, and I feel the urge to pull off his sunglasses to see them better.

You don't know him, Bri!

The crimson deepens as I step over and grab a coffee collar for my cup, hands shaking a bit from my nerves. I grab my coffee and slide the cardboard covering on before thanking Mark and Cheryl and hurrying toward the library, releasing the breath I had been holding.

It takes me almost an hour to calm myself down enough to focus on my paper. I already completed the outline for it days ago, or I would still be sitting here with nothing to go on. I lean over, flipping a notebook page to double-check a fact.

I keep throwing more words into my document and hoping I have the correct information since my brain isn't cooperating.

"Excuse me," a masculine voice begins, "You're Brielle, right?" I glance up, hoping to politely tell this person I'm too busy for whatever they need when the words catch in my throat. I tense, unable to form words, looking up into the most beautiful storm-gray eyes I have ever seen. I nod, intentionally checking to ensure my mouth is closed as he continues.

"Great! I'm Cain. I'm in your Global Business Strategies class with Professor Horwin...."

"No, you aren't," I blurt, cursing myself for interrupting him. "I mean," I stumble over my words, "I'm taking Professor Horwin's class, but you aren't in it." I rephrase, looking at him in confusion.

He grins, setting his coffee down on the table, and crosses his arms over his defined chest, which immediately brings my attention to his tattoo-covered biceps.

Did this guy live in the gym? Is that an animal on his shoulder?

"Is that so?" He says, his smirk growing as he notices my attention and uncrosses his arms, grabbing the chair in front of him. "So you know my schedule better than I do, is that it?" He chuckles a bit. The sound seems foreign coming from him due to his hard exterior.

"I'm sorry, but," he cuts me off this time.

"No need to apologize. You can't be right all of the time." He states matter-of-factly and shifts his weight, sliding into the chair like this is his office before grabbing one of my notebooks and moving it closer to him, flipping through the pages casually—*the audacity.*

"No," I restate firmly, flustered to have him close, talking to me, looking at me and my things.

"You have never come to class. I would have noticed you there," I snap, pulling the notebook from his hand and swatting it away as he tries to grab it a second time.

"You would have noticed me? I'm flattered," he remarks, his grin firmly in place and his eyes lit with a fire that makes them look like the ash that burns in the embers. He slowly pulls a pack of gum from his pocket and slides out a single piece, unwrapping it before throwing it into his mouth. My attention remains wholly entranced in his motions.

"That's not what I meant." I'm completely flustered, tomato red now, and trying to regain control of my emotions which have decided that now is an excellent time to go haywire. I sigh deeply, steeling my resolve.

"What can I do for you?"

"I thought you would never ask," he responds, tipping his head. The look on his face turns sexual as his eyes sweep my body with desire before they meet mine again, and he shakes his head as if trying to focus.

"I have been taking Professor Horwin's class virtually due to some unexpected travel I had to complete." He looks down, quickly regaining the notebook as he continues. "Because of this, I have fallen a bit behind, and he recommended you as an option for a possible tutor to get me back on track." He finishes pulling his eyes back up to mine and throwing on a million-dollar smile that doesn't quite reach his eyes.

"No," I respond firmly, not bothering to explain myself, and begin typing on my laptop again, not attempting to recover the stolen notebook a second time.

"No?" he repeats, sounding thoroughly confused, as if this may have been the first time someone who looked like him had ever heard the word.

"But you haven't even heard what's in it for you yet," he announces, changing tactics and turning into the ultimate salesman, "and before you say no again, which it sounds like you're about to do, hear me out." He is rambling a bit now as if knocked off his game, and the thought of that brings me more joy than it should. My eyes slide back over to him.

"I'm sure you can flirt your way into another tutor. I'm not interested," I deadpan resolutely. Proud to be standing up for myself for a change.

"I don't want another tutor," he growls the words, the rumble going straight to my core, and I can see he is battling to keep his anger down; his hands are clenching and unclenching. There is desperation on his face, and I pause as I can almost see the gears turning as he looks for another compelling argument.

"Professor Horwin said you're the best in the class. I need the best." He pauses as my eyes meet his, and his voice drops so I can barely hear him, which has me leaning closer to him without even realizing it. I see the defeat in his eyes for only a moment before he covers it with determination. Staring right into my soul, he whispers, "I need you, Brielle. Please."

I don't think I've ever been wetter than I am now. With his eyes on me, the words rolling off his lips take me back to my shower and a vivid self-made memory of his hands between my thighs. I clench my legs together, fighting my baser instincts while I bite my lip to focus on the pain, centering myself in this reality. He closes his eyes, inhaling deeply as if he can smell how much I want him.

Don't be ridiculous! He is probably just trying to calm down from how rude you were!

Embarrassment floods me as I struggle to think. I grab my coffee and take a long drink, buying myself a few precious moments.

"Look, I get that you need help. I just can't be the person to do that for you. I don't have the time. I work full-time and have my classes and interviews for jobs after graduation. Hell, I have two papers to finish today that you are keeping me from working on. I already have too many balls I'm juggling. I can't add another one." I finish trying to add conviction to my voice.

I am busy and don't have time for one more thing. Today I'm going to have a backbone. I lift my chin and look at the hard lines on his face and his firmly set jawline. He throws me a smile that says he has just won something.

"I thought you might say that," he responds, bravado returning to his posture. "I spoke with the Professor before coming here, and he told me he is willing to extend your deadlines for the next few weeks while you get me caught up. So those papers," he points to my laptop and notebooks, "aren't due until the end of the term. Additionally, I'll pay you a thousand dollars a week." He pauses, letting that number settle in before continuing. "Come on, Brielle. I'm a quick study, and hanging out with me couldn't possibly be so bad." He drops his smile into a sexy smirk, which I assume he uses to make every girl swoon. I can't lie; it was kind of working on me too.

Stop that!

I take a breath and lean back, considering his proposal. There were five weeks left until the final exams. Five thousand dollars would go a long way toward getting me to Boston, Knoxville, or Charlotte. I flip through my notes, looking for course requirements to see what work I have remaining in my classes.

Three papers in Global Business Strategies, including the two I'm working on, one essay and a presentation in International Marketing through Social Media, and two tests and a group project with a demonstration in Brand Strategy and Positioning. It isn't as much work as anticipated, considering I had taken five classes a semester leading up to this one to get as many credits as possible.

I pull open my phone to look through my work schedule as he sits patiently, watching me consider. He doesn't try to speak or throw anything else my way. He just lets me work through his offer. His gaze is intense, and I get the feeling he is memorizing me.

My calendar shows I have three shifts this week, four next week, and four the week after, leading into my vacation time, which corresponds with my birthday. That takes me right into study time for finals, giving me time to avoid being overwhelmed.

"Ok, let's say I agree, and I'm not saying I am. How often do you expect me to meet with you, and for how long?"

He doesn't even pause before responding.

"Every day."

I pull back, shock evident on my face.

"You can't possibly believe I have enough time to tutor you every day?"

Who does this guy think he is?

"Ok then, Firefly, give me a counteroffer." He suggests raising an eyebrow and crossing his arms again as he leans back in the chair, looking less distressed than he had moments ago.

"Firefly?" I question, wondering where the nickname came from, along with the presumption he had to give me one at all.

Not that I hated the sound of it rolling off his tongue. Don't think about his tongue!

"Ya, Firefly." he points to the doodle on the notebook page in front of me and then moves to lean over the table. His hands grab my wrist with more tenderness than I would have expected from someone with his size and strength, and he slowly slides the sleeve on the hoodie up, exposing my forearm and the small watercolor tattoo I had gotten for Sammy when I turned eighteen.

How the fuck?

I inhale audibly, partly because his touch is warm and my body responds in ways I can't control and partly because I feel exposed. His eyes trace the veins in my arm slowly until they lock onto mine; his hand travels delicately to my chin.

Oh my God, he is going to kiss me.

I panic, my heart racing, and I begin to wonder what it would feel like if I let him.

You don't even know him, Bri!

My body doesn't agree with that thought, and my lips part in anticipation as I tip my head back slightly, never breaking from his stare.

"Not to mention, these eyes of yours seem kissed with flames of orange, so it seemed fitting, Firefly." He taunts quietly, the sound barely loud enough for me to hear. His eyes flick to my lips momentarily before mine close, leaning in slightly in anticipation.

He pulls away, and my body feels the absence of his heat and minty smell. I open my eyes in surprise.

You idiot. He doesn't want to kiss you. He wants you to tutor him.

My crimson blush returns, bringing with it my anger. Not at him, but at me for thinking someone who looks like he does would be interested in someone who looks like I do.

I am perfectly ordinary. I can effortlessly blend into the background with my mousy brown hair, plain brown eyes, and a height that takes me out of the running to be a model while making me too tall to really be allowed to wear a solid heel. My weight fluctuates, occasionally carrying extra curves through my hips and thighs, but never have I been confused for someone dainty or petite.

Freckles splatter my face, which never looks sun-kissed or dewy, but instead embarrassingly paints itself tomato red at every opportunity. Top that off with a powerfully crafted inability to be carefree like so many others my age, and I fall right out of the running to be pursued by a man whose features should be memorialized in stone and placed in a museum.

"It's a lightning bug," I reply, clearing my throat and pulling my sleeve back into place.

"I want two thousand a week, and I can't do every day. It isn't feasible with my schedule. I can do four days a week, two hours per session." I counter, sitting up straighter, awaiting his response.

Was that too much? Had I pushed it?

He doesn't seem like a guy with tons of money, but what did I know? He could pad my savings if he wanted me to make time for him.

"Every day. That's non-negotiable. I'm willing to work around your schedule, filling hours before or after your classes and work, but I get you every day." His response sounds more intimate than I expect due to the proximity of his body, which never retreated.

He wants me every day.

I must remember that he needs my brain and my services, not my body, despite how much my body seemed to be volunteering as tribute.

Calm down. He is a means to an end.

"Every day for at least two hours will cost you more," I state, trying to get him to walk away from this crazy deal.

"Try me," he retorts, not looking fazed by the talk of thousands of dollars flying around.

"Three thousand, and you get me two hours every day" My confidence falters as I think about the fifteen thousand dollars, no one would pay that for a five-week tutor.

"I'll give you five grand, and I get to have you as much as I need, respecting your class and work schedule, of course." He offers, looking rather amused by the back and forth.

"Deal," I spout before I can even rationalize that kind of money, and I continue speaking as my logical side catches up with my hormones, "But I want there to be ground rules. First, you flake on a session, and it is over. I won't waste my time waiting for you to grace me with your presence. Second, I'm your tutor, nothing more. I'm not a puppet or paid escort going to events with you. If you can't accept those terms, I'm out," I finish, huffing a little at the end, which gives away how flustered he and his deal are making me.

"If we agree on a session, I'll be there. Additionally, if I request a session outside of your scheduled conflicts, you'll show up regardless of what other things you have planned." His eyebrows crease as he concentrates while waiting for my response.

The jokes on him, I don't have a social life, what would I need to cancel? Studying while Liv watches serial killer documentaries? Listening to Keith try and untangle some bug in his code while I read a book? Grocery shopping? Ha!

I stick my hand out in a gesture of good faith before stating, "I want it in writing. We start tomorrow. I can meet you after *our* ten o'clock class and work with you until one. Then I have to get ready for work. I'll send you a list of my prescheduled work and school obligations, so you can schedule our future sessions as you would like around them."

"Why can't we start today?" He asks, confused and looking around before continuing, "We're already here." His tone aims to challenge my decision, and I know he is baiting me.

Talk about a guy who is used to getting his way.

"Because I have no contract to sign, I'll use my last bit of free time to finish these essays." I throw back at him pointedly before getting back to my work.

"But you don't have to turn those in for weeks." He appears perplexed that I would want to complete work when I don't have to.

He must have been born with a silver spoon in his mouth with that work ethic. He won't last a week.

"I can work on it now or work on it later. I already planned today for these to be done. Delaying them postpones the work I'll have to do anyway, inevitably putting me further behind, which I don't need, especially since I just took on Nathan Scott as a student." I point out, rolling my eyes, knowing he would miss the OTH reference.

"My name is Cain, not Nathan. Cain Mingan." He spits out, clearly offended, thinking I forgot his name.

I imagine no one forgot his name. Not when he looked like that.

My eyes raise to meet his as I smirk, feeling like I finally had the upper hand, liking the feeling of rattling him, even if just for a moment.

"Aww, you get all cute when you're mad. Calm down, Candy Cain. I didn't forget your name. It was a reference to a show I used to watch." I laugh a bit as I explain, shaking my head. "Now, would you go? I need to focus, and you are a distraction." I wave my arm, shooing him away as I try again to continue my paper. He stands up, adjusting the backpack straps on his shoulders, and grabs his coffee cup, his eyes drinking me in for a moment before he leaves.

"See you tomorrow, Firefly." He promises, a half grin on his mouth as he walks toward the elevator. I attempt and subsequently fail not to watch his retreating backside.

"Not if I see you first," I mumble, under my breath, knowing his distance prevents him from hearing me recite the corny line. I drop my head into my hands.

What the fuck did I get myself into?

Chapter 11
Bri

"Shut the fuck up!" Liv shouts for the tenth time since I arrive home and tell her about my day. We are holding planks in the living room, finishing up a forty-five-minute full-body HIIT workout which wasn't as bad as the butt-and-thigh-focused routine we had on Friday, but I still know I will be sore tomorrow.

Not the walking funny I was hoping for.

"Can you please stop saying that? It makes me feel a hundred times worse about the whole thing. What the fuck was I thinking? I can't do this. I couldn't even sit with him for ten minutes without having three sexual fantasies, thinking he would kiss me, and completely embarrassing myself a handful of times. How will I make it through hours of looking at his face?" I rant, my breath coming out in grunts as I struggle through the last few seconds of the hold.

"Time," Liv calls at last, and we both fall to the carpet, entirely spent, breath huffing out of us. "Tell me, why isn't he having someone else tutor him for free? I mean, no offense to you, Bri; you're brilliant. Still, you aren't exactly walking around with a banner advertising your services," She asks, honestly concerned but with a curious sparkle in her eyes as she tries to picture the scene.

"No idea," I pant, flipping over to lay on my back, sweat coating me and causing my hair to stick to my forehead where it escaped from the bun. "He says my professor pointed him to me, which is strange since I didn't even know Professor Horwin knew who I was. I mean, yes, I have an A in that class, but there are almost fifty of us." I reach for my water, thinking about that information as I take a long swig.

"Well, I see this going one of two ways." She starts while getting up and heading to the kitchen. "One, he flakes on your first meet-up, and you don't have to worry about doing any of it. Or there is option two, he is amazing, and you two fall in love over your shared passions for global marketing strategies and have little business school babies, which you can spoil with all of his money." Her gusto as she finishes makes me laugh out loud.

"Liv, there is no way I could end up with an arrogant, entitled, self-righteous asshole like him." I retort, picturing his face as it fell into a frown today when he thought I had refused him.

"She doth protest too much," Liv giggles as she pulls out a pan and begins to make us an egg-white scramble for dinner.

God bless her energy levels.

"I'm serious, Liv. He may be a literal walking wet dream, but he is so pushy and intrusive, and he made me seem rude, which we both know I'm not!" I argue while tenderly walking to the table to wait for my food.

"That I can say without question. In fact, often you are too nice. I like that you have a bit of backbone with him. Maybe he will be good for you." She turns, giving me a give-it-a-shot shrug as my phone pings, alerting me to a new email. I pull my phone from the small leg pocket of my olive green workout leggings, thinking that I hadn't heard back from Keith since I messaged him earlier this afternoon. I make a mental note to call him tomorrow if he isn't on shift when I am and open the notification. I find an email from Cain with a document containing our contract. I read the included message.

Hey Firefly,

Attached is the contract outlining the agreement we came to today, with a small addition I took the liberty of adding. Additionally, I have included a schedule for our first week working together that I hope you will find acceptable. Please respond with the signed documentation in addition to your preferred banking or cash app information, and I will see you at ten.

Respectfully yours,

Candy Cain

XX

> PS. I looked up the Nathan Scott character, and I must tell you that I have very limited basketball skills.
>
> PPS. I need your phone number so we can stay in contact should anything come up last minute.
>
> PPPS. Why are you still reading this instead of signing the papers?

I laugh a little at his final remarks causing Liv to look over at me. I shake my head to let her know it is nothing and refocus on the email.

So he does have a sense of humor. That I can work with.

I click open the document, noticing immediately how official it looks.

This guy spent some time on this—points for effort.

I scan through, noting the key points I asked for and the one he added. Underneath the three stipulations we had set forth is an additional topic that hadn't been covered.

Line item 4: All items addressed with the above signing parties are confidential and cannot be discussed with any external parties without prior consent.

He had added a non-disclosure agreement to our tutoring contract.

Why would we need that? What could we cover that would require such measures?

I lean back in my chair, brows drawn together in concentration.

"What does it say?" Liv asks, causing me to jump as I realize she is standing right next to me, sliding a plate down onto the table that smells like heaven.

"He added an NDA to our contract," I respond, still baffled that he felt we would need one.

"I imagine that would be pretty standard in most contracts. Maybe he doesn't want anyone to know he needed help or required tutoring. Or maybe he has a filthy rich family and will lose his inheritance if they find out he couldn't finish school without help. Or maybe, he's a secret mafia boss, and it may come up when you're together, and this NDA means you wouldn't be able to testify against him." Liv rattles off with a completely straight face.

Someone had been watching too many crime shows.

I snort. "Don't be ridiculous," I say, taking a big bite of my eggs and moaning before continuing. "It's probably just something standard on the contract template he used," I explain, trying to convince myself as much as Liv.

What have I got to hide?

I think flippantly before remembering the video I took two days ago.

Well, I will just have to keep that bit to myself.

After finishing my dinner, I thank Liv profusely for making it. She waves off the appreciation and continues with her show as I head into my room to shower and go to bed. My brain checked out early today. Not only had it taken me twice as long to complete my essays because Mr. I'm Too Sexy For My Everything decided to crash my library session, but I was missing one of my notebooks. Thinking back, I remembered to bring it with me because it had some information I needed that instead had to be looked up.

Venturing into my bathroom, I give my shower an evil glare and mentally threaten it.

Tonight will be all business, damn it. No sexy Cain. No world-shattering orgasms. Just water and soap!

Holding to my resolve, I get my teeth brushed and shower with only a tiny memory flash of Cain's eyes on mine as he licks his lips before I can snap out of it.

Damn, if he wasn't delicious looking.

As punishment for my sexy thoughts, I dress in my most un-flattering pajamas and return to my room. I pull my laptop into my bed, open the contract email again, and reread his message with a dopey smile. I electronically sign it and place a copy on my hard drive. Then, I see the second document, which hadn't shown up on my phone, and open it as well. It is a detailed calendar of the upcoming week with color-coordinated blocks showing my classes in blue, my work hours in purple, and burnt orange my tutoring sessions with him.

Aww, he color codes. Don't think I didn't notice the color choice for our time together.

I shake my head, disregarding that thought altogether.

There is no way he thought about it that much.

The schedule had an obscene amount of orange.

Firefly Schedule Week 1

	Day	Start Time	End Time	Activity
1.	Monday	10:00 AM	11:30 AM	Class A
2.	Monday	11:30 AM	1:30 PM	Tutoring
3.	Monday	1:30 PM	2:00 PM	Prep for Work
4.	Monday	2:30 PM	11:00 PM	Work
5.	Tuesday	11:00 AM	1:00 PM	Class B
6.	Tuesday	1:00 PM	2:45 PM	Tutoring
7.	Tuesday	3:00 PM	5:00 PM	Class C
8.	Tuesday	5:00 PM	8:00 PM	Tutoring
9.	Tuesday	8:00 PM	10:00 PM	Studying
10.	Wednesday	10:00 AM	11:30 AM	Class A
11.	Wednesday	11:30 AM	1:30 PM	Tutoring
12.	Wednesday	1:30 PM	2:00 PM	Prep for Work
13.	Wednesday	2:30 PM	11:00 PM	Work
14.	Thursday	11:00 AM	1:00 PM	Class B
15.	Thursday	1:00 PM	2:45 PM	Tutoring
16.	Thursday	3:00 PM	5:00 PM	Class C
17.	Thursday	5:00 PM	8:00 PM	Tutoring
18.	Thursday	8:00 PM	10:00 PM	Studying
19.	Friday	10:00 AM	4:00 PM	Tutoring
20.	Friday	4:00 PM	8:00 PM	Tutoring
21.	Saturday	10:30 AM	1:30 PM	Tutoring
22.	Saturday	1:30 PM	2:00 PM	Prep for Work
23.	Saturday	2:30 PM	11:00 PM	Work
24.	Sunday	10:00 AM	12:00 PM	Studying
25.	Sunday	12:00 PM	10:00 PM	Tutoring

I look forward to hearing your suggestions.

XXX

The new and improved Nathan Scott

I sit there slack-jawed as I count the hours he set aside for tutoring.

Ten hours on Friday and Sunday?!? What did he think I was a machine?

All totaled, he wants thirty-five and a half hours. It is almost a full-time job! On top of the twenty-four hours I'm doing my actual job, and the eleven hours of classes I have to attend. These totals don't even include getting any outside reading or work done.

I type up an email reply to him with a heavily revised copy of his outrageous schedule and attach the signed document.

> Cain,
>
> I would call you Candy Cain, but as your schedule shows you have lost your ability to be sweet, I will leave it at that. I have attached the signed contract, NDA included. I have also sent back the revised schedule for you to peruse at your leisure.
>
> Please be advised that I'm a human, not a machine. No tutoring session over three hours will give you any benefit. Don't believe me? Look it up. I have changed the tutoring times to reflect a more balanced ability to teach you what you have missed.
>
> Disrespectfully my own,
>
> *Firefly*

> *PS. Try to remember I have a life that doesn't include you.*
>
> *PPS. I included the payment information and phone number in the signed contract.*
>
> *PPPS. Nathan Scott is a legend; not sure you can measure up.*
>
> *PPPPS. Why are YOU still reading this?*

By the end of the message, I'm pounding the keys on my laptop in anger at his audacity.

Almost thirty-six hours the first week? He is nuts.

I slam the laptop closed with an enthusiasm which makes me feel a bit better, and place it back into my bag only to remember my lost notebook and look through my desk area to see if it has fallen out.

Maybe it was in the car.

Absently I add looking for it to my to-do list for tomorrow before crawling back into bed.

After adding an alarm on my phone for nine to give me time to get ready and wake up before my day begins, I set my phone on my nightstand to charge for the night. Almost instantly, it dings with an incoming text message. Assuming it is Liv reminding me to grocery shop tomorrow, I pick it up and flip it open, only to find an unknown number flash across the screen.

> **Thanks for getting the contract back so quickly, Firefly.**

I stare at the text for a long moment before fully processing it from Cain, remembering that he now has my number.

> I thought you needed my number for emergency schedule changes, not waking me up in the middle of the night.

He hadn't woken me up, but he didn't need to know that. I quickly save his number before he responds.

> My apologies. I assumed since you sent over the documents this late that you were still up and may want to negotiate some of your rather drastic changes

> They aren't drastic! They are necessary!

> Wow, two exclamation marks. Now I'm thoroughly convinced

I can almost hear him laughing at me as I read his sarcastic words.

Ok, buddy, you want to go?

> Since you are obviously ignorant of what average, everyday people do in a week, let me educate you. I must: Eat. Shower. Grocery shop. Exercise. Travel from one event to another. Do laundry. Feed the damn cat. And occasionally unwind and relax. None of which I have time for with your crazy schedule.

> So if I'm paying you to eat, shower, exercise, and unwind, does that mean I'm allowed to join you in those pursuits? I do like to see that I'm getting my money's worth.

He counters and includes a devil emoji to emphasize his point.

I'm pretty sure I'm fanning myself without realizing it.

He is flirting with me... He wants to shower with me...

Suddenly I feel out of breath and overheated in a way I wasn't moments ago. Never in my life had I responded to a man on such a visceral level.

I guess this is what they mean when they say a bitch in heat.

One part of me is panting over the idea of him wanting me naked, and another part is seething at his nerve to think he is entitled to my body because he is paying for my time. Responding, my thumbs fly over my screen, hitting them like the extra effort will show through in the message I send.

> I'm not a hooker! At no time did I agree to sell MYSELF to you. TUTORING. That's what I agreed to offer. My KNOWLEDGE and EXPERTISE.

> Oh, I'm very well aware, Firefly. I'm simply offering to supplement our time with some of MY knowledge and expertise.

I sit there gobsmacked, my mouth wide open, staring at the message and the winking face that accompanies it. Unsure of what he is insinuating, and entirely too chicken to ask him to clarify what HIS expertise might include.

I can think of a few things I would love for him to educate me on, like the size of his...

Shutting the thought out as I feel my pulse beating between my thighs.

> **As I recall, no one asked for or is paying you for your knowledge OR expertise in whatever dirty activities you are hinting at.**

> **Dirty activities? Little Firefly, where is your head tonight? I happen to be very knowledgeable in the gym, an expert at folding laundry, and exceptional at ordering food. Not to mention how helpful I am at getting others to unwind.**

Internally flustered and practically screaming into my pillow to keep from alerting Liv to the madness of our exchange, as APPARENTLY I'm no longer even allowed to talk to her about it, I can't help but laugh at his brazen attempt to make me seem like the one with the dirty mind.

> **I'm not even going to entertain that. If you have an issue with the revisions, I would happily listen to your new concerns tomorrow during our SCHEDULED time together.**

My fingers end by sending an eye roll emoji, a sleeping emoji, and a skull and crossbones emoji for good measure.

> **Can't wait.**

Oh, I bet you can't.

Rolling over to place my phone back down, I try to force myself to go to sleep, all the while knowing as riled up as he has made me, it will be hours before rest will find me.

Game on if he wants to pretend he isn't flirting with me. The slightly inappropriate outfit, coincidental. Unintentional touching, whoops. Double talk and innuendo; count me in. You don't know who you are messing with, Mr. Mingan.

You've met your match.

Chapter 12

Cain

E arly the following day, I wake wanting to run on two feet before starting the day. It would be unwise to bring out my wolf, knowing he'll take me straight to her house and probably try to break his way through the door.

She's our Mate.

He's been pulling me toward her since he recognized her scent, and as much as I hate to admit it, I'm getting tired of fighting him about it. I want to be near her too. This feeling of needing someone is such a drastic change for me. I spend most of my life seeking solitude over the company of others, and while I enjoy time with my pack and Dante, I have never felt like I need them to be content. Brielle makes me feel like life without her is meaningless. I barely know her, and already, the emptiness I feel when I'm away from her is too much.

I've barely slept the last two nights and need to get my head straight before I meet with her today. My mood is irritable and overbearing on a good day; being sleep deprived, horny, and unable to touch her while in her presence is a recipe for disaster. What is Dante thinking? How can I possibly do this job?

He isn't thinking anything because he doesn't understand the gravity of the whole damn scenario.

Keeping something this big from my best friend is excruciating, but I have no idea how to handle something of this magnitude. This information is life-altering, and I'm not ready to be pushed into a decision. I just want to see her, get to know her, and find out if the fates are correct in their choice.

What if I'm not ready? What if she rejects this life or me?

The thought alone gives me a pit in my stomach, causing me to slow down my stride. I have a plan. Spend every minute with her, and ensure she keeps our secret. It isn't a solid well-thought-out plan, but I don't have anything else. I hate having to do it under the guise that I need tutoring for a class that was already completed four years ago while working on my Business Degree with Dante to solidify our front as a legitimate company. The only difference is I focused on the entrepreneurial side instead of the marketing as Brielle was doing.

Worse than lying to her about needing tutoring is having to pay her to be around me. Initially, I had planned to ask her out, but every time I tried the words, I sounded like an idiot. Presley was right. Erik was the one with the game. I tended to rely far too much on my looks and put minimal effort into getting women.

At six foot two, two hundred ten pounds of lean muscle with stormy gray eyes, even saying I put in a little effort is a lie. I put in none. Zero. If I want to get laid, I spend a minute looking for someone hot and nod to the back. Done-deal. Fucking is a means to an end with them, and when I finish, I leave. Alone.

Instinctively I know that none of that would work with my Firefly. She is feisty and combative and tried to brush me off multiple times. Her lack of interest in me actually makes me want to work harder. She has to be at least a little interested, or she wouldn't have taken the picture, but the minute I try to turn on any charm like I have seen Erik do a million times, it is as if her bullshit meter goes off, and she is less than impressed with my effort.

What strikes me most are the few moments I had when she seemed to be reading me. When I started to think I wasn't going to be able to convince her at all, she seemed the most open to it. So that gave me my new plan. Be as authentic as I can while lying to her face about why we were spending time together, convince her to provide me with all the copies of the video, and hope she can forgive me later.

Seeing her respond to me last night while I texted her gave me hope. While she may have been coy and abrasive in her messages, she was anything but in her facial expressions. Watching her from the hidden camera we placed in her room gave me the other half of the story. It revealed her attraction to me underneath all of the hostility. She even lied about falling asleep when she hadn't even tried lying down.

I have enough respect for her privacy to ensure she had gotten dressed before watching her but, man, did it take everything in me not to have that feed on her every minute of the day.

I'm not a sick stalker. I'm her Mate. She is Mine.

So today, I want to change her mind about me. Today, I want her to admit to herself that she might like the idea of being more than my tutor.

I finish my run and head back to my apartment. It isn't much. A two-bedroom unit just under the penthouse floor that Dante inhabits. It has a seventy-inch television, an oversized couch, and a few end tables. It is modern and functional and looks every bit like a single man decorated it. At least, that is what my mom tells me every time she visits and tries to convince me to add a painting, throw pillow, or a rug to the space. She is always trying to domesticate me, which makes no sense when she chooses to live in an RV and travel the United States year-round.

Putting down roots wasn't her or my dad's thing. After they retired from working for the pack, when dad lost his best friend and Alpha in one fell swoop, they only come back for holidays or my birthday. The last update I got, they are somewhere in Montana enjoying the wide-open spaces.

Walking down the hallway to my bedroom, I peel my sweat-soaked t-shirt off, before launching it at my hamper and continuing into the ensuite to start the shower. I need to get into a mental space where I can be present in my time with Brielle and not spend every minute trying to claim her.

My cock is already throbbing from the beatings I gave it in the last twenty-four hours. It took getting myself off four times before I realized my body wanted the real thing and wouldn't settle for anything else. I was beginning to feel like a pubescent teen again, jerking off over and over and having it just pop right back up.

Now is so not the time to be thinking with our dick.

I shower quickly, not giving my cock the attention it so clearly desires, and get dressed for my study session. Opting for black jeans and a belt to serve as a vice for my dick and hoping it'll camouflage my apparent need for her, I top it with a light gray t-shirt and some Nike Jordans. I shave to remove the five-o'clock shadow, which takes me no time to grow out, and spray on my YSL cologne for good measure.

Maybe the goal here should be making her want me as much as I need her.

Exiting my apartment, I grab my wallet, the keys to Dante's car, and the stolen notebook I had flipped through thoroughly last night, looking for clues or insight into my girl. Unfortunately, besides a few rather well-drawn doodles, the entire thing was full of class notes.

Before we study, I can sneak it into her bag today. In an effort to cover my tracks, I grab a few decoy notebooks and leave the apartment just after nine, texting Dante to let him know my plans for the day.

> **Headed to our witness's class. Then I have a date with her in the library before she heads to work. Taking your Vette. I can't have her linking me to the video yet with another Tahoe sighting.**

Sending it off while remembering how close we had gotten to getting caught with Lucas tailing her home from the party the other night. If we hadn't had access to her messages, we never would have known she saw him and knew she saw the car following her. Thankfully, she had texted her roommate, allowing us time to call him off and send someone else to the apartment in his place. Not that we needed a physical person there. With all the cameras, the phone tap, and the GPS tracker on her car, we had the place covered, but technology could fail; our guys didn't. My phone dings, alerting me to Dante's response.

> **Glad to hear it. Don't fuck this up. Marlo is too far up our ass right now to be fighting wars on two fronts**

> **I can handle one girl, D**

> **Let's hope so. Knight's game tonight?**

> **Ya. I'll be over by puck drop**

I throw my phone into my pocket, glad to be able to hang out with my friend tonight instead of my Alpha. It is hard on Dante to lead us all and still try to be twenty-seven. He has an entire company, a pack, and a sister to take care of, which I know gives him more stress than he could have imagined when he took over.

Sometimes I wish we had taken the Europe trip we planned the summer his dad died in the accident. At least then, Dante would have had time to live his life with no one depending on him, but with the pack in turmoil, he had needed to stay, establish himself as its new leader and begin the political bullshit that came along with it.

When I get to campus, I head straight for the coffee cart, hoping to use bribery to my advantage after memorizing my Firefly's order yesterday. According to her bank statements,

Thank you, Presley, for unfettered access to my girl's life.

She uses the coffee cart sparingly as a reward for studying or logging hours in the library. The same barista is working today as I start my order.

"Hey there, handsome, another dark roast black today, Cain? Is it? She spouts off absent-mindedly, grabbing for a cup.

"How do you memorize everyone's order?" I ask, surprised by the apparent talent while glancing at her name tag to try and remember her name and mentally thinking back to be sure I hadn't slept with her. Cheryl. She is pretty with big brown eyes and short pixie brown hair. She has large boobs and a matching ass that normally would have caught my attention, but since finding my Mate, no one even remotely piques my interest.

I definitely hadn't slept with her.

The realization relieves me.

"Only the ones who look like you, baby," she flirts, batting her eyelashes more than necessary to send the message while continuing to write my order on the large cup. "That'll be $5.50," she rattles off and turns to make my drink.

"Actually, I was hoping to get a second drink as well," I state and see the glint in her eyes fade as she takes in my lack of a companion.

"Of course, Sugar, grabbing something for a girlfriend?" She asks, clearly fishing for information.

"Something like that. Can I get a large caramel macchiato with no foam, stirred?" I list off, hoping I remembered it correctly. She pauses a moment eyeing me as she mentally puts together who the extra drink is for.

"I'll get those right out for you," she finishes, forcing a polite smile that doesn't quite reach her eyes in the same way, but I can see the wheels turning.

Once I grab the two drinks, I thank her and head for Beam Hall for the ten o'clock lecture. As I enter the building, I casually gaze at the reflective windows trying to blend as much as possible. Turning down the first opening on the right, I make my way to the classroom.

At the top of the lecture hall, I pause, scanning the area for Brielle's signature messy bun, and come up short.

There is no way she would be late for class. She's too much of a goody two shoes to be tardy.

I check the time on my phone, noting it is still seven minutes until the start time.

The class is rather crowded, with more than forty people scattered throughout the hall. I'm grateful to have lied using a course with enough students to pop in without the professor's notice.

We haven't made it through the class just yet.

It is then that I spot her. She is seated in the middle of the room, just off the central aisle.

Funny, I had you pegged for a front-of-the-class girl. Full of surprises.

Her hair is down in full wavy curls. She is wearing a low-cut orange crop top that shows off her cleavage and pierced belly button. Her pale, freckled legs are beautifully on display in her cut-off jean shorts accompanied by a pair of checkered vans.

Holy fuck!

My mouth waters at the thought of licking my way up those long porcelain legs to where they met in the middle.

Damn it, get it together.

I shake my head, trying to clear the thoughts of taking her right here in the middle of class while mentally trying to yell at my cock to stand down as I grow hard at the mere sight of her.

Scanning the area around her out of habit, ready to fight anyone too close, I find she is taking up the three seats around her. She has it set up almost like a self-imposed barrier between her and everyone else in the class.

Good girl, no one gets close to you but me.

Straightening my spine, I walk confidently down the middle aisle, notebooks under my arm, readjusting the coffees into one hand as I move her oversized bag from the edge seat and plant myself in it before she can utter a rebuttal.

"What the.." she starts to say, looking up confused and half awake as she pulls the AirPod from her ear, a pop country hit playing.

"Good morning, Firefly," I state cheerfully, leaning over to keep my voice down while sliding the coffee in front of her.

"Umm... is this for me?" she asks, eyeing it like it contains poison.

"Yep!" I assure her my voice is a little peppier than I intend as I wait for her to take it.

Too much, dial it back.

I shift forward in my seat, going for causal as I set her bag beside me and simultaneously slip the stolen notebook back into its intended place.

"You didn't need to get me anything," she pauses, looking a bit nervous, "and while I appreciate it, I don't drink regular coffee. I have a weirdly specific way of ordering coffee, so it tastes nothing like coffee," she explains, her face apologetic as she pushes it back toward me without trying it or thanking me.

"I imagine Cheryl did just fine remembering your order," I respond sternly while offering her a believable lie and lounge back in my seat, throwing my arm over the back of hers. Her eyes widen in surprise before carefully grabbing the cup, removing the lid, and inhaling deeply. She closes her lids and moans. I don't think I have ever heard a sexier sound, and neither had my cock, which strains painfully against my belt. I try to adjust myself without drawing her attention.

"It's perfect," she remarks after taking a long sip and letting her head fall back as she enjoys it. My eyes trail the line from her jaw down her neck appreciatively and land on her slowly rising breasts.

"Least I could do after waking you up last night," I say seductively, my eyes flicking back up to hers, so I don't get caught staring. She looks over at me, heat filling her gaze as she flushes pink up that delectable neck. The golden flecks in her eyes are more pronounced today with the shirt she has on. I lean closer to her, tucking a rogue strand of hair behind her ear before whispering, "I would hate to think you lost any sleep because of me."

I shift my weight back as I see her pulse increase and hear her breath hitch. My focus slides from her to the older gentleman setting up his laptop at the front of the room. I grab my decoy notebook from its place on the floor at my feet, ready to look like an excellent student.

Brielle eyes me as I open it to the first blank page, just as I realize I have absolutely nothing to write with.

Fuck I forgot a pen.

A small giggle to my left tells me she also noticed my lack of writing utensil. She grabs her bag and pulls out a notebook with a couple of colored pens before setting herself up and turning her attention to the professor.

Not interested in sharing Firefly. I guess I'll take what I want.

I wait until the professor begins speaking before swiping a blue pen from the far side of her desk area. Her head whips toward me, astonishment and a little anger flash, but I know she won't interrupt the lecture to get it back.

I grin at her triumphantly and turn to focus on what is being taught. I needed to take key moments from today into our tutoring session, so I didn't seem completely inept.

"You should really stop your music," I whisper twenty minutes into the lecture while the professor is helping a student with a document on their laptop, "It's distracting to those of us who are here to learn." I finish feigning a serious face and tone.

"My what?" she responds, confused, as I point to the earphones on her desk, still playing music faintly in the background. "Oh, I didn't realize they were still on. How can you even hear that?" She asks, surprised as she tries to hear them before bringing them up to her ears and back down several times to test when she can no longer listen to them.

"You know what they say about wolf hearing," I retort without thinking

Fuck!

I immediately regret the phrase and begin to scramble at what I can say to make that sound more normal.

"Actually, no. What do they say?" she asks, confusion lining her face now that she has the headphones away.

"Just that they have good hearing." I shrug noncommittally, hoping she'll think it is just an expression, and I flip intently back through the notes I have been taking along with the scribbles that occupy most of my attention on the two pages.

"Is that why you have a wolf tattoo on your shoulder? Because you have good hearing?" she asks, spinning a strand of her hair idly around her finger in a way that makes me want to wrap it around my fist as she looks up at me from her knees.

"Checking out my tattoos, were you, Firefly?" I question, turning up my flirtation to guide us away from the previous conversation. I have several pack tattoos, but the largest is my wolf which spans from my back onto my shoulder. She drags her eyes down my body in blatant perusal and shrugs one shoulder, trying to appear aloof.

"Just trying to figure out who I've gotten into bed with," she finishes and immediately flushes crimson. "With tutoring, I mean, not as if we are getting into... it's an expression. I wasn't thinking about... Oh fuck, never mind," she finishes, throwing her hands over her face to cover her growing embarrassment. I pull her hands from her face and grab her chin roughly, forcing her eyes to mine as the professor continues.

"Trust me, when you fall into my bed, you will know exactly who put you there," I promise, using every bit of self-control I have not to kiss her. This is the second time I've had to fight my instinct to claim her lips as my own.

There won't be a third.

I promise myself as I allow my attention to appear on the lecture again, but the only things I'm thinking about are all the ways I'll make Brielle mine.

Chapter 13
Bri

*G*et it the fuck together, Bri!

Mentally I chastise myself while splashing cold water on my face to cool me down. The last ninety minutes of the class had been pure torture. Cain acted sweet and friendly, and I completely embarrassed myself. In fact, I can only imagine he is back there now, trying to get the name of a different tutor.

Maybe it's for the best.

Stress is all I have felt since getting ready to come to class today. I picked my outfit specifically to try and distract him. In the end, it only made me self-conscious and cold, if I'm being honest.

This semester is supposed to be me coasting to completing my degree. I've taken fewer classes, dropped from working five days a week to three or four, and instead of feeling more at ease, I said yes to stupid McSteamy on his too-good-to-be-true deal, which is only bringing me stress and anxiety. How can I go out there and face him for the next two hours of tutoring?

Maybe I can cancel?

Think of the money... you can do this. You need this money. Even if we only make it a week. Five grand will be more than two months working at the call center.

Staring back at my reflection, I mentally give myself a pep talk. If I can think of it one week at a time, maybe I can make this thing work. After a quick fix to my face and hair, and a gentle tug on my outfit, I leave the bathroom. As I turn down the hall, I pull my phone out of my pocket, nearly dropping my purse in the process, wondering if we are meeting in the library or somewhere else when a voice sounds behind me.

"Running away from me already?" he asks, a hint of flirtation laced in his words as he grabs my bag from my shoulder like it weighs nothing and throws it across his.

"No, I was just about to text you on the location for us to study since I have to stop by the quad and grab something to eat before we begin," I answer, trying not to sound out of breath due to his proximity.

"I have a better idea. Let's take our studying on the road today. I know an excellent Mexican place just off campus, two birds, one stone, and all that. Don't worry, as it's a working lunch; it is on me, of course," he finishes with a big smile.

"I think staying on campus will be better for you to focus on the content," I say hesitantly as my stomach betrays me with a large growl.

I knew I shouldn't have skipped breakfast today.

"Your stomach and I disagree with you. Come on, we have to work out the schedule today anyway, and maybe we can try to get to know each other so you, what was it you said earlier," he looks at me with unabashed heat in his stare, "So you know who you are getting into bed with."

Even now, the embarrassment of that moment creeps back into me. I sigh, defeated.

"Fine, where are we headed? I parked off Maryland, so it'll take me some time to get back to my car, but I can meet you there," I offer, looking up at him through my lashes.

"Better idea, we can take my car. I can return you to your car when we finish so you can get ready for work," he counters, already turning us west toward the student parking without waiting for me to agree.

He steers me toward his car, which turns out to be some fancy sports car that is bright orange. Halting, my jaw drops, leaving me to gape like a fish.

"Please tell me this isn't your car," I inquire, hoping he'll tell me it is the seen-better-days jeep behind it, but knowing deep down that Mr. five thousand a week isn't driving a beat-up old off-roader.

"Technically, it's my best friend's, but I'm borrowing it. Well, I guess we are," he finishes before opening my door and waiting for me to get in.

I stand there frozen, unsure how to respond to such an ostentatious display of wealth. After a moment, my feet begin to move, one in front of the other, and I robotically sit on the seat like it is the most dangerous thing in the world.

It truly is a beautiful cage.

Cain runs around the car and jumps in. The interior is small to begin with, but with his large frame seated next to me, taking up all of the space, I feel trapped, surrounded by his smell and feeling the graze of his arm as he shifts gears. My heart rate starts to increase as we take off down the road.

His eyes glance over to me as he drives with complete competency out of the college area and off toward the east side of town. I try to distract myself by looking out the window at the city as we drive, hoping to keep tabs on where I am, but my eyes keep coming back to the interior of the car, how small it feels, how hard it would be to get out of, how unlikely I would be to survive.

"You should relax. It's an amazing ride," he comments, looking over at my hand white-knuckling the door handle.

"Oh, yeah, I'm relaxed," I spit back the blatant lie before sighing and continuing, "I just don't like riding in cars much because I was in a pretty bad accident," I explain, my heart rate escalating, my breath coming out in short pants. His eyes light up, a flash of understanding before he pulls into a parking lot. He sits there a long moment, a war happening behind his metallic irises before he turns his focus to me with nothing but sincerity in them.

"I'm so sorry. I should have asked. I just assumed since you drive every day," he rattles out, letting the words linger in an unasked question.

Surprised by his reaction to my fear, I stare at him. He had no way of knowing that I had been in a car accident that should have killed me. He had no idea I was trapped in that car for hours while they attempted to tear the door off while I floated in and out of consciousness. He had no way of knowing that that accident took the life of the only person who had ever cared about me in this world, a person who was alive and talking for almost an hour while he bled out before they could get to him.

He had no way of knowing, yet as I look into his eyes, I see nothing but understanding, and it breaks my resolve. Tears begin to form before I can stop them, and I try to force them back with sheer will.

"I'm so embarrassed," I murmur, throwing a hand over my face as I fight back the emotions of that night. "Most of the time, I'm ok, and I thought I would be, but it's just so small in here, and it makes me feel a little trapped." One tear escapes rolling down my face, and I shake my head violently, throwing it off. "I'm sorry I'm freaking out," I repeat, pulling the door open before stepping out and breathing in large gulps of air.

This can't be happening now.

I try to think back to what the therapists told me to do if I start to have a panic attack.

Count backward from ten, focus on something that can ground you in the moment, and take deeper breaths.

"You have nothing to apologize for," he whispers in the gentlest, most soothing voice I have ever heard. He had gotten out of the car and is now standing behind me, close enough that I can feel the heat emanating from him, but he doesn't touch me. His breath tickles the hairs on the back of my neck as he exhales and the scent of his cologne wafts around me, drawing me in.

I turn around, removing my hands from my eyes to look into his deep slate ones. He lifts his hand onto my cheek and wipes away a stream of new tears with his thumb. He speaks, and I feel his words resonate in my bones.

"I never want to do anything to make you feel unsafe, Firefly. I want to protect you from everything in this world." The sincerity of his words has my mind spinning, and the touch of his hand on my cheek grounds me in a way I can't explain.

I lean forward, unable to stop myself from the pull I feel to him. Closing my eyes, I lose the fight and gently touch my lips to his. He stills for a moment before responding, pressing back against my kiss, his hand wrapping around to the base of my neck, his fingers tangling themselves in my hair. It isn't tender or sweet. It's rough, intense, and hot in a way I haven't ever experienced.

He brushes the tip of his tongue along my lips, begging permission to penetrate them as he tugs slightly on my hair to tilt my head back, allowing him more access. My mouth parts, letting him inside, and my tongue massages his in a frantic rhythm as my hands reach for places to grab him. He tastes minty with a hint of sweetness that urges my body to delve deeper and explore more.

He is hard everywhere. Muscles cover every surface of his body. I can feel the length of him now pressed against my hip.

Jesus!

I moan, unintentionally pushing myself more onto him, and he releases what sounds like a growl as he slides his mouth down my jaw and onto my neck, licking and biting his way around my ear to the exposed meaty flesh of my shoulder. His fingers remain, circling at the base of my neck, keeping me attached to him and holding me steady. I whimper, the feel of him on my neck driving me closer to orgasm as I grind my body into his, hating how much clothing he has between us.

A car door slamming on the other side of the parking lot pulls me from my ecstasy, knocking us back into reality and causing my eyes to fly open and my brain to turn on again.

What the fuck was that?

My eyes ask the silent question while we stand there breathless for a long minute, trying to figure out what the hell just happened. Cain's steel grays never leave me, desire swirling in their depths as he struggles to reign in his rather apparent intentions.

I break our contact first, glancing around and reminding myself first that we are in public and second that I'm just supposed to be his tutor.

"I'm sorry," I utter, dropping my face toward the ground as I realize I basically attacked him with my mouth and then dry-humped his leg for the last two minutes.

"Firefly, look at me and listen. I will only say this once," he commands, waiting for my gaze to return to his before continuing. "You may apologize to whoever you want about whatever you want, but never apologize to me. I regret only that it took this long for me to get my lips on yours, so I'll hear nothing of this being a mistake, an impulse, or a series of unfortunate circumstances. I have wanted you since the moment I laid eyes on you, and this thing between us isn't going away. It may not be today, this week, or in the next five weeks, but I will have you, Firefly. You will be mine." He finishes by placing his lips back on mine for a short but resolute kiss that promises his sincerity. "Let's get you fed," he adds, turning and handing me the keys as he strides to the passenger side. He closes the door and rolls down both windows to allow more space.

"Wait, I'm supposed to drive this thing?!?" I question, shock on my face as I count the years it would take me to afford it if I crashed.

"I figure you'll feel more control if you're behind the wheel. Don't worry. It's insured," he replies without missing a beat before leaning over and flipping the radio to a country station I love. His ability to be utterly casual after the earth-shattering, life-changing, single-hottest kiss of my life makes me slightly angry with him. It also makes me feel more daring.

When will I ever get to drive a brand new fire orange corvette?

I doubt myself for a moment before straightening my shoulders and walking to the driver's seat. I adjust the settings to fit my much shorter frame, reset the mirrors, and buckle myself in before I look over to see Cain completely relaxed with a smile.

The stress from my panic attack, the overwhelming hormones and emotions when he kissed me, and the flood of thoughts and questions I have from his declaration fade in my mind as I rev the engine, and a full laugh escapes my lips. I smile with my entire body as I turn to him.

"Where to Candy Cain?" I shout over the music.

"Anywhere." He answers with a challenge looming in his tone. "Take me anywhere."

Ok, McSteamy, anywhere we go!

Shifting into gear, we ease out of the lot. With my hair flapping in the wind, my body feels lighter than it has in months.

Chapter 14
Bri

It feels like hours before I turn back onto Maryland parkway and head for Cafe Rio to grab food before work. I had driven a loop through the city with Cain silently cruising along. It took just over ninety minutes, leaving us no time to study or even look at the schedule for the week. I park the wildly expensive car and walk around it, double-checking that it is still in perfect condition.

Cain gets out, stretching his legs after the long stint on his butt. The smile he had after our kiss never left his face. Even as we drove, I felt him watching me with an unbridled amusement that is so polar opposite of the complex, dangerously sexy guy I glimpsed from across the party.

"How do you feel now?" he asks while casually walking up beside me and pulling the door open before I can grab for it.

"Starved, actually," I avoid his actual question. I don't want to talk about my panic attack or car accident, and I absolutely don't want to bring up that kiss. Just at the thought, heat pools in my center, and I'm turned on again. A blush creeps up my neck as I see Cain's eyes flare with desire before he responds.

"Me too." He licks his lips, bringing my attention back to them, heat rising within me before I can stop it.

Calm the fuck down. That was a one-time emotional breakdown moment. A mistake.

Even though he said he didn't think it was a mistake.

How could it not be?

He doesn't know me, and I don't know him. I'm supposed to be his tutor, so I have to put my foot down and set some clear boundaries.

"So let's quickly grab some food. I need to get back to my car and head to work. It's getting late," I quip and hurry past him, purposely avoiding the hand he is trying to wrap around my waist. Hustling into the line, pretending to decide what to eat today, I evade his gaze and intentionally place distance between our bodies. I'm painfully aware of the space created between us as I aim for a more professional relationship.

I grab my tacos, he gets his burrito, and we head back to the car. As we return, I glance at him, hoping to see his casual demeanor from the extended test drive he gifted me, but instead find his dark, hard exterior firmly back in place. My heart drops, despite knowing this is the right decision in my gut. He is paying me to be his tutor.

Then why does it feel like I'm fucking this whole thing up?

I tear my eyes away from him, focusing on returning to the car, pulling the keys back out of my shorts pocket, and unlocking the doors before sliding back into the driver's seat. As I'm trying to see where I can set my food and still be able to steer, he reaches his hand toward me to grab it.

The sudden movement of his arm causes me to flinch involuntarily. His eyes instantly harden, and his voice comes out through clenched teeth.

"I was trying to help with your food. I would never...." He gently pulls the bag from my hands, shaking his head without finishing. I sit there for a moment, frozen in embarrassment, not understanding why I thought he might hit me. I feel safe with him. I'm sure of that, but some habits are more challenging to kick than others, and with his tenuous mood, I had my guard up. He clicks his seat belt and stares out the window, intentionally turning himself away from me and any response I may have tried to come up with. I sigh, feeling defeated, turn the key in the ignition while fastening my safety belt, and drive the three blocks to my car.

By the time we arrive at my Kia, the silence in the car is deafening. I want to apologize, explain, to fix this tension between us, but I find myself at a loss whenever I try to find the words to make it right.

"I'm sorry we didn't get our study time for today. Why don't you look at my revised schedule and find a few hours to add to replace today," I suggest, sheepishly avoiding the actual reason for the tension. I intend it as a peace offering while I busy myself moving my bags from the trunk to my car.

"We don't need to make up the time. Today was supposed to be about getting to know each other, and I think we did plenty of that," he scoffs, a forced smile plastered on his face as he holds his hand out, silently asking for the keys. Unwilling to relent to him, I stand my ground.

"We had an arrangement, and today it wasn't fulfilled. I want to make up the time," I insist, lifting my chin defiantly, hoping he can see this as a business deal and, because of that, a contract. He stands for a moment contemplating my statement before his eyes land on mine again, and I see something I'm not expecting. Pain.

Or am I imagining that?

He moves faster than I thought possible, pulling me into him, his arm wrapping around my waist, his hand diving into my hair. My breath catches, and I lean into the embrace taking in his masculine scent. I can hear his heart beating frantically in his chest. My mind is spinning, trying to find a way to get back to the light-hearted flirting and banter we had in class today before I screwed everything up. He pulls back to look at me again before giving me an answer.

"This stopped being just an arrangement the minute your lips touched mine, Firefly. Tell me you don't feel this pull between us." His eyes dive into my soul, pulling the truth from my lips without any chance of me stopping them.

"Of course I do," I reply, feeling a little dizzy from his touch, "but I can't do this." I shake my head and step out of his arms, lightly pushing his body away from mine to allow space to think. "I don't have the emotional capability of investing in anyone. I'm fucked up. Broken beyond repair. I'm the one you walk away from. The one you leave behind. Sure it'll be great at first, but this feeling will fade. It always does. My only superpower is my ability to ruin any good thing that comes into my life. My relationships don't work. Everyone I care about leaves. Not that it would matter because I leave in six months. This thing," I pause, pointing my finger between us, "can only be tutoring. That's all I can offer you. I need to focus on my future right now. I know that sounds selfish, but I won't be just another woman who gives up her dreams to chase after a man. I won't be trapped here. I can't be." My words come out in a rush, and my heart is breaking by the end.

He takes a step back, his hands falling to his sides. I feel their absence immediately, and it takes all of my resolve not to reach back out to him. Uncertainty storms in his eyes as he processes my explanation. He releases a sigh, sets his jaw, and nods curtly, a mask falling into place.

For the first time, I can't read him. I feel detached from him. Our connection no longer hums with electricity like it usually does.

I lift the keys toward him, and he grabs them gently from my hand, careful not to touch me, before spinning on his heel and retreating to the Corvette without a word. To his credit, he waits until I get into my car and pull away before leaving himself. I look down, and the clock reads 2:14 pm.

Shit, I guess we are going to work wearing this.

I glanced at my outfit, cursing myself for trying to ooze sex appeal today, especially considering my work dress code. It is casual, but this outfit won't even pass for that. I turn onto the freeway, hoping to have enough time to throw on the clothes I packed before logging in.

Talk about a shit start to a long shift.

***

My car flies into the parking lot with only four minutes to spare. I grab all of my bags and hurry toward the employee entrance. My eyes swing over to the warehouse alley, briefly reminding me of Friday night. One part of me is grateful I haven't heard anything more about the incident, while another part wonders how that is even possible and if no news really is good news. Thankfully I didn't have time to dwell on it before I rush into Citi's employee entrance, a smile plastered on my face. I hurry past Cynthia and Sydney, heading toward my cubicle, hoping to avoid any managers. Once at my desk, I quickly clock in and boot up the computer, willing it to load faster.

In the last two years, I have never been late, never missed a shift, and I don't even think I have ever called out of work. I did everything possible to fly under the radar and be an exemplary employee. I need this work history to stand out against my peers when interviewing for new positions to show that I'm reliable and committed. The last thing I need in the remaining few months I work here is anyone starting to think I'm slacking.

I slide into my seat, throwing my bags under the desk while Cynthia's face appears over the divider above my head, causing me to jump as she takes in my outfit and silently fans herself in a message telling me how hot I look. My cheeks flush, and I slap a hand over my eyes, unable to talk to her but wanting to explain my wardrobe malfunction of the day.

Thankfully my system loads quickly. I enter the queue and place myself on hold to run to the bathroom before my first call.

Finally, something was working in my favor today!

I grab the bag containing my work clothes and bolt toward the restrooms just through the employee lounge. I hurry around the corner into the break area, glad my manager, Steven's door is closed, and I slam right into a broad chest, causing me to fall to the floor and sends my bag and all its contents flying around me.

"Oomph"

"Whoa, slow down, Elle!" A familiar male voice cries out. I look up to see Keith's face grinning back at me, surprised. "What's with the outfit? Lose a bet with Liv? I don't think I have seen you out of leggings and hoodie at work, like ever." He scrunches his eyebrows in confusion as he reaches out to help me. I take it, heaving myself back off the floor, a little out of breath.

I definitely need to work out more.

"I was heading to change. Time got away from me today, and I didn't get home after class," I inform him, gathering my scattered articles of clothing.

"You wore that to class?" He whistles slowly. "I didn't take you for the fuck a professor type, Elle." His eyes are dancing with mirth as I smack him with the back of my hand.

"Gross, no." I roll my eyes dramatically. "Just wanted to change it up," I finish hoping he won't push me on it.

"You thought a cropped tank top and booty shorts was a good choice in November?" he asks, amusement dancing in his crystal blue eyes. He is one hundred percent making fun of me.

Laugh it up, buddy.

"Yes, no, I don't know, but I have to go. I'm already late, and my handle time is suffering." I point out, flustered by the time crunch, and I try to get around him.

"I'll take care of that, looks like your system needs an update. I'm actually just heading that way," he tells me, winking as he heads for my cubical.

"You're the best, Keith. Thank you!" I shout, continuing to the employee restroom, glad to know I have a few minutes to get myself together while Keith pretends to fix my system for me.

Quickly I strip out of my clothes and throw on my black leggings and lavender Roxy hoodie. I take a moment to throw my hair into a messy bun before changing my mind and pulling it back down to let my curls free. It's a rare occasion that I leave it down these days, and the feel of it reminds me of Cain.

I'm proud of myself for standing my ground against him today. He has been trouble from the moment I laid eyes on him, but I never expected to enjoy spending time with him as I had today on our drive. He took a moment in the car where I usually would have completely lost it and turned it into one of the best afternoons I have experienced in years. He made me feel comfortable with him in a way I hadn't felt in a long time.

Then why did I push him away?

Well, that answer is simple. Because he makes me feel things that I didn't think I could. He has wrapped himself entirely around my brain in the last twenty-four hours and taken over. I need to get control, and the only way to do that is to deny myself the sexual pleasure he promises for the small price of losing him altogether.

It's called self-preservation, and it sucks.

I don't even know if I'll see him again. He left today without saying a word. I don't know where we stand now, which makes me uneasy. I have spent too many years establishing set boundaries and building walls to protect the broken pieces inside of me. I don't know how to feel about the way he was able to waltz right through them without a second thought.

It doesn't matter because he knows it is just a job. No relationship. No sex.

I frown a little, thinking about the last part. I want to cut these feelings off before they become more, but I also secretly want to know what it would be like to be taken by him fully.

One no-strings-attached night could fix that.

But I know better. My heart will always get tangled up in my vagina's conquests and lead me astray. I'm not a hit-it-and-quit-it kind of girl. Not like Elaine, who gave herself away at the slightest bit of attention, drugs, or money.

I splash my face with water to focus my thoughts on the work I have to complete and hustle back to my cubicle. The entire wardrobe change took less than ten minutes, and Keith is still sitting at my desk chatting with Cynthia when I get back. His eyes glance over to me as I walk up.

"There she is," he states conspiratorially. "I was just telling Cynthia that you got some bug in your system, and it should take me about thirty minutes to sort it out."

"Is that so, huh? Good thing it was only my system," I remark with a grateful smile. "By the way, thanks for texting me back to let me know you were alive after Liv's thing," I accuse, sending him a look with a disappointed eyebrow. His face pales slightly before he recovers, flashing his smile that is oozing with charm.

Interesting. Keith never uses that one on me.

"Yeah, sorry about that," he scrambles, " I lost my phone after Liv's party. I looked for it in several places yesterday but couldn't find it anywhere, so I didn't pick up a new one until right before I came to work today. I haven't even finished syncing everything yet." His mouth finishes and sets in a firm line, making him appear to add the rest in his head. I can tell there is more to this story that he isn't telling me.

"Wow, I had no idea. Could you have left it at Mila's? Or in the Lyft?" I ask, genuinely concerned because I know how much information Keith has on his phone; how much we all do these days. "Do you think someone stole it? Has any of your other information shown any suspicious activity," I rattle off questions thinking about the banking information, Apple Pay, Venmo, CashApp, and so many other personal accounts I have stored on my phone.

Not to mention the murder video. Shit, I have to delete that. What if someone got ahold of it? Could I be charged as an accessory? Or for not providing the information to the cops?

My mind spins in a million directions at the idea of losing my phone. Keith watches me closely, trying to read into my reaction.

"No, Apple told me the phone hasn't been on to ping any towers since I left Liv's. I'm guessing I dropped it somewhere, and it's dead, so I can't locate it," he explains, bringing my mind back to the conversation in front of me.

"I think it would be nice to be unplugged for a few days. You, young people, love being connected to everybody all the time, but in truth, it's nice to have some peace and quiet now and again," Cynthia pipes in before tapping her earpiece, falling into her phone intro, and taking her seat on her side of the divider.

Keith moves to get out of my chair and holds it as I sit down. I lift a questioning eyebrow, pulling his arm to bring him back to my level.

"I have known you for over a decade, and you have never lost anything, nothing, not a Post-It note, not a single playing card, not once. Plus, I know you don't drink, so you wanna tell me what actually happened?" I whisper-shout at him.

"I was working a side job. It went sideways. I have a new number I'll send you. Not sure what kind of people I got mixed up in, but I can't imagine they haven't cracked into it yet. Don't send anything to that number; block it for me on your phone," he insists, speaking quietly in a rush. My eyes must have looked like saucers as I take in the information.

"Are you OK? Do you need a place to hide out? You know our couch is always available. Just say the word," I affirm. Panic slowly overcomes me as I think about my best friend in trouble. "I warned you about getting in with that group Anonymous."

"Thanks, Elle. This particular incident has nothing to do with them. This came from my old school buddy K. He needed me to figure out an encryption code, which for the record, is impossible without the right hardware, and even then, the code I got my hands on was some of the most technical shit I have ever seen. Every backdoor was booby-trapped. Every pathway had tripwires. I couldn't comb through even a quarter of it before they took it back, along with my phone." He looks lost in thought and simultaneously a little shaken up.

"Well, I'm glad you're done with that job then. You shouldn't be doing this black-market hacker bullshit. You have all the credentials to go legit. Why do you stay here for shitty pay when you could do real coding or code security for a hell of a lot more money with an upstanding company?" I admonish him with the same thing I have been asking since I came to work here. I always thought Keith would leave and start his real career once he graduated, but he never did. I never understood what was holding him back.

"And throw you to the wolves? Who would save your half-naked ass, then?" he jokes, changing the tone of the conversation. I reach out and smack him again.

He is insufferable.

"Well, promise me you won't do any more jobs with this guy." I push, wanting to hear him say it, but his eyes drop to the floor. "Keith...what aren't you telling me?"

"When they took the code, they took everything I had on-site, but I made a copy to my home server before heading back to work. I have to find out more about this code base. I need to know what it does or who wrote it," he finishes before looking back up at me. "But they don't know I have it, or I would already be dead. So no need to worry."

"No need to worry!?! That's exactly what I need to worry about. What the hell have you gotten mixed up in?" I chastise him and try to wade through the information. "Could you give it back? Or not look at it again?" I ask hopefully.

"Come on, Elle, you know I can't do that. It's a puzzle," he concludes, finally pointing to my screen to show my login ready. "Looks like your time is up," he states firmly, ending our discussion.

"We aren't finished with this conversation. Text me your new number. You have no idea how mad I am at you for being so stupid. You are supposed to be the smart and stable one, remember?" I smack him again for good measure before grabbing my headset and completing my login.

I don't know how I expected to get through this night. Between the panic attack, my kiss with Cain, my outfit fiasco, and Keith's shady side business, I'm distracted for the entire shift.

I answer call after call and respond robotically to everything I can, placing customers on longer wait times than ever. I even forget I have a customer on hold as my mind falls down a rabbit hole of losing Keith to some Russian hackers. My sales and pitch numbers are abysmal, and my daily handle time is the highest I have ever seen.

By the time eleven comes around, I'm exhausted. Cynthia left at nine, and Sydney has three more hours, making up for her missed shifts the last few days by pulling a double. So I'm the only one from our team who is leaving now.

I'm a bit apprehensive when I think about walking out to my car alone tonight after how Friday night had gone down. As I grab all my bags, pulling my notebooks back into my school bag, which had fallen under the desk. A red cover catches my eye.

Where have you been?

I reach for the once-missing notebook and flip through its pages. I'm sure I looked in my bag yesterday when I couldn't find it, and it hadn't been there.

He couldn't have... He wouldn't have...

I turn to my last page of notes and notice two small lines written in handwriting that isn't mine that reads:

In my darkness.

You are the only light.

I stop breathing; my heart beats loudly in my ears. He had written it next to a random doodle of the firefly I had drawn during the lecture last week—my brain stalls, unable to fully comprehend the meaning he placed in those two lines of text.

I'm not anyone's light. If anything, I'm darkness. The girl everyone leaves behind.

My head is spinning as I slowly exit the building, keeping my head on a swivel, looking for anything that could jump out at me on my way to my car. The walk ends up being uneventful, and I can get all of my stuff in and drive home without any gangsters with baseball bats or large wolf dogs coming after me.

Liv is in bed when I get home. I drop my stuff in my room and walk to the fridge, hoping for cold water, only to find Liv had picked up some groceries for us, and included in that haul were more energy drinks and the ice cream I had asked her about earlier.

Bless her!

I 'd completely forgotten I was supposed to go today after class before work, what with the new crazy tutoring schedule I have laid out before me. Hopefully, my revised hours for tomorrow will hold, and I can see Liv before she is out for the night again.

Jumping into a quick shower, I don't think at all about Cain. Cain in the shower. Cain dripping wet. Cain covered in soapy bubbles.

Ok, maybe one time or two.

Before getting into bed. I look at my phone for a minute, feeling an overwhelming need to text him. To see if we were still on for tomorrow. To see if he would respond. To connect.

That would only muddy the waters. We are PROFESSIONAL; professionals do not send late-night texts to sexy men.

It takes everything in me to place my phone on the charger and set it on the nightstand for the evening.

Rolling around for over an hour, I can only think about the chaos of my day. The stress in my life is overwhelming, and each trigger runs its worst-case scenario through my thoughts. I must find a way to remove the excessive amount of chaotic energy from my life and focus on what is most important—finishing this school year strong. The last thing I remember before falling asleep are the words Cain whispered during my panic attack.

"I want to protect you from everything in this world."

Why did I suddenly feel like I needed that protection?

Chapter 15
Cain

Hours, that is how long I have been running, pushing my wolf until I can't run anymore and then going farther just to feel the pain. The hockey game with Dante ended a while ago without so much as a call or text from me, and I didn't watch a single minute of security footage from Brielle's apartment. I hadn't even taken my phone.

After leaving the study session, I drove straight to my apartment and dropped off the orange corvette before jumping on my motorcycle. My only thoughts were to get as far away as physically possible, so I could no longer feel her drawing me in. I rode up to Mount Charleston, hoping distance would allow me the ability to breathe. Every fiber of my being wanted to shift, to leave behind my humanity and give the reigns to my wolf.

When I made it up, I pulled off on a small hiking trail, stripped down, tucked my clothes into my bag on my bike, and let go.

My wolf is wild. Even after hours of punishing speeds, I can't take back over, his pain sinking in with mine as we run from it all. Her words cut deeper than she could have imagined. The things we feared most from the beginning, she said out loud.

"I need to focus on my future." Her future. Alone. Across the country.

She doesn't want to be ours. She doesn't want to be stuck with us. She wants to live out her dreams. Dreams that have nothing to do with being Awakened, belonging to a pack, or being mated to me. Dreams that take her far away without so much as a backward glance.

The logical part of me knows she doesn't have the mating bond like I do because her wolf is Unawakened, but I know she wants me. I know she thinks about me; she has even screamed my name, not that she would ever admit it. I don't know why I let myself believe she would want me over everything she had chosen for her life.

I don't want to be the one who holds her back from her passions or life pursuits. I want to live those plans with her. The mating bond pushes me to make her happy in every way, and I know from the stories of mated wolves that those feelings only grow stronger once the bond becomes official.

Never have I heard of a wolf whose mate rejected the bond. It is unheard of among our kind because we believe mates are blessed to us by the fates as our perfect match. I do know two wolves who had lost their mates. They went feral and were put down within a year. I can't imagine losing her, and she isn't even mine to lose yet. Brielle is supposed to be my match.

It doesn't matter if she wants nothing to do with us or our lifestyle.

Stop!

The yell is filled with Alpha command and sent directly into my mind. My wolf stops running, sensing Dante's wolf nearby. He must be close for me to hear him so loudly.

What do you want, Alpha?

I send back through the mental link struggling to find the words with my wolf in such control while I stand panting, clouds of crisp air wafting out from me. Dante's wolf walks out into the clearing. His ruddy copper-brown pelt gleams with the light of the moon. Dante's wolf's size and stature match my own. He doesn't appear winded as he walks confidently forward.

He stops in front of me, nuzzling the side of my cheek in greeting before backing up a step to shift into his human form. My wolf eyes him wearily while he pulls a pair of sweats from his bag and stands before me with concern etched on his brow.

"I can feel your pain for miles," he remarks before commanding me, "**Shift back**."

My wolf yields to him, allowing me to return to my human body. Dante tosses a second pair of joggers and waits while I pull them on. Every movement is strained by the overused muscles.

We stand there for a long while, not talking as he waits me out. Clouds of frosty air floating silently into the distance as I pant, still catching my breath from the miles I have run. It is much colder up in the mountains than down in the city, which my wolf prefers and is my main reason for driving the extra distance to run up here most of the time.

Well, that and the fact that I currently couldn't trust him closer to her.

"What happened, Cain?" he finally asks. The voice coming from my best friend, all traces of his Alpha, pulled back. I cross my arms over my chest and let out a long sigh before dropping my head and finally answering him.

"She's my Mate." The words leave my mouth dripping with unbridled emotion. The pain of her rejection stings intensely. My statement hangs between us, filling the space with a weight I wasn't aware I had been carrying.

"Who is?" Dante asks, his face giving away the shock he feels from my statement before the realization hits him. "The witness." It isn't a question, and I can see the gears turning in his mind as he processes my predicament. "This should be good news. Why do I only feel anger and pain from you? Does she know about us, about her?"

"No, she is still in the dark about what she is and about us, and I'm not sure we should tell her. She has plans to move to the east coast," I reply, avoiding my pain altogether.

"There are packs on the east coast she could join. She wouldn't have to stay with us, but that's not why you don't want her to know. You'll want to go with her or keep her here as her Mate. Why are you struggling with those options?" Dante asks, confusion marring his face as he quickly deduces the turmoil I face in that decision.

"I've sworn my life and loyalty to this pack, and I won't cage her here for my desires. She dreams of moving away, and I don't want her to lose that choice to the Mate bond that will pull her to me," I state firmly.

"So you would take away her ability to make an informed decision about her lineage, her future, her life? You know how rare Unawakened wolves are at her age, and you know that if a rogue wolf or an unaligned pack were to get ahold of her, she would be Awakened against her will and used for illegal breeding. Leaving her unaware is leaving her defenseless, especially if she is on the other side of the country where her Mate can't look out for her," he spits back at me, forcing my wolf to the surface.

"Only those with Alpha blood would know what she is. That's less than a few hundred wolves in the hundreds of thousands in this country alone. I'll take that chance. Awakening her will mean she will feel the bond. She'll want me from the moment she scents me. It'll force her to want me when truly she doesn't. It'll force her to choose between the life she has always wanted or me." I seethe, anger flowing with my words. Dante's eyes light with understanding as we stand squared off.

"You think she'll reject you. This is your fear talking," he states plainly, calling me on my bullshit, as only he has ever been able to do.

"She already has!" I shout, feeling my eyes shift to the bright silver of my wolf a moment before I strip back out of the sweats and call over my shoulder. "I've made my choice. Once she has given up the video, it's over. I'll be back for Pres's debrief on our hacker's phone tonight. **Let me go.**" I add my own command into my voice, and to his credit, he does.

I'm off, not looking back. Anger drives my paws as my thoughts spin out of control.

She has been safe as a human her whole life. Telling her puts her at risk.

I tell myself, trying to beat out the voice of my wolf, who wants nothing but to claim her and protect her himself.

***

After another hour of aimless running, I circle back to my motorcycle. It is still on the side of a hiking trail near the main road. I pull my clothes out of the bag strapped on the back and head back to the office. Dante's words still swirl in my mind. The idea of Brielle in one of the archaic breeding programs turns my stomach.

They have been outlawed for decades by the Lycan Legal Council, LLC, but some of the original North America packs still haven't fallen in line despite the council pushing for better enforcement. The originals still believe females are property to be used as they see fit, and they use breeding programs to fill their ranks. When the laws changed, those packs merely moved their operations underground and kept them secret. Like any society, we wolves have our share of criminals and even a whole crime underworld but cut off one head, and three more will pop up.

Dante petitioned for his father's seat on the LLC when he took over our pack, but the board wouldn't allow him to take it due to his age and lack of experience and instead handed Nevada's seat to the head of the Marlo pack. To Deacon.

Just one more reason to remove him from power.

We are undoubtedly documenting everything we can use against him for the next gathering, which will happen next summer, though I doubt he'll be in power that long. We also have a few of our best-pack members inside their ranks as enforcement officers. They work for them, but they are loyal to us and give us any information they can. One day our pack will be back in power, and we can eliminate those enslaved packs and free their members.

I get to headquarters before ten and stroll back into the conference room we met in just two days ago to plan our tech retrieval mission. It is crazy how much has happened in just forty-eight hours. I pull Brielle's mirror phone out of my pocket and scan through it for any new messages missed during my extended run, but not seeing anything of note. She was at work, so it shouldn't surprise me. The only message she sent since leaving me was to her roommate Liv about ice cream and whether they had any more.

I can think of better ways than ice cream to cure her sorrow.

Pres walks in a few minutes later, dancing to her headphones. She is singing to herself and bopping along, unaware I'm already in the room. I clear my throat loudly to let her know of my presence, and she jumps in a shout. "Aaahhrrrggggg. What the hell, Cain? The meeting isn't for another fifteen minutes. Why are you in here?" She pulls the headphones off without turning down her music and glares at me.

"Sorry to interrupt the concert you were putting on, but I'm eager to see what you found out about Mr. Anderson," I reply casually, refusing to show any of the emotions I have been dealing with all day.

"Well, I'm not going over it twice, so you can wait until we start, Neo." She huffs, rolling her eyes as she makes the Matrix reference which is far too fitting for the situation than it should be, and logs into the computer to bring up the projector again with her newly acquired information.

"Someone is in a shit mood. Let me guess, our hacker is better than you, and you have nothing?" I ask, baiting her with her ego, hoping it'll push her to start spilling, if only to distract me from my own thoughts.

"He is NOT better than I am, and with some time, I'll be able...." She stops abruptly and looks up, realizing she has played into my hand. "You ass! Manipulation is a terrible friendship-building skill." She flips her copper-red hair over her shoulder and slaps me before blatantly placing her headphones back over her ears, effectively ignoring me until the meeting. I grin at her attempt at immaturity until she finishes her thought. "Must be why our girl wants nothing to do with you."

My smile drops immediately, and pain fills my chest, causing me to flinch involuntarily. My drastic change in mood is broadcast all over my face before I have a chance to throw my walls up. Presley stills, and I can tell she can read me like a book. Her face falls, remorse evident in her reaction. I look away, throwing my walls firmly back into place and distracting myself by pulling up the surveillance feeds of Brielle's apartment.

We have four cameras inside her residence placed in different rooms. Because we didn't know which room was hers initially, we set one in each bedroom, one in the kitchen, and one in the living room. Once they were connected, only four people had access to the streams. Presley has been screening the footage of the apartment in addition to looking into the hacker's phone. Also authorized were two of our other female pack members, Jess and Quinn. This came at my explicit command because I'll be damned if any male is going to watch my girl undress. Even the thought of that had my wolf raising his hackles within me.

I have only gotten the chance to watch a few minutes of the recordings so far, most of which are of her studying in bed or reading, but I did manage to hear her moan my name in her sleep last night, which made me harder than I have ever been. I don't know if I have ever heard a sexier sound. I had to jerk off several times before I was able to fall asleep.

While I focus on the footage, Presley steps out and returns several times, grabbing various items and stalling for time while eying me for some sort of hidden answer to my reaction. I give her nothing and avoid her eyes with practiced nonchalance.

The last time she returns, Dante is with her, and he seems more distracted than usual. He locks eyes with me as he enters, trying to gauge where my head is. I drop my chin in a silent message that I'm fine, but I hope he kept what I told him between us. I don't need Presley's smart mouth tearing open wounds I haven't healed yet.

"It's just us for this one. I have Jake and Erik following a Marlo lead," Dante advises as he sits down. "So what is the news on this hacker? You said he isn't one of Marlo's wolves?"

"The building wing's lease belongs to one of his many shell companies, but I can't seem to find a connection with the actual hacker, who is one hundred percent human." Presley snarls, clearly pissed that she didn't have more information.

"He is our witness's best friend. I feel that is too close to this whole thing to overlook as coincidence," I add, not wanting to bring her up but knowing it is a detail we need.

"Could she have been a plant? There to oversee the transfer and report back?" Dante asks, his eyes flipping between the two of us. He is careful to not imply anything in his tone now that he knows about our connection.

"No," I state firmly. "She isn't a part of this."

"It's possible," Presley says at the same time as my denial. My eyes fly to her, rage bubbling, barely contained as she questions my Mate's intentions.

"Your head is clouded on this," Dante asserts. "Think about this logically. They agreed to the location for the drop. She happened to be there recording from her car. She panicked when shit hit the fan. Maybe she is working with her friend as allies down here in Vegas. If Deacon has never met her or her friend is the one who brought her in, they wouldn't know about her lineage. Only direct contact with Deacon, Wyatt, me, or you would tell them that," He finishes, and I hate how logical he sounds in his reasoning.

Our Mate!

My wolf doesn't care about logic or coincidence. He just wants her, but I need to be clearer headed.

What if she was working for Marlo? What if all of this is a trap?

Presley pipes up as I spin through the ramifications, "I hate to say this, but I am leaning toward coincidence on this one. None of her communication indicates any connection to anyone we have identified in the pack.

"What if the hacker is her connection? It's possible he brought her in, and Marlo has no idea, or that the hacker was trying to pull one over on the Marlo pack and brought her in as reassurance that the deal would go down?" Dante rattles off more theories that only have me spinning.

Could she be in on this?

"All I can say is that she hasn't made any connection between the video and Cain. At least not in any public communication in her home, email, or between her and Keith, our hacker," Presley adds before continuing, "and while I can't pull much off his phone because, yes, he is good. I got into his public accounts, and the messages with her seem legitimate. He has several encrypted communication apps that are impossible to hack into without a face or the actual password. I'm guessing that is where his pack connection is held, so it is possible they are communicating there, but she doesn't have any of them on her phone," she finishes looking between us, frustration marring her face.

Dante and I sit there staring at her, perplexed. She always finds a way in when it comes to tech, so if she says there isn't a way, then there really isn't.

"Don't look at me like that. I'll figure it out," she asserts with conviction in her tone.

"We know you will," Dante reassures her before turning to me. "We need you to dive in on our witness. It'll help if you can get her to trust you enough to confide in you about her friend. We need to know if this is a loose end," he finishes with concern etched on his brow, "Can you do this?"

Before I can answer, Presley interjects, "We have another issue. When I scanned our girl's computer to ensure we knew where all her copies were, I found one transferred to an external device. So we have two copies that are unaccounted for. One to the unknown email and one on a flash drive somewhere. We need both before we can clear her. I should be able to break into the email in the next day or two, but I can't touch the external device."

"You two are asking me to lie to her, get her to trust me, and then betray her, all before we maybe tell her that everything she believes is a lie and she is another species? Do you hear yourselves?" I turn to Dante, "There must be another way."

"Short of kidnaping her and interrogating the information out of her... which, by your wolf's arrival to this conversation, I see isn't your favorite choice. This is our best option of getting her away from this clean." My eyes shift while a growl rolls from my throat at the mention of her interrogation. My claws tear out of my hands, shredding the arms of the conference chair.

Dante continues with his Alpha voice pressed, "We are asking you to get to know her and get her to confide in you. The rest we can figure out later. Now **calm down,**" he ends strong, but my wolf rises to the challenge instead of yielding to him, and Dante's eyes go wide, surprised by my refusal of a direct order. "Cain, I won't fight you here. Relax." Everything in me wants to attack him. My best friend sits looking at me like I have lost my mind.

Maybe I had?

Several moments pass, all three of us silent as I pull my wolf back into submission. Presley never takes her eyes off me; I can see she is trying to work through what is going on with me.

"I'll continue my fake tutoring until we develop a better plan, but I stand by my previous statement that she is innocent in all of this." I glare at Dante, and my Alpha voice comes out without any chance of me stopping it, "**No one will touch her for interrogation or anything else unless I give the order. She is MINE.**" Presley's eyebrows shoot all the way up into her hairline as she processes the fact that I just gave our Alpha a directive, and Dante is visibly fighting his wolf against the challenge I issued. Anyone else in the pack would have been on the ground submitting to him.

Dante and I had always known it would have been a tough battle for the Alpha position, our wolves were well-matched, and neither of us was willing to kill the other for the job. It was why I had decided to let him take the reigns. I never wanted to lead despite my lineage, but I won't yield on this, and he knows it, so he is trying to hold back.

"Fine." The one word comes out through ground teeth and takes everything in him. So I get up and walk out of the room. I'm halfway down the hall when I hear Presley's footsteps behind me.

"I don't know what's happening between you two, but you need to pull it together. Now isn't the time for an internal war. He needs you on our team, Cain," she announces carefully as if trying to read me as I slow my stride.

"He has my loyalty Pres," I declare without a second thought.

"Even against her?" she asks defiantly. My head whips around, and a snarl comes from my throat. "That's what I thought," she continues shaking her head as if disappointed in me. "You need to ask yourself if it turns out she is somehow involved in all of this, are you with her or with us because you won't be able to choose both." She concludes, turning on her heel and walking away from me.

My brain is spinning as I enter my office.

Would I choose her?

I shake my head, trying to throw away the idea of it all but coming back to the same realization no matter how many scenarios I run through—*Every. Single. Time.*

Chapter 16
Cain

I sleep like shit. Again. My dreams run rampant with scenario after scenario of Brielle moving away. In one version, she leaves for Boston. In another, she takes a job in South Carolina. In some, she is Awakened first; in others, she remains human. The worst one happens when she leaves without telling me where she is going, and I spend months trying to track her down, only to find her enslaved with one of the elder packs.

The only thing they all have in common is her leaving. So, needless to say, my mood is atrocious, and I leave early to try and work through some of my aggression in the gym before meeting up with her today.

After an hour in the UFC facility beating the life out of a punching bag, my attitude improved. I picture hitting her hacker friend more than once during the session and grin a little at the thought of being able to bring him into an interrogation.

Maybe I can see what Jake gets out of it after all.

After showering at the gym, I throw on gray sweats and a black t-shirt to meet up with Brielle. She is in class right now and will have a second one later this afternoon, so I swing by Jimmy John's on my way to campus to grab us some sandwiches for her break. I spend almost twenty minutes standing in the sandwich shop trying to figure out what she might enjoy. I buy six different subs, everything from vegetarian to meatball, so I get something that she will eat. Knowing her, she won't take any of them.

Once I arrive on campus, I hover around the door of her lecture hall for about ten minutes before the students begin to exit, holding my breath. My chest feels tight as I realize I'm nervous about seeing her. After the way we left things yesterday, I'm not sure how today will play out.

She pops out of the door, juggling her arms full of bags, completely distracted. She attempts to throw a notebook into an already overstuffed bag on her shoulder. A chuckle falls out of my mouth at how unbelievably adorable she is without even trying. I note that her outfit today isn't nearly as revealing as it had been yesterday, which confirms my suspicions that she had worn the short shorts and crop tank for me.

I see you, Firefly.

Today she wears black workout leggings and a pink Roxy hoodie that hangs down to her mid-thigh. Her hair is back in its knot on the top of her head, and she isn't wearing any makeup. Honestly, she looks even sexier today. I imagine her rumpled look, climbing out of my bed in the morning, and I have to adjust my sweats.

I catch her in stride. "Hey there, Firefly. How was class?"

"Aahhh! Jesus, why do you have to sneak up on me like that? You should wear a bell. It's creepy." She collects herself, huffing as she readjusts her heavy bags, and heads out of the building before stopping to face me directly. "I thought you got my updated schedule? We don't meet until 5:30 pm today." She raises her eyebrow as she questions, caution evident in her tone.

"Yes, I remember that we were supposed to make some changes to that schedule yesterday, and the day got away from us." That is an understatement of epic proportions. The day not only got away but so did my feelings, which I'll have to work harder to keep ahold of.

"Have lunch with me, and we can discuss it before your next class?" I offer, forcing a casual tone though my heart is going a mile a minute. "I brought sandwiches. We don't even have to leave campus. Come on. You have to eat?" I smile fully, hoping she won't push me away.

"I really can't today. I have a phone interview at two o'clock that I can't miss, and class right after that." She sighs, looking almost upset that she is telling me no.

"No problem, let's get you fed, so you are ready for that interview. You can even practice with me," I finish without waiting for another rebuttal and throw my arm around her back, guiding her toward one of the tables outside the quad, which is currently vacant. Surprisingly, she lets me.

There's my girl.

"I should apologize for my outbursts yesterday. I didn't mean to be unprofessional or rude," she explains as she sits down and looks across the table at me with an expression that matches her words. I can tell she is trying to see where we stand. "Honestly, I'm surprised you wanted to continue tutoring with me after yesterday." An uneasiness crosses her face as she waits for my response. Her hands clench in front of her while she plays with the strap of her bag absentmindedly.

"Trying to get rid of me already, Firefly?" I challenge, not wanting to bring up her resolution to stay away from me. "Well, you'll have to get used to the idea that I'm not going anywhere." I smile a genuine smile, hoping she sees the truth in that statement. "Now, what sandwich would you like?" I present the six sandwiches, laying them out like a buffet in front of her.

"Did you have to buy the whole store?" she laughs a little as she tries to understand why we would need all this food.

"I couldn't have you going hungry." Which is more than the truth. My wolf constantly wants to care for her, and feeding her is a big part. "So we have one with meatballs, one like a BLT, a ham option, a turkey and swiss, an Italian with everything, and if none of those sound appetizing, a vegetarian option," I finish opening my arms up wide in front of all of the subs while she giggles a bit and starts clapping at my display. I may have overdone it with the six sandwiches, but I needed her not to turn me down.

"Where to begin? Well, I'll take the Italian if that's ok with you." She smiles, grabbing the sandwich and sliding it to her side of the table. I open the meatball, allowing a bit of silence as we start eating. She dives right in, getting mustard all over her face as she takes large bites before wiping her mouth with a napkin. There is a visible moment when I see the tension in her shoulders relax, and I enjoy how the breeze blows strands of her hair out of the bun on her head. She looks perfect just like this. My wolf begins to stir, my need to claim her growing with every minute I spend with her.

"Thank you for this," she points to the array of food on the table, "I haven't had time to grocery shop the last few days and didn't even bring anything for lunch today."

"So, you're saying I'm your hero? That I saved your life today by providing essential nutrients?" I reply with a false sense of bravado and even go so far as to sit up straighter and place my fisted hands on my hips, Superman style, before cracking a grin and returning to my sandwich. She throws a napkin at me, laughing.

"Absolutely, Sandwichman. Another life saved." Her sarcasm is one of the sexiest things about her. That smart mouth gives me ideas that I need not have.

Making her submit beneath me would be a challenge I was happy to take on.

I'm hard again. It seems a constant since I found her, but I'm tired of trying to cover my boners like a teenage boy.

Claim her.

If only it was that easy. She still doesn't know what I am, hell, what she is. There is no way I could fuck her without claiming her, and I won't force her into being mine without her consent. I'm not an animal. Well, I am, but not that kind.

"So what's the interview for?" I ask, trying to refocus my horny brain onto something that would tame its urges.

She's leaving.

"It's for a marketing firm in Boston. Boston Digital. They specialize in social media marketing and data-reliant strategy. I passed the initial HR screening interview, and now one of the department managers will be calling to do a more content-focused interview," she answers, her face lighting up as she explains some of the more significant projects they have tackled and some of the pro-bono work they do for small businesses and community programs.

"Wow, that's impressive," I answer honestly because they seem like an excellent opportunity for what she wants to do. "What happens when you nail this interview?" I ask, not giving failure on this step a second thought. "Do you move out there? Do some test products to show your skills?"

"Not exactly. From what I hear, the next interview would be on-site with the entire department. Kind of a trial-by-fire scenario, and if that goes well, they'll offer me the position. All that being said, I don't want to count my chickens. I have to get through today's first," she replies, nervous energy entering her tone.

"You'll crush it. I know from what you shared with me today. You know the company, understand the brands they represent, and are passionate about its causes. They are going to love you." I wish disappointment didn't sneak through a little in the last statement. If she got this position, she would leave. There is no doubt in my mind that I'll lose her, and selfishly, I'm not too fond of the idea despite seeing how much she wants it.

Her phone lights up on the table, a call coming in from a 617 area code, and she immediately sucks in air. Her eyes flit to me, their fire flecks shining as her fear slips out. I give her a nod and a thumbs up, locking eyes with her to try and give her strength. She answers with a more than chipper hello and then adjusts her voice to more natural octave as she continues the call. I can hear the questions and see Bri's confidence build as she handles each with ease and enthusiasm. By the end of the interview, she sits comfortably with an arm wrapped around her knees, both feet on the seat, while she laughs alongside the manager, Ethan.

While I don't like her getting all chummy with this Ethan guy, my heart surges seeing her excel in what she loves. They'll be asking her back; I don't doubt that. She is precisely the type of marketing associate any company would love to hire. Hell, as I listen, I think about hiring her to head up marketing for us.

She hangs up the phone and lets out an exaggerated sigh. Her eyes met mine several times throughout the interview, small glances looking for reassurance, but the look she wears now is pure joy. She appears lighter somehow, as if a considerable weight has lifted from her.

"That felt good," she confides while stretching out her shoulders. "I'm sorry you had to listen to half of the conversation. You could have left," she says as a statement, but I can hear the question underneath.

Why did you stay?

"Just trying to provide moral support, plus we haven't gone over the schedule since the call came in early, so I thought I would hang out and see what changes you were making to the week," I end with a smile, hating the fact that it was one hundred percent a lie.

I could have texted her or emailed her with changes. I want to be here with her. I want to watch as she bites her bottom lip when considering a question or how her nose scrunches when she makes a joke, as if she is laughing at herself.

"Oh, of course, let me get it out, and we can talk details," she replies, a slight disappointment sliding into her voice at my response.

Wishful thinking much. She isn't disappointed. She is relieved.

She continues with the schedule in front of her now. "Well, I had taken the time between classes off for today, but I guess we kind of had that. We are supposed to meet again tonight from five-thirty to eight, and then tomorrow, we have class together and a session after before I head to work. The only big changes I made were to your proposed Friday-Sunday schedule." She looks up at the last word fumbling a bit, and I smile, thinking about what it might be like to propose to her. She would want it small, with no stadiums or restaurants—something personal that linked us. I shake my head as I get way ahead of myself.

"Seeing as we haven't exactly gotten into any content this week yet, I feel like the time this weekend is necessary. If you have errands to run or groceries to get, we could add those into the time, and I could go with you. You could quiz me along the way?" I offer, hoping she'll keep the weekend the same.

"Ok, let's meet in the middle. We keep Friday morning the same, but I get Friday night. Saturday can stay as is since I work half the day, and we do the second half of Sunday, so I have my morning to complete my assignments." Her counter takes almost eight hours away from me over the weekend, but hopefully, I can spend that time figuring out what she did with the video so I can get rid of that complication.

"I guess I can make that work. Friday at your place, Sunday in the library?" I ask, trying to find a way into the apartment to look for the missing USB copy Pres told me she made.

"We could do both at the library, so we have space and quiet," she responds, her voice hitching up an octave like it does when she is nervous.

"I would hate for you to come all the way to campus when you have the entire evening to yourself. I'll come to you," I push, making it a statement in hopes she'll relent. "But as for today, let's get you to your next class."

While she was on her call, I began cleaning up the trash from the two sandwiches I ate, the meatball and the turkey and grabbed her wrapper from the Italian sub. She sits there as if trying to convince herself to argue. Once I gather everything, I lean into her, grabbing her chin lightly and turning to me. My need to feel her overrides my better judgment.

"It's just studying, Firefly." I lie, knowing fully that her heart sped up when I touched her. I take a deep breath, memorizing her scent before letting her chin go to help her with her bags. It takes her a minute before she moves. She seems puzzled and shakes her head as if throwing away some thought.

I walk her to her next class, feeling the tension like electricity between us. My arm swings just a breath away from hers, and the almost touch of it holds all my focus. I want to grab her hand and pull her into me. Hell, I would take her right here in the quad if she would have me, but I know she is battling with her emotions as much as I am, and I can almost see her wheels turning in her head as we try for small talk.

"Elle!? Hey Elle. Wait up," a masculine voice calls from the south side of the courtyard. We turn, and my hackles go up as I place my body in front of hers, protecting her from the man approaching. It is then I recognize him.

Shit.

I knew this would happen eventually, but I was hoping it would be after the job part of this was done. I turn my face away from him, trying to seem nonchalant.

Maybe he wouldn't recognize me? Perhaps the drug took that part of his memory away?

"Hey Elle, I hadn't heard from you since work...." He stops, fully seeing me next to her, recognition dawning on his face.

"Hey Keith, sorry I meant to call you last night, but you never sent me your new number." Keith's eyes flash to mine, anger and panic warring in them.

She doesn't know how he lost his phone. Interesting. I guess they aren't as close as they let on.

"Oh, this is Cain. I'm tutoring him for our Global Business Strategies class," she introduces me, not noticing the staredown Keith and I are having. I raise an eyebrow at him before extending my hand in his direction.

"Nice to meet you, Keith," I taunt, seeing how he'll play this, though his name came out through gritted teeth.

"Likewise." He takes my hand, both of us squeezing harder than necessary in a show of dominance.

You've got nothing on shifter strength, man.

Bri stops and looks at us in our exchange, confusion ghosting her expression. I relent, letting his hand go and turning on my smile for her.

"Well, you should get to class. I'll see you after?" I assert, pulling her into a hug, all while glaring over her shoulder at Keith.

Let him think there is more here because there is. She. Is. Mine.

I pull back, and she seems dazed and a little embarrassed that she let me hug her when we are just supposed to be study buddies. Her eyes glance at Keith before landing back on me.

"Yeah, at five-thirty, I'll meet you in the library. The same table as before," she turns and starts to walk off. Watching her leave with him is pure torture, but I can't exactly get into an all-out brawl with her best friend right in front of her. Besides, he was the one who stole from me. Keith falls into stride with her before she turns around, "Oh, Cain?" I hold my ground. "Thank you for lunch and the pep talk. It helped."

"Anytime, Firefly," I shoot back with a wink knowing full well he can hear me. She gives me her million-dollar smile before tucking a rogue hair behind her ear and walking off with Keith. Let's hope that guy knows how to shut his mouth because I don't need him in her head.

When they disappear, I pull my phone out, calling Pres.

"Hey, what's up, Cain?" she answers cautiously, gum-smacking as she speaks.

"What have you gotten off the hacker's phone?" I ask, forgetting all preamble through my seething anger.

"Well, hello to you too. So far, I have only been able to get into one of the encrypted messaging apps. The bad news is the messages erase themselves every twenty minutes. The good news is whoever he has been connecting with sent him a message to meet tomorrow. More bad news, we have no idea where, and if he has gotten a new device, then chances are we won't be getting any new communication on this device at all," she concludes, leaving me with more questions than answers.

"Does Dante want to bring the hacker in?" I ask, hoping I'll get a chance to interrogate him myself, take out my aggression over his relationship with Bri all over his face.

"Not yet. He thinks it'll compromise you since he saw you at the office building before he was drugged. My best advice is to avoid him if your girl is going to be hanging out with him because otherwise, he'll become a loose end we have to take care of." Her voice holds a warning in it that I don't much appreciate.

"And, hypothetically, if I had already been in contact with him?" I throw it out there because, at some point, they would need to know he is aware of me.

"Then hypothetically, he and your girl might need to be brought in because who knows what he's telling her... hypothetically." I can hear the condescending tone of her entire response. "Do I need to notify Dante?"

"I'll get back to you on that. I meet with her again at five-thirty and will get a feel of the situation then. Keep looking into that phone, we need the location, or we won't have his ties to Marlo," I end the call and walk back to my SUV. I have a pit stop to make before my meet-up at the library, and I hope to clear my girl because this week might take one hell of a turn if I can't.

Chapter 17

Bri

After my interview and lunch with Cain, I'm in the most fantastic mood. He is so easy to talk to, and just having him sit with me gave me immense confidence. As I walk to my last class, I try to focus on whatever Keith is talking about.

"How did you meet that guy?" he asks, turning us out of the quad.

"My professor sent him to me for tutoring. He just showed up in the library wanting to pay me to tutor him," I reply, remembering how he tried to flirt with me to get me to take the job. His eyes were stormy as he waited for me to fall to his charm, and I had. I just didn't let him know it. He is too hot for his own good, and the last thing a guy like Cain needs is an ego boost. He is one of those cases where people say he's a ten, but... and fill in something unbecoming. Well, I would fill it in with ....
but he knows he's a ten. I laugh a little as we approach my next class.

"Are you hearing me? That guy seems like bad news," he states, grabbing my shoulders to face him to ensure he has my attention.

"Don't be ridiculous. Cain is just a guy who needs some extra help with a class. I think you are reading too much into this," I deflect, unsure why he seems so invested.

"I know guys like him, and if he is trying to spend time with you, it's because he wants something." Keith declares, growing angry at my lack of belief in him.

"Well, thank you for that... I guess that shows exactly what you think of me. He can't possibly think I'm smart and capable of giving him the knowledge he needs. No. He must want to sleep with me because all women are just sex objects for men, right Keith? All of us are my mom? Objects to be used and thrown away?" I'm yelling now and don't realize it until I finish the thought. I glance around to see several people looking our way. Keith's face drops immediately, apologetic at his tactless misogynistic comment.

"You know that's not what I meant, Elle," he tries using the pet name to calm me down. I'm nearly shaking at this point.

"Look, I don't care what you think of him. He is a client. I'm tutoring him for the extra money I need for my move. I'm not sleeping with him; it would be none of your business even if I were. I'm not like you, Keith. I don't do half-way, wishy-washy, noncommittal bullshit, and I know I'm leaving, so it's not even an option." I realize by the clenching in his jaw that I struck a nerve just like he had, but for some reason, I don't care. I find myself growing defensive of my relationship with Cain, no matter how platonic it is.

"I'm just asking you to be careful. You just met this guy. Keep your guard up, Elle. Not everyone is a good guy," he finishes throwing his hands up as if in defeat, sighing. "I didn't mean to upset you. Look, can we hang out this weekend? I only work Saturday, so otherwise, I'm free."

It has been ages since we have been able to spend time together. Not since our trip last summer, unless you count seeing him at work or Liv's party. He has always been a big part of my life, but recently we have grown farther apart. Keith had been the older brother I always imagined Sam would be, so maybe I need to let this go. He is only trying to protect me. I have known him for over a decade, and we hardly ever fight. I don't want to start that right before leaving for the other side of the country.

After calming down and trying to justify my anger toward Keith, I respond. "I guess, yeah. I don't have much time because I'm tutoring Cain, but we can find something. Could you text me? I have to get to class." I give him a quick one-arm hug before turning and heading into the building. "By the way, what brought you to campus? You graduated, remember? You are supposed to leave all this behind," I joke, trying to lighten the mood between us.

"Had to see a man about a horse," he replies with a completely straight face, and I laugh because he uses that line far too often for it to make sense.

"Ok, mystery man, keep your secrets," I shout over my shoulder and send up a wave, feeling better having left things on a lighter note. I hope he texts me, but I wonder when I can squeeze in time to hang out with him with everything else I have on my plate. I need to make time. Keith is important to me, and I only have a few months left here.

"Bye, Elle!" He waves as he turns and heads back toward the courtyard.

My class flies by, and I can barely pay any attention to the notes I'm taking. My mind is elsewhere, thinking about Cain, Keith, Liv, and Boston. I don't particularly appreciate that I'm so attracted to Cain or that he occupies more of my thoughts than he should. I hate that being around him makes me relax and feel centered. But most of all, I hate that I don't hate it. That I want to want him. I need him to be more than a client, even though I know he is out of my league. He is the walking, talking reincarnation of Damon Salvatore, and I'm no Elena.

I sigh, looking over at the clock for the fiftieth time, and I see I still have ten minutes to go until I see him again. My pocket vibrates with an incoming text message, getting my hopes up that a particular grumpy sex dream is checking in. I pull it out, feeling my stomach clench in anticipation. My mood drops a little when I notice it is from an unknown number, and the message lets me know it is Keith. I send him back a thumbs-up emoji and put my phone back away.

The professor wraps up our lecture with some reading to complete before our next class and a reminder about our upcoming project. I groan internally, knowing I'll do the entire thing myself because I can't put my grades into anyone else's hands.

One more thing to add to this never-ending to-do list of mine.

I pack up my notebooks and throw my bag over my shoulder before heading to the library, where I'm determined to complete some content with Cain, so I can be paid for doing my job.

***

When I arrive at the library, Cain is already taking up residence at my favorite corner table behind the elevators. He is spread out with his feet on the chair across from him, still wearing his gray sweats and a black shirt that looks like it is made for him. He has a notebook and a pen with him but nothing else.

No wonder he is failing; he doesn't even have the book.

I roll my eyes, knowing I'll be lending him mine to ensure he can complete all of the reading material before class tomorrow, especially since I have already finished it and completed my notes.

"Hey, good looking. You come here often?" I ask, throwing a deep masculine tone to my voice and trying not to laugh before he answers.

"Not often enough. It seems I haven't swept you off your feet yet," he responds without missing a beat. I chuckle and throw my books onto the table before kicking his foot off the chair I'll inhabit for the next few hours.

"We have much to cover before class tomorrow, so let's get started," I suggest, all business in my tone despite the fluttering in my stomach. "I know you missed quite a few classes at the start of the semester. What work do you need to do for the first four weeks? We can start with that." I look at him, my syllabus in front of me, ready to note what we have to tackle.

"All of it," he admits. "It took a lot of convincing to be allowed to stay in the class despite my inability to attend the weekly lectures. That's why I need you. I'm half a semester behind with little chance of catching up without expert help." He looks me straight in the eyes as he speaks, and something tugs inside me when he says he needs me.

"Why did you have to start so late?" I ask, genuinely curious why he didn't just push the course to the following semester.

"I had a work opportunity out of state that went longer than expected. This class is the last one I need to complete, so I didn't want to put it off another semester." He shrugs, twirling his pen in his fingers lazily.

"Wow, that's awesome that you are so close to being done. It has to be a little less daunting knowing you already have a well-paying job on the other side of this. What do you do that allows you to afford a five thousand dollar-a-week private tutor?" I dig in, hoping to learn more about what makes him tick.

"My best friend and I run a small but profitable security company. We work with all kinds of clients. Some more prosperous who take outstanding care of us." He smiles and shifts his weight to open his notebook, clearly signaling he's ready to start.

Got it. No more personal questions.

"I feel safer already. Why don't we start at week one, and we can see how far we get." I go into full-on tutor mode, passing him notes and explaining critical elements mentioned in the lectures. He nods along as I speak, asking questions occasionally, and writing down things I tell him are pertinent to exam one and the first essay. It is well past ten when we complete all the week one assignments and readings.

"I'm sorry I cut into your study time for tomorrow," he apologizes, with sincerity written on his face.

"It's ok. I'm glad we got to a clear stopping point. I think you have a grasp of the key concepts and are on track to be able to make up the first assessment early next week." I beam at him, proud of his ability to comprehend complex theory without much effort. He makes me feel like I'm doing well with his tutoring even though I had my doubts coming in.

"You're good at this. It's a wonder you aren't going into teaching instead of marketing. I think you'd make one hell of a professor." he states with no humor in his tone. "Can I ask you a question?" he continues looking at me with a more serious face.

"You just did," I joke before realizing he's being sincere.

"Sorry, I use humor to deflect compliments. It's a defense mechanism. I'm working on it," I reply, embarrassed to explain my shortcomings to a man with no confidence issues.

"Why didn't you tell me you had a boyfriend?" The question hangs in the air as I consider how to answer it.

On the one hand, I could lie and say Keith is my boyfriend. It would place a barrier between us that we desperately need to have.

On the other hand, I'm not too fond of the idea of misleading him. I'm not sure why but some part of me is connected to him, and that lie feels wrong. So I go with option three.

"Would it matter if I did? You asked me to be your tutor, not your date. I don't think my relationship status is pertinent to what we're doing here," I reply with false confidence, not answering his question and flushing with the implication that he cares whether or not I have somebody else.

"Does he know that you kissed me?" his voice is deeper, darker somehow, as he asks, leaning toward me with an intensity that radiates off of him. My mouth falls open for a moment before I force it back shut. I search his stormy gray eyes, wondering why this line of questioning. For a moment, he has me exposed, seeing past the bravado and sarcasm to the darkest parts, the broken pieces, and lost battles that have left irrevocable scars.

Breathe.

"You kissed me back," I state plainly when I regain my ability to talk, though my answer has absolutely nothing to do with his inquiry.

"That's because I don't have a boyfriend," his reply is dead-panned, but his tone is playful as he examines me, waiting for my answer in this cat-and-mouse line of questioning.

"Well, neither do I, not that it's your business because, as I said, I'm your tutor." At this point, my heart is racing, and I swear you can hear it beating out of my chest. I busy myself by putting away my papers and notes, anything to calm down the tension between us.

Is the air not on in here? Why am I sweating?

"So, who is Keith to you?" his eyebrow raises slightly with the question, and I notice his jaw firmly lock as he waits for my response.

Is he jealous of Keith? That's ridiculous.

"He's my best friend." It is the truth, yet I can see him flinch subtly at the words weighing their meaning. "And if you must know, he told me to be careful with you. He told me he got the impression you weren't a good guy and you have an ulterior motive for this tutoring." Emotion flashes on Cain's face, and it surprises me, but it's gone before I can genuinely analyze it.

"Warned you about me, did he?" He laughs a little, taking away some of the electricity flying between us as he wipes his hand down his face. "He's probably right to do just that," his gaze finds mine again, making my breath catch as he continues, "I do have ulterior motives."

My eyes widen in surprise, and my heart picks up as I try to decode the message he is sending me.

I shake my head, "Cain, we talked about..." he cuts me off before I can finish the statement.

"I know, Firefly, just tutoring. I remember," he stops short, standing up to move into my space, slowly crowding me until I have to sit on the table to avoid touching him. He places his hands on either side of my thighs, forcing his body between them before finishing his statement. "But if you ever want to revisit that hotter-than-hell kiss we shared, I'll be happy to amend our arrangement." He winks, leaning forward to slide his lips a breath away from my skin, descending slowly down the column of my neck. Not touching me but making me feel him all the same. My skin responds automatically, straightening the tiny hairs in an attempt to close the distance he is purposely leaving between us.

Yes... No... Yes... No. Fuck!

Every nerve ending in my body is on high alert, straining slightly in hopes he'll touch me. My eyes fall closed, and I give in to my desire leaning my forehead onto his shoulder and letting out a strangled moan. His hands move to my thighs, squeezing them firmly before sliding them up until they reach my hips, where he grips me roughly, hard enough to leave light bruises on my skin before he pulls away from me completely.

When I open my eyes, he has his back to me, grabbing his notebook and placing the pen behind his ear before turning back to face me, his eyes still swirling with desire. He clears his throat.

"Let me walk you to your car."

"Oh..." I respond, still shaken from the almost moment in the middle of the library. "You don't have to do that. I can find my way."

My voice is a little breathier than I intend, as I'm still warring with my insides.

I grab my bags, avoiding his gaze, hoping he'll leave, so I can think clearly and gather my bearings.

"Firefly." He pauses, waiting for me to look at him, and damned if it doesn't take a minute to set my resolve before peering back into the storm of his eyes.

"It's late, dark, and unsafe for an untrained female to walk alone. For my peace of mind, let me escort you?" The sincerity in his eyes finally sways me.

I like him protecting me. I'm safe with him.

The realization that I trust Cain hits me like a freight train to the heart. I spend several moments second-guessing it, and every way I look at it, I get the same result. He makes me feel safe. I can't remember the last time I felt at ease with a man. I'm not worried about his temper or his lascivious intentions. Though they are certainly there. He just proved to me he has the ability to respect my wishes, stopping even when my body certainly wasn't protesting his actions. Thinking about it now, even with my boyfriends, I always had my guard up to some extent.

Maybe that's why it never worked out.

I was certainly young and naive once, but growing up in the system tears that right out of you. I learned fast to avoid the foster dads and older male siblings for fear they would overpower me. It was a lesson I had learned the hard way, to the tune of several broken ribs and a fractured eye socket in an attempt at my virginity. It was the first and last time a man put his hands on me without permission. I had made sure of that.

"I would hardly say I'm untrained. I have taken self-defense classes for years, I carry pepper spray in my bag, and I can run extremely fast when necessary. I would hardly classify myself as an easy target," I quip back, strength lacing my words with the confidence I feel.

"That may be true, but unfortunately, I have a mother who would kill me if she found out I let you walk back to your car late at night. Humor me?" He ends by reaching out his hand to take my textbook bag from me.

"Well, we can't have you dead before finding out if you were able to learn anything today," I throw back, heading toward the stairs and allowing him to escort me despite knowing I can handle myself.

"Certainly not! And from the sounds of it, maybe I need you out here protecting me. Pepper spray and Karate master." He jokes, walking out into the crisp November air.

The campus is deserted at this time of night. Students have long since retreated to their dorms and parties or are off at the clubs on the strip. There is a peaceful silence as we walk to the lot where my Kia waits to take me home. It's dark out, but the light poles illuminate our way keeping us from getting lost as we stroll unhurriedly through the lushly landscaped paths.

I look over at him, occasionally wondering what it is he is thinking about as he stares out into the night. He appears at ease, carrying my bags with calm confidence. My mind takes me back to the notebook and the message he left on its pages.

"So, are we not going to talk about the fact that you stole from me?" I ask, trying to keep my tone casual while studying his reaction.

"Stole from you? Now Firefly, that's quite the accusation. And what, exactly, did I steal?" His tone mocks surprise and innocence while his face gives away an entirely wicked intent.

"My Global Strat notebook," I respond resolutely.

"Now, what may I ask would I need with your notebook? I have the expert herself at my beck and call. Translating your notes sounds tedious and time-consuming. I can't imagine I would take such a thing." He grins, continuing his pace as we get nearer to our destination.

"And yet I don't hear a denial anywhere in there." I laugh, enjoying his theatrics as he so blatantly feigns offense.

"Word choice is such a significant detail, Firefly, and as I believe you have your notebook in your possession. I find the idea that it was stolen to be a bit far-fetched." He rolls his eyes as we take the final steps to my car. Amused by the easy conversation, I shake my head, and begin an internal battle with myself.

Should I ask about what he wrote? What does it mean? Would that kill this normalcy we have found?

As I go back and forth on whether to ask the question rolling around in my head, Cain speaks, taking the decision away from me.

"Thank you for today, Firefly. You know your stuff. Will you do me a favor and text me that you made it safely?" He asks, setting the bags in my backseat.

He cares about my safety. Swoon.

"I will, and hey, great job today. I'm impressed with how quickly you picked up European digital strategies," I add lamely, knowing I'm stalling to spend another moment with him while turning this encounter back to what it should have been. Two people studying. Two friends even.

"Well, I had a brilliantly beautiful tutor that I couldn't take my eyes off. She made things hard to forget." He winks his signature, 'I'm a sex God, and I know it' wink, which has me melting again as I climb into the driver's seat. He walks to my window. I start my engine and roll it down, country music wafting softly from my speakers. He grabs my chin and tilts my head toward him. For a moment, I think he might lean down and kiss me. For a moment, I think I'll let him this time, but he just stares into my eyes as if he is looking for an answer.

Part of me wants to give him that answer. To throw caution to the wind and allow him past my walls. But the other part knows that the minute I take down even one brick, the whole thing will crumble, and I'll be his to shatter.

Never again.

"Goodnight, Firefly," he whispers, understanding shining through his stare.

"Goodnight," I echo as he slips his calloused hand away and turns off toward wherever he is parked, a saunter in his gait as he walks off. I sit in a haze momentarily, trying to understand my warring feelings. The duality of my emotions is pulling me in opposite directions. Heart and mind are at odds over the right choice.

To fall and risk a devastating heartache, or to shield myself and spend forever wondering what it could have been. I don't know which would hurt more. My body for sure feels as if not touching him again will be the death of me, but I remember what it is to shatter. I'm still gluing back the pieces of losing the only person who ever truly loved me. I never want to feel that helpless or lost again.

I look down at the tattoo on my forearm, reminding myself why I got it.

I haven't forgotten, Sammy. I won't be like her. No one will trap me.

Emotions are warring inside me, and I'm taking deep breaths to keep the pain that washes over me at bay. I want to be impenetrable. Strong. Fearless. But deep down, I know Cain is starting to mean something to me. With his intense gazes and comfortable conversations, he is slowly working his way into my life and, in doing so, my heart.

I press the palms of my hands into my eyes, feeling a headache starting to form behind them.

Just get through this week—one day at a time.

After a deep calming breath, I pull out of the lot, heading for home, knowing deep down that even one day at a time will slowly kill me. Maybe I need a distraction from tall, dark, and dreamy. It hits me then what I need to do. I just hope Liv is still awake to help me.

Chapter 18

Bri

Ten days later

    What the fuck am I thinking? I wasn't thinking. That's the only logical reason I came up with this hair-brained scheme. I bend over the sink, splashing cold water onto my face to try and calm my nerves. Whoever came up with the saying the only way to get over someone is to get under someone else was an idiot of the highest order.

    Why did I think I could do this? I don't do casual sex. Hell, I barely dated. And I certainly don't go on blind dates to try and get a very overbearing and pushy man out of my head.

    Breathe Brielle. Calm down.

    I glare in the mirror, questioning every decision I have made in the last two weeks. My hair is still shining with its perfect beachy curls, but my eyes look tired, despite my attempt at mascara.

    Thank goodness for waterproof!

The skirt Liv picked out for me is a wrap-around mini similar to the one I wore to her birthday, but it is deep crimson-colored, and the spaghetti-strapped black top I wear with it hugs my curves and shows off a little cleavage. God, I look like I'm asking for it in this, and now that I'm here, I'm not sure I can follow through.

It's Friday night, and the last week and a half have been eerily uneventful. I did catch myself daydreaming about taking Cain's clothes off and fucking him on the library table on more than one occasion. I dream of him and get lost thinking about him in the shower and during class. There isn't a time of the day my mind doesn't try to wander straight to him, and if I'm not thinking or dreaming about him, I'm coming up with a reason to text him.

I've sent him more memes along with random marketing information, trying to get just a few minutes of his time. Every time we get together to study, it is all almost touches and discreet glances while he works. My body can practically feel how far away from me he is; it tingles and comes alive anytime his arm brushes against mine or his thigh presses up against me under the table. I feel like I'm genuinely losing it.

My only saving grace coming into this stupid idea of a night had been that Cain had to cancel this morning's study session because of work issues. He asked if we could switch it to tonight, but because I'm trying to distance myself from him, his smell, and his soul-sucking storm eyes, I already devised this ridiculous plan to distract myself by going on a blind date with some guy Liv knew. To be fair, it is a double date. Liv is here with Jason? Or is it Jeremy? I'm not sure, but he is her new obsession and has been since her birthday two weeks ago.

Has it only been two weeks? How was I going to get through three more?

So much has happened since the night I saw those guys get murdered.

I never thought that would be such a casual sentence.

Not the least of which is that I deleted all evidence off my phone and email. I even pulled the USB out from my floorboard and wiped it clean. I certainly didn't want that getting traced back to me now that it seemed I'm in the clear. I still feel uncomfortable walking in or out of my car at work. I constantly look over my shoulder to ensure no one follows me. And now, like the genius I am, I'm here on a date with a guy named Hudson.

Don't get me wrong, he is delicious to look at for sure, over six feet tall, with deep caramel skin, built like he never misses a day in the gym, but unfortunately, aside from a pretty face, he has nothing going on intellectually. The guy is your typical frat boy. All drinking, cars, and girls. He did say he spent a lot of time in the mountains doing outdoorsy stuff, which sounds good in theory, but aside from lightning bugs, I don't get along with wildlife much.

I stare at my reflection, trying to give myself a pep talk to go back out there and endure another hour of Hudson and *Jacob?* go back and forth about parties, drinking, and weights.

Liv is so enamored that she just giggles at all the stories. As much as I love her, these guys aren't my crowd. I find myself missing Cain, and I pull out my phone for the fifteenth time to see if he has messaged me. Not since this afternoon, when he offered to swing by after my dinner with Liv.

Did I lie to him about what I was doing tonight? No. Did I leave out the fact it was a date? Yes. I don't know why it bothers me so much to keep this from him. I don't belong to him. We aren't together. I'm his tutor, and if I want to continue as his tutor, I need to get my head out of the clouds and find something or someone else to fantasize about.

I return to the table with more resilience than I feel possible. Hudson is in the middle of a story about raiding some warehouse with some buddies. His eyes find mine as I sit down next to him, and his hand slides onto my thigh as he continues. His thumb lightly circles as he speaks. I stare at it for a moment, unsure how I feel about it. It isn't particularly intimate, but it doesn't give me the electricity I feel when Cain is even in my proximity.

Stop comparing them! You are here to have a good time. Hudson is precisely the easy, no strings attached good time we need!

I paint on a smile and reach for my margarita.

"It was crazy how in sync we all became. We were like a military unit, clearing rooms and kicking in doors." His eyes dance with enthusiasm as he tells the story, and he grins at me in a way that appears confident, like he is proud.

"Was this through your job?" I ask, curious about what kind of profession had people clearing warehouses in the middle of the night. I briefly wondered if he worked on the air force base in some SWAT capacity.

"Umm yeah, I work for an independent security company in town. We do all kinds of interesting jobs. I once got to escort Conor McGregor out to his fight, and man, do people either love or hate that guy! It was all panties in the air on one side and beer bottles being chucked on the other. We never knew what was coming at us." He laughs, downing the rest of his beer. Liv looks across the table, smiling at me, which I assume means

See how great he is.

I nod at her and salute her with my drink. I'm going to need all the liquid courage to get through tonight.

After dinner, we all pile into an Uber to head home. I spend the ride clinging to the door handle with the window open, trying to maintain control while everyone laughs and jokes. Hudson has his arm casually around me, but he is feeling the alcohol, so he isn't picking up on my anxiety or reluctance. I'm starting to panic about what comes next. I have never done the one-night stand thing.

Do we go straight to the act? Do I offer him a beverage?

The apartment is stocked with groceries in part thanks to my tutoring installments from Cain hitting my account.

Why does every train of thought lead back to him?

Just as I think of him, we round the corner into the apartment complex, and my heart stops. He was here. Sitting on the stairs outside my apartment in jeans with a sexy-as-sin white shirt stretched across his chiseled chest with a brown take-out bag sitting at his feet while he runs his fingers through his untamed hair. I see the moment he realizes it is me climbing out of the car. His face is flush with concern like he has been worried, even though I told him I was having dinner out tonight. Relief washes over him, and his shoulders relax as he gives me that smile that makes my panties wet.

It feels like slow motion because just as I meet his eyes with a smile to match his own, delighted to see him despite my best efforts not to be, which I assume is at least partly due to my three margaritas. Then, his steel gray eyes flip over my shoulder, and he sees Hudson climb out behind me, holding my bag. The air becomes tense as I look between them, wondering how this will play out.

"Cain?" Hudson speaks first, surprising me and making my head snaps toward him.

Does he know him?

"Hudson," Cain responds, his voice strained.

Do they know each other?!?

The two men stand there like statues as I feel Cain reading the scene, his face hardening and anger filling his eyes. I attempt to diffuse the situation.

"Cain, what are you doing here? I told you I couldn't meet tonight." My voice is weaker than I intend. I barely finish the statement before his eyes slide back to me, all the previous warmth wiped from them. A scowl is now firmly in place.

"Clearly," he grinds out, "though you left out the part where you were taking my," he pauses as if searching for the word, his eyes again briefly lifting to Hudson, "employee with you." The venom in his voice washes over my skin as I try to understand what is happening here.

Why is he so angry? I'm not his. I don't belong to him.

But even as I consider the words, I know I'm full of shit. Though not the brightest bulb, Hudson takes this moment to plan his escape.

"Well, I'm going to head out, Bri. Thanks for hanging out tonight." He reaches out as if to hug me, only to stop halfway, faltering as a menacing growl escapes Cain's throat, which is threatening and more wild animal than civilized man. I turn to him, the hairs on my body standing on end, and see his frame primed to fight. His upper lip snarling. While that in itself is terrifying and makes me shuffle backward a step involuntarily, what gives me pause are his eyes which appear to be almost glowing.

That can't be right. How much did I drink?

In an instant, Hudson is back in the car, and the three of them are off to *Joshua's? James's?* Oh hell, Liv's plaything's place to finish the night. I feel paralyzed at the base of the stairs. Barely able to raise my arm to wave at a very drunk Liv, who has completely missed the entire interaction and is shouting out the back passenger window, "Night bitch!"

When I pull my focus back to Cain, he has regained some composure. Gone is the wild look in his eyes and the soft glow that seemed to emanate from within them. His shoulders slump down, and he is breathing heavily. He stares in the direction the car has just left for several long moments in silence.

"I'm sorry I ruined your evening," he muses so quietly I almost miss it, and he starts his descent toward the parking lot. His eyes no longer meet mine, and the casual, confident gait he walks around with is now missing.

"You didn't. It was over anyway." I reply in a voice that feels still smaller than it should have.

I didn't do anything wrong. Why do I feel so guilty?

I start up the stairs, carefully blocking his path, unsure if I should provoke him after the scene that just played out. "Is that ice cream?" I ask, pointing to the Baskin Robin's bag forgotten at the front door. He laughs. Not his typical deep rumble but more of a scoff as he runs his fingers through his disheveled hair.

"I thought you might like dessert after your dinner," he replies, swinging his arm out absently toward town. My heart pitter-patters at the romantic gesture while cursing myself for messing this whole thing up.

"Well, let's get it inside before it melts completely," I order, hoping he won't leave things like this. I nod my head with more authority than I feel and grab the bag as I walk past him to the door. As my body slides by him, my skin begins to tingle with its signature hum, the connection between us just as palpable as before, but the mood is undoubtedly less alive. My eyes flash up to his momentarily, and I can see him respond to it as well. I turn the lock and push into the apartment, heading directly to the alarm to turn it off and toss my keys into the entry basket. Cain closes the door behind us and stands awkwardly in the entryway.

You can do this. Just explain it to him.

I enter the kitchen, throw the ice cream bag into the icebox to refreeze, and then grab two beers from the fridge before returning to him. The buzz I had when I left the restaurant is now completely absent. I offer him one and tilt my head toward the living room, indicating he should sit. I kick off the heels I'm wearing and curl my legs under me on my spot on the loveseat across from the TV, and he sits on the other side as far from me as he can. It is like one of those romcoms where the couple sits down for the movie on opposite ends of the couch, and all the while, you know they will end up meeting in the middle. I smile at that, hoping he and I could both literally and figuratively meet in the middle tonight.

For the first time since we met, the silence between us isn't comfortable or easy. It is loaded with unasked questions and unanswered pleas—eyes that are avoidant and words that go unsaid. There is no banter, no back and forth, no laughter.

Have I lost him already?

I study him as he tries to process his emotions, occasionally letting some of them appear on his face—anger, pain, lust, sadness. As he slowly drinks from the brown glass bottle, I see them all in flashes. He won't meet my eyes, instead looking anywhere else in the room that he can. It is several minutes before he finally speaks, but it feels like hours as I wait to see what he will say.

Is he mad that I lied? Jealous that I was with someone else? Irritated that I blew him off for Hudson?

My mind is spinning, and trying to brace myself for every possibility. The same question bounces around that I can't escape.

Was this it?

"Why him?"

The words seem to echo in the small living space and are clear as day though laced with unfettered torture.

"Why is it ok for you to be with him and not me?" His eyes finally lift to mine, and my resolve shatters. I can feel his anguish as he holds my gaze, and for a moment, the world stops turning, and my heart stops beating because nothing hurts more than feeling like I caused him pain. I struggle to find words.

"Because he doesn't mean anything." I let the words hang in the air as I fight to find a way to make him understand. Hoping he hears the truth behind what I leave unsaid.

Because you do.

I don't know how to explain without showing him my cards. Without giving away how much I'm falling. How much I'm beginning to rely on his connection to get through the day.

I'm not entirely sure when I start to cry, but I feel the first tear hit my thumb as I sit staring at my hands, fidgeting with my fingers as I turn over all my reasons.

Damn alcohol! Always making me cry.

More tears slowly slide down my cheek as I struggle to regain my composure.

He lets out a deep sigh that sounds like he is giving up and closes the distance between us, reaching up to wipe the salty moisture away while wrapping his other arm behind me and pulling me onto his lap. I don't fight him. Hell, I lean into his chest, letting his scent fill my senses as his racing heart beats to a rhythm that matches my own. The hollow thumping centers me, and I glance at him through tear-drop-covered lashes.

He studies me, his eyes showing the war he is fighting with himself as he tucks a strand of my hair behind my ear, leaving his hand to linger on my jaw.

"Do I mean anything to you, Brielle?" he asks, holding my stare while his metallic gray irises swirl, waiting for my answer. His jaw clenches, his breathing becomes uneasy, and I feel him trembling with physical restraint as he attempts to respect my limits after our last kiss. His stare is wild and penetrating, silently asking my consent to give in to this unfulfilled need between us, and as I sit there in his arms, surrounded by his warm, masculine scent, something inside me surrenders.

"Firefly." It comes out breathy, but the demand I place behind it rings true. "You don't call me Brielle. You call me Firefly." His face softens first, and a small smile forms. Then the tension begins melting slowly from his body as his lips descend, landing in the center of my forehead before trailing a line of soft kisses to my eyelids, stealing my tears before going on to the tip of my nose. Then he pauses, hovering over my lips, only a breath away, and my entire body screams to kiss him. My pulse is racing as I reopen my eyes and look up at him through my dark, wet lashes.

"Do I mean anything to you, Firefly?" he repeats his question amending the name as his breath dances over my lips. The sweet hint of toothpaste mixes in the air.

"Everything. You mean everything to me." It comes out as a whisper, and despite every argument my brain throws at me, I let down my walls, reach up, grab him at the base of his neck, and capture his mouth with mine.

My kiss isn't gentle or polite, but instead, is a total release of every emotion I have bottled up since he walked into that party. I can feel his surprise for an instant before he falls into the kiss, slowly tilting my chin and sliding his tongue across my lips, demanding access. I part them, sucking his tongue deeper inside while my fingers thread through his hair to pull my body even closer to him.

Too many clothes.

His hands are moving, one skimming the side of my top and the other sliding down to my ass. He lifts me slowly, allowing me to guide my leg over him so that I straddle his lap, causing my red skirt to slide up my thighs. A moan escapes his lips as I land squarely on his hard length, and a thrill runs through me as it hits my core, causing me to grind my hips deeper into him, loving the friction it provides my clit with only a tiny strip of fabric between my heated slit and his jeans.

Still too many clothes.

I'm unsure if I say the words out loud or if he reads my mind, but he sucks my bottom lip, nipping and biting at it as he begins working my shirt up my sides to my shoulders; electricity tickles my skin where he touches. I lean back, throwing up my arms to allow him to pull the shirt off. He breaks our kiss only to enable the fabric to free itself from my body.

He freezes for a moment, completely still, as his eyes skim over my body, feasting on my exposed chest. Lust swirls in his hooded eyes as he leans forward, taking my left breast into his mouth, suckling it a moment before dragging his teeth off the nipple, causing me to gasp with the bite of pleasured pain.

"Mine," he growls out before switching to the other side and teasing my nipple with his right hand. My body is alive in a way I don't think I had ever felt. Every graze, caress, grab, nip, bite, and scratch feels amplified and sends a never-ending wave of heat to my core. I'm soaking through my thong as I ride his cock over his clothes. I moan quietly, still frustrated by the layers between us, and I fumble my hands, trying to grasp the hem of his shirt.

His mouth leaves my chest as he wraps both hands underneath my ass and abruptly stands up, causing me to shriek a little and grab his shoulders to steady myself as he begins walking towards the hall, his mouth kissing a trail up to my neck and back down my shoulder.

"On the right." I direct him, fully panting as I throw my head back and hold onto him like a lifeline, so I don't fall. He grapples with the knob before pushing us over the threshold and flipping on the light. My breath catches, and I panic briefly at the illuminated space, knowing he will be able to see everything without the filter of darkness and shadows. He tosses me onto the bed before pulling off his shirt.

For a moment, he just stands there, breathing heavily, raking his eyes over my body. I can almost feel them as they trace a path over every inch. Goosebumps pop up on my arms, and I feel exposed under their stare. I lay there sprawled awkwardly on top of my comforter, breathing heavily, my skirt pulled up around my stomach, revealing the black thong from underneath.

As casually as possible, I roll to my side, attempting to cover the scar on my ribs and throw an arm over my breasts. I send a small thank you to Liv for forcing the workout sessions over the last month. I'm not fit by any means, but my curves sit firmly on my ass and chest while my stomach is flatter than before.

"Don't," he commands, his voice is deep gravel as he steps up to the bed. "Don't cover yourself. I want to see you. All of you." He locks eyes with me, and my heart skips a beat.

This man is built like Adonis, and he wants to look at me?

He steps up to the edge of the bed, turning me while he drops his knee to the mattress. He slides his hands up the outsides of my thighs, placing his body between them and dropping kisses slowly as he ascends. I'm trembling with anticipation as he locks eyes with me and hooks his fingers on the sides of my underwear, sliding them off before he grabs my skirt and tosses it away too.

"Open for me," he demands while pointing at my now-closed legs. I obey him instantly and without hesitation, surprising myself. His smile widens, and his eyes dilate, taking joy in knowing I'm letting him lead.

"Good girl."

He kneels there momentarily, slowly taking in every inch of my now wholly exposed body before meeting my stare again. He swiftly pulls off his jeans and boxers, standing to kick them away.

Oh. My. God.

I don't think I have seen anyone with a more perfect body. He is hard everywhere.

Everywhere!

His abs lead down to a sexy v lightly dusted with dark hair that leads right to his long thick cock, which at the moment is standing at full attention. He fists the base as he pauses for a minute, letting my eyes take him in, confidence oozing from him.

What's not to be confident about when you look like a sex ad? I'm so fucked...

Insecurity begins to flare up in me even though I know he wants me.

Why? He could have anyone...

He slowly climbs onto the bed, laying his chest on mine and diving in for another kiss. His hands slide along my skin. Digging in and gripping where he can and tracing lines in between. He plays me like an instrument, and I can feel my body sing as he builds me back to the intensity I was feeling on the couch.

All thoughts of my body are gone as his hand slides from my hip into my slick center. I gasp, breaking our kiss in surprise as he moves his now wet fingers rhythmically around my clit. Every nerve in my body is electrified and sends signals to my core. His eyes are intent on my face, watching my reactions as he gauges when he should speed up or slow down, keeping me from my orgasm while massaging my breast and rolling my nipple with his free hand.

I lift my hips into him, reaching for more friction, urging him faster and harder as I need release. I'm so close, and I know he can feel my hips shaking, my breath barely able to keep up. He swirls firmly, switching to his thumb while he slides two fingers into me. In an instant, I cum. My nails dig into his shoulder and neck as I ride the pleasure he draws from me. I meet his eyes, seeing his desire and his triumph in bringing me to the edge and pushing me over it.

In a single motion, he is gone, and he moves my legs to allow his shoulders room between them.

Oh, God.

"I need to taste you," he moans between the kisses he places on my inner thigh. He breathes me in, groaning loudly before descending to my core. His tongue is gentle as he caresses my now overly sensitive clit, sucking and licking as if he is enjoying every minute. I stare at him, unable to take my eyes away as he worships me.

My hands dig into his hair, trying to keep a hold of this reality as he builds me back up and has me teetering on edge.

This must be what drugs are like. He's my addiction. My brand of cocaine.

It takes only a few minutes, and I reach my peak again, writhing as he drinks me in, not leaving anything behind. When my tremors stop, he sits up, licking his now glistening lips with a smile that is sexy as sin. I'm desperate to touch him, to feel his connection again. My hands reach for him as he climbs back up my body, licking a nipple as he passes.

"I need you inside me," I whine, my body primed and ready to receive all of him. My hands claw at his back to pull him back to me, and then he is gone again. Grabbing his pants and pulling out his wallet to retrieve a condom before rolling it on his exceptional cock. He is back on me in a flash, his weight shifting the bed before resting on top of me. He claims my mouth once more, filling me with an instant desire as I taste myself on his lips.

He lines himself up, teasing my slit with his tip before locking eyes with me and thrusting inside me full to the hilt. My breath catches as I adjust to his size. A moan escapes me that falls somewhere between pleasure and pain.

Oh, God. Oh my God.

"You can just call me Cain," he jokes, his eyes lighting up.

Did I say that out loud?

My eyes dilate in surprise before I forget all about my words and can only focus on the pleasure building within me.

"Fuck, you are so perfect, Firefly," he whispers into my ear before slowly rocking in and out of me. My head falls back as he gradually increases his pace until he slams into me full force, my bed hitting the wall. I lock my ankles around him while arching into his thrusts, needing him closer, faster, harder. I'm determined to take him with me this time, and I drop my lips to his shoulder, trying to distract myself with his taste, kissing, sucking, and biting his neck until I can't hold out any longer. Everything in me clenches, seizing under the force of this peak, and forces Cain's release as my muscles tighten around his cock.

His weight falls on me as we both struggle to catch our breath for several minutes. Eventually, he gets up, kissing my forehead before walking to the bathroom to throw away the condom and clean himself up. As soon as he leaves the room, my head begins to spin. Question after question.

What does this mean? Where do we go from here? What if this was all he wanted?

This is precisely why I don't have one-night stands. I don't understand the expectations, and my heart is too invested to have taken this leap. I throw a pillow over my face and silently scream into it. Just my luck, I would have the literal best sex of my life and then not even be able to enjoy it before I overanalyze everything. *Maybe it was just sex? Maybe it wouldn't change anything? What if it wasn't a one-off? What if he wanted more than I could give him? What if I wasn't enough?*

He returns with two bottles of water from the fridge and sits back in the bed behind me, handing me a bottle before opening his own. We lay there in silence for a few minutes, neither of us wanting to break it by labeling what had just happened. After finishing his bottle he throws his arm over me, spooning me to him and kissing the back of my shoulder.

I lay there, searching for the right thing to say, wondering what this all means. His fingers skim lightly over the exposed skin on my hip. They circle toward my belly button, absentmindedly playing with the gem on my piercing.

"Get out of your head, Firefly," he commands lightly, causing me to sigh and release some of the tension in my shoulders.

Why is it always so easy to listen to him?

I turn to face him, finding the strength to look him in the eyes. His face appears serene and is probably the calmest I have ever seen. His eyes are gentle as they take in mine.

"I don't know how not to be freaking out right now," I respond in a voice that comes out more controlled than I feel. "What does this mean?" I ask hesitantly. He pauses for a long moment before answering. The fear I experience in the moments before he answers is all-encompassing.

"What do you want it to mean? We are going at your pace on this Firefly, though if you tell me I'm not going to get to fuck you again, I might not survive it," he finishes by throwing a dramatic grin. I giggle despite my unraveling inner dialogue and playfully slap his chest.

"Yes, I'm sure you have a terribly hard time finding anyone willing to have sex with you." I whip back at him sarcastically. His face drops his joking smile, becoming severe in an instant. His hand comes up to my cheek, and he plants a deep kiss on my lips before holding my gaze while he explains.

"You aren't just anyone. You've never been just anyone to me. I know you feel this pull between us too. This isn't normal or ordinary. This is electric, once-in-a-lifetime chemistry that I'm not ready or willing to walk away from. I know you have plans for your future that don't involve hanging around me or this town, but you can't tell me I'm the only one feeling this." His eyes are begging me for reassurance that I feel the same way he does.

"It doesn't make sense, Cain. You barely know me. I don't know anything about you. We just met two weeks ago." I ramble, trying to identify how I could be this invested in that short of a time.

"Then I guess it's good that we have the next few weeks to work all those things out. We don't have to have all the answers tonight." He places a kiss on my nose to lighten the moment. "Let's get cleaned up, so you can get to sleep," he insists, climbing up out of bed and pulling me with him.

He carries me into my shower and washes us both clean before literally making my dreams come true by fucking me boneless against the tile wall. I may not have many answers after this crazy night, but the one thing I know is that my imagination had nothing on Cain.

Not. Even. Close.

Chapter 19

Cain

Perfect. It is the one thing that keeps playing on repeat as I watch Bri sleep. She's so fucking perfect. Everything makes me want her more, her body, her smell, the sounds she makes before she cums. Even now, I can't stop my hands from gliding along her alabaster skin, tracing from freckle to freckle, sliding down the ridges of her uneven scar. My wolf hates seeing the pain etched so clearly on her skin, and it riles us that she had to endure it.

It took everything inside me to stop my wolf from claiming her and making her officially ours tonight. She deserves better than to be forced into a life, a partnership without any say. I won't force that choice on her. Hell, I'm not going to give her that choice at all.

I was utterly lost in the moment tonight after recovering from the shock that she had been on a date. It took all the resilience in me not to wolf out on the steps and charge at Hudson. Her calm demeanor became the only thing capable of reeling me back in.

I knew coming to see her tonight was a risk. We have only been meeting on campus as she continued to finagle her way out of having any sessions at her apartment. This frustrated me because I wanted her alone, and I knew I was supposed to be finding the damn copy of the video. Pres was already able to find out she deleted the copy from her phone and that she hadn't contacted anyone else about the video. My only guess is she ended up in the wrong place at the wrong time and has no idea what she is privy to.

On the other hand, Dante doesn't like the lack of progress we have made to clear her, and my gut isn't enough to sway him otherwise until we clean up this whole debacle. We haven't found the traitor, we haven't found the tie to her friend Keith, and we haven't seen her copy. So far, we are losing on all fronts.

We backed off the security detail on her house, but we have added a tail on her friend to see what he is up to. I even canceled my tutoring session today to attend a recap meeting with the council to brainstorm a new angle.

Honestly, I wanted to be near her at this point, so I came up with the dessert excuse hoping I would get some time back that I had lost. I would never have guessed she was on a date, and even less chance of me thinking it was with Hudson, of all people. He is one of our younger pack security at only twenty-one, and I hadn't spent much time with him, but I know he isn't her type.

I'm her type. She is Mine.

My phone lights up with a text message as I hold Bri, memorizing her body. It is now a little after one in the morning, and she had fallen asleep after our shower. I loved seeing her dripping wet and clinging to me. I couldn't keep my hands off her even as I tried to get us clean. Even now, my cock is waking up, hoping for another round.

Not tonight. She needs sleep.

I grab my phone, seeing Presley's name on the message.

> **Meet Jay at the door in five. He has a USB drive you need to put in her computer. It should take about three minutes to get the backdoor installed. Then remove it and take it with you when you leave.**

> **I don't like this**

> **Pres: You don't have to like it, but we need to be protected. He's there.**

> **Fine.**

I slide carefully out of her bed and pad lightly to the front door. I disable her alarm and open the door to find Jay standing there. He hands me the USB and nods before walking off. I reset the locks and alarm before grabbing her laptop from her bag in the kitchen and powering it on. I keep my ears tuned to her room to listen for any movement.

Once the laptop loads, I add Presley's tech and wait, wondering how long the download would take. I don't like deceiving her. I want to tell her everything, but I also want to protect her from this life. I know she is leaving. The only thing I don't know is whether I'll be strong enough to let her or if I'll be following her to the other side of the country.

A small download icon appears on the screen and gradually increases its percentage. It starts at 6%, jumps to 13%, then 26%.

Come on. Come on.

It is another few minutes before it hits 100% and then disappears like it was never there in the first place.

My phone buzzes in my pocket, and I remove it to see Pres's message.

I'm in. Thanks.

No problem.

BTW excellent performance tonight *wink*

Presley...

It's been deleted from the server, and I was the only one here. I left for an extended break once I realized where you two were headed. Enjoy your night.

Thanks.

Finished, I close the laptop, thankful we are one step closer to being done with the covert mission side of this arrangement. I know in my gut Bri has nothing to do with our missing tech or the Reno pack's involvement in its disappearance. She's too good to be a part of that. She's too moral for this lifestyle. Letting her go is the only way to keep her safe and away from the dangers of being part of a pack.

I sigh deeply, rubbing my hand down my face as I gingerly walk back into her room, stopping briefly in her bathroom to quickly flush the toilet as an excuse for being gone in case she noticed my absence. As I re-enter her room, I stop to stare at my Mate.

She's tangled up in the sheet, one freckled leg out completely and thrown onto the side I was on. Her deep brown hair is tangled in a loose bun that falls just off her pillow, but what strikes me the most is how peaceful her face looks. She walks around with so much stress on her shoulders and face that seeing her entirely at ease as she sleeps calms my wolf in a way I wouldn't have thought possible.

My Mate.

Letting her go will kill me, especially now that I have tasted her and heard her sounds when she cums, but she deserves more than a life shackled to me. A life without danger or pain. A life I don't think I can give her.

I crawl into her bed, gently wrapping myself around her and allowing her sleeping form to curl into mine. She is warm and smells like the apple-vanilla combination of her body soap with a subtle underlay of sunshine. I breathe her in deeply in an attempt to memorize her unmistakable aroma and attempt to freeze this moment in time.

My mind wanders, thinking about what our life could look like if she stayed here. Suppose she chose her wolf and me instead of choosing Boston. What a life we could lead. The pain hits me right in the chest as I see her give up her dreams in an attempt to be mine. I imagine the fire in her eyes dimming, and I know I would hate myself for forcing her into a life she didn't want. The rumble in my chest would have to take a back seat on this one because I know that Brielle DelaCourt will get everything she wants out of this life, even if that means a life without me.

***

Hours later, I wake to an empty bed and the smell of bacon wafting into the room. Sunshine slips in through the blinds lighting up the space. It takes me no time to remember where I am, but I'm surprised that Bri climbing out of bed didn't wake my wolf or me.

I haven't slept that well in months, maybe ever.

Rolling myself out of bed, I head into the bathroom to relieve myself. After washing my hands and splashing some water onto my face, I borrow her toothpaste, working it with my finger to rid myself of morning breath. A moment of stretching out my muscles helps me feel relaxed, which is a nice change of pace to my usual demeanor, and I mentally search for the last time I let my wolf run.

We can take care of that today while she works.

I amble into the living room, following my nose toward the sounds of the soft sizzle on the stove. Bri has music playing in her AirPods, dancing around in a tank top and some tiny running shorts that do everything for her shapely ass. My cock stirs immediately, hoping for a replay of last night. I slide my hands onto her waist, pulling her into me while she jumps in surprise.

"Ahhh, Jeez!" she giggles and pulls out her AirPod to hear again. Her heart rate increases momentarily at the shock of me being awake and in the kitchen.

"Sorry to startle you," I chuckle before kissing the space between her neck and shoulder. "I woke up alone and hungry." I let my tone imply that I'm not just hungry for the breakfast she is making, and she blushes furiously, turning her skin the color of a sun-ripened peach. She smirks while turning to take the last bacon from the pan and places it on a rack to dry and cool.

"Well, I guess it's good I got up early to cook," she replies, looking over her shoulder with humor glinting in her honey-brown eyes. She purposely avoided responding to the sexual undertones I sent her way. I grin back at her, happy that she hadn't attempted to leave my grip while my fingers lightly circle her hip bones, and she even leans back into me, melting into the embrace.

"Did you sleep ok?" she asks, moving to grab some plates before I can answer.

"Better than I have in a long time," I respond truthfully, watching as she dishes out the bacon before bending to open the oven, pulling a stack of pancakes out, and placing those on the two plates. I take the plates from her and walk them over to the table while she grabs the syrup and a couple of coffee cups. It all feels domestic and routine, and the sense of rightness it gives me is instant and overwhelming.

Home.

She was that for me—more than the woods, more than my pack, more than anyone else had ever been.

"Now, don't expect too much, they are box pancakes, but I got pretty good at making these in my third foster house," she states, flicking her eyes away as if she is embarrassed to have let that little tidbit slip out. I tilt my head, examining her and giving her a minute to recover before I ask the question that I already know the answer to.

"I didn't realize you were in the system,"

Lie.

"My buddy Jake bounced his way through a few foster situations before turning eighteen, and he has some stories that sound more like warzones than family homes. His mom died having him, and his dad never knew he existed. What happened to your parents?" I ask, only genuinely curious about what she knows of her dad since I had read enough about her mom to know she is a junkie without many redeeming qualities.

"They died in a car accident along with my older brother," she lies without hesitation. While she avoids my eyes by cutting into her pancakes, her heart rate remains constant.

This is a lie she has told before, too many times.

"You were in the car," I state, remembering her freak out from Dante's sports car. "How old were you?" I ask though I know the answer.

Only ten.

I have read and reread her file a hundred times, trying to know her, to understand how she ticks.

"I was ten," she replies before changing the subject completely, "This is a little heavy for this morning. Why don't you tell me what you are up to today?" She shovels a large bite into her mouth to punctuate her point that she isn't discussing her past anymore, so I let the conversation flow away from that topic and onto lighter things.

"Well, I had planned on repeating several of the activities we engaged in last night and maybe coming up with a few new ones just to spice things up," I reply, my eyebrows dancing up and down suggestively. I'm incapable of keeping the grin off my face as I watch her turn even deeper crimson as she laughs, nearly spitting her food everywhere. "But as I woke up alone, and you mentioned yesterday that you have work today, I guess I'll have to rain-check that for... tonight?" I finish turning the last word into a question and hope she wants to keep this going with everything in me. Her face turns seductive, and I swear my cock responds immediately.

She is going to be the death of me.

"A bold ask, but it's interesting how you insinuate that there will be the next time. I'm not sure that it was really memorable enough to give it another go," she finishes shrugging one shoulder, fake doubt dripping into her statement and causing my wolf to flare up.

Unmemorable?

A growl slips out of my throat as I lose all of my humor. I push myself back from the table as I rise, leaning toward her in a predatory manner. She giggles, biting her bottom lip as I get closer. I love this playful side to her.

"Be careful, Firefly. I might just carry you back into that room and fuck you until the only thing you can remember is my name." I lean in and kiss her. It's rough, possessive, and thorough, and I end it by pulling her bottom lip through my teeth with enough pressure to barely not break the skin. I open my eyes to see hers still closed, her breathing labored, and her hands tangled in my shirt. I laugh a little darkly at how much she responds to my touch.

Oh, what I would do to this body if it were indeed mine.

I take her empty plate from her and stroll into the kitchen to place everything in the sink. I have to adjust my once again rock-hard cock, which is now straining against my jeans, while I begin rinsing everything and putting it in her dishwasher. She sits watching me over the brim of her cup of coffee, and I see our entire lives play out for a moment.

She is made for me.

I revel in that moment before allowing reality to sink in with the knowledge that she can't be mine. The loss I feel is excruciating.

She will never be mine.

Just as I try to bring up the enormity of what I'm feeling, wanting, and needing, her phone lights up, buzzing as it vibrates on the table. She sets down her coffee and reaches for it, her eyebrows shooting up when she looks at the screen.

"It's Boston," she gasps, eyes wide. My heart pounds more urgently in my chest as I steel my resolve.

Breathe.

"Answer it, Firefly. Let's hear the news," I try for a supportive tone, but it feels like it comes out more like a command than a request, so I add a forced grin and a nod of encouragement. She clears her throat and lets out a puff of air before accepting the call.

"Hello?" she answers as she places her phone to her ear. I lean on the counter, casually eavesdropping easily with my enhanced hearing.

"Brielle? It's Ethan from Boston Digital," the man on the line begins.

"Hi, Ethan! How are you?" she asks brightly.

"I'm doing well. We just got another storm, so it's cold but looking beautiful." I can hear his casual tone and my gut twists.

She got through.

"I will have to take your word for it, we don't get much snow here in Vegas, and when we do, it's brown and melts pretty quickly." She laughs while easing out of her chair and begins to pace the room, playing with her shirt's hem.

"How would you like to come to see it in person?" he asks, causing her to freeze in her spot, mouth agape. He continues, "You were very impressive in your interview, and we would love to have you fly out to meet the team, sit down with everyone, and see if you would be a good fit." I struggle to hear because of the pounding pulse in my ears; my wolf fights to take control and protect what is ours. I use every bit of focus I have to try to appear nonchalant while doing the mental gymnastics of what this timeline will look like, what it will do to our tutoring schedule, and what it will mean for us.

There is no us. There can't be.

But I desperately want there to be an us, and I curse the timing of everything. She turns to me with the most beautiful smile lighting up her face. She shakes her head as she responds, stuttering as she wraps her head around the offer.

"Oh my goodness! Wow! I would love to come to meet everyone." The relief and joy that is humming through her makes me soften.

This is what she wants.

As much as I hate the idea of her leaving, all I ever want is her happiness.

"Great! Well, I know you have classes, and you mentioned work. How do your next couple of weeks look? Do you have any availability to spend two or three days? If possible, we would love to get you here just after Thanksgiving."

"I think I can make that work. I don't have any shifts scheduled from the 25th of November until the 5th of December." She rattles off and goes over to her bag, pulling out her laptop and starting it up before going back to pacing.

"Perfect! I'll have Sofia, our HR coordinator, email you with details for flight and hotel information, and we'll see you soon. Congratulations, Brielle. We are excited to meet you in person." He ends the call, and she sets down her phone, turning to me immediately.

"I made it through! They picked me to move on to the physical interview in Boston. The last step." Her eyes are wild as I see the wheels turning in her head. I walk over to her wrapping her up in a hug before picking her up and spinning her around excitedly.

"I told you they would love you, Firefly. I never had a doubt. What are we doing to celebrate? Dinner? A night out?" Maybe I'm getting ahead of myself, but I want to be a part of her joy.

"I don't ... I don't know. I have work tonight, so I can't really do anything, but I'm off tomorrow, and we already have studying scheduled, so why don't we try something after that?" She rambles, and I smile at her, a genuine full smile that gives away every bit of how wrapped up in her I am.

She locked eyes with me, and those fiery flecks usually hidden within the brown seemed brighter. I lean in to kiss her. Softly. Slowly, and with the promise of more to come. I can feel the moment she gets into her head. Her body tenses slightly, and her shoulders stiffen. I pull myself back and search her face for a moment.

"Everything will work out exactly how it is supposed to, Firefly. It always does." I let her go, and I walk back into her bedroom to sit with her while she gets ready for work. It's quiet between us as I give her space to process the upcoming interview, her school and work schedule, and me. It isn't uncomfortable like our living room silence was last night, but a dark cloud has shifted its way over the whole ordeal, and I know we were both overthinking it.

"How come you have a two-week vacation scheduled at work?" I ask, trying to lighten the mood as she finishes putting small hoops in her ears.

"I always take time before finals to ensure I'm ready," she responds, her eyes not quite meeting mine, and she paints on a small smile.

That isn't the whole truth.

I nod, allowing her the ability to tell me her real reason in her own time.

"Alright. I'm ready. Let's get out of here before Liv rolls back in, and we have a lot of explaining to do." She laughs as she changes the subject.

"No worries there, we have an NDA," I reply, winking her way before opening the door and following her out. Her face drops in surprise as she registers what I just said.

"I completely forgot about that!" she exclaims, her face mirroring the shock in her statement.

"Oh no, Firefly, have you been spreading our secrets? Well, at least now, your account of my overwhelming sexual prowess will be accurate."

I quip as we approach her car. She places her bags in the passenger seat, and I note how messy her vehicle is, a striking contrast to the organization in her apartment.

"I didn't realize you need reassurance so often, Mr. Mingan. Asking for compliments should be beneath you." she retorts.

"No, you should be beneath me." I shoot back, leaning her onto her car door before kissing her until she's moaning, her knees tremble, and her body calls out for mine. She laughs. The sound warms my heart with its innocence. "Call me when you get home tonight. And maybe come home alone this time," I ask her before walking her to the driver's side and helping her in.

"I think I can manage that. At least the calling you part. You never know who I'll bring home these days. I must be dropping my standards." She smiles, scrunching her freckled nose with her sass.

"Yeah, Hudson is a shady character. You should definitely avoid him." I remark and back up, so she has room to drive off. She bites her lip as she gives me one last look before pulling away, taking my heart with her.

I text Dante as I walk back to my SUV. Now that I know Bri will be out of town, I know just who we should pull in for some questioning to further our investigation. I hate lying to her, but the sooner we solve this mystery, the sooner it will all be behind us.

> Set up a council meeting for tonight, and tell Jake to prepare his office.

Chapter 20
Bri

I'm on cloud nine all day at work. I'm nicer to my clients, friendly with my coworkers, and even remember to text Liv to ensure she is alive and well today. Everything in my world is finally falling into place. I have nearly completed all my classes, I have a job prospect at the most incredible firm in Boston, and I'm sleeping with a man who gave me five orgasms last night.

Five!

Just thinking about him turns me on all over again.

I'm not allowing myself to dwell on the what-ifs of what will happen next with us. I'm sure the idea that I won't be around long is undoubtedly one thing that entices Cain. It makes this a whirlwind romance that we know has an expiration date. For once, I'm allowing myself joy in this one facet of my life. I'm doing everything in my power to hold onto my heartstrings, so that I won't be devastated when it ends.

Yes. When. Not if.

Cain Mingan can break me. From only the last two weeks, I know his easy charm, overbearing nature, and firmly opinionated thought processes have me in knots. I spend hours analyzing moments, rereading texts, and trying to get him out of my head to no avail. The draw is even more compelling now that I have opened up to him. He has been sweet and vulnerable while also being dominant and insisting.

He knows how to push me and when to pull back. He can read my body like a book and play it like a violin. I know what I'm doing is dangerous, Russian roulette with my heart, but I can't walk away. Every piece of me needs him. Every piece of me craves him. Every piece of me will need an endless supply of glue to put me back together when this ends. I have no illusions about fairy tales. Life doesn't work that way, but I'm hanging onto my joy.

I roll my shoulders after disconnecting with my customer, happy that we are slow tonight because it allows me to prepare for this week's classes and tutoring sessions.

"Hey, stranger. Where have you been?" I turn at the sound of Keith's voice, and I reach over and put myself on hold, so I don't get a call.

"Hey! I haven't seen you around here lately. You have been off my shifts, and most of my other time has been spent tutoring." I reply, and his face falls a bit.

"You're still tutoring that guy?" he asks, his voice dripping venom as he says, "that guy." I have to laugh at his reaction to Cain. Keith has never been the type to interfere with my dating prospects, though he did make sure he intimidated them whenever possible to ensure they treated me right, and while I don't date often, I have never seen this side of him.

"Yes, I am," I respond truthfully, crossing my arms over my chest.

"Is he why you never called me back last weekend to hang out?" Keith's tone has shifted, and I can hear the irritation in it. I pause, remembering our last conversation and my promise to try and hang out with him.

"I'm so sorry, Keith, the weekend got away from me. It's the end of the semester, so I have a lot of work to push through, so I don't fall behind. I never intended to forget about you." I apologize earnestly. His face softens, and I can see he is trying to calm down.

"I know, Elle, you always have the best intentions. I'm sorry I got upset the other day. There is just something I don't like about that guy, and it sets me on edge. I'll try to withhold my opinion. I mean, he is just a tutoring client, not your boyfriend, so it's not like he will be around long." He finishes his sentence with an easier smile and leans against my cubical. I try to set my face, not giving anything away, especially now that I have been reminded of the NDA.

"Exactly, and thank you. Actually, what are you doing tonight after work? I'm going to meet with Liv to get a drink to celebrate."

"I'm off at ten. What are we celebrating now? Your birthday isn't for another...twelve days?" he asks, curiosity crossing his face. It consistently surprises me that Keith remembers my birthday. He always does something special, especially after I told him about Sam's birthday shenanigans. Elaine was usually too high to know what day it was, let alone to save any money for gifts. To compensate, Sam always found a way to make it memorable by building a blanket fort to tell stories in or creating a scavenger hunt that led to my favorite places.

"I made it to the next step with Boston Digital. They are flying me out to meet the team and see if I'm a fit." I tell him, excitement leaking out of me as I repeat it. His long arms come up at his sides as he responds.

"That's amazing, Elle! That's the dream job, right? The company that the philanthropist guy you were always raving about started?"

"Vince Gordon, Yeah. This job would be everything I have ever dreamed of." I shrug, shaking my head a little as I realize the enormity of the situation while also feeling a small tug in my gut that tells me it's no longer my only dream.

I'm making my dreams come true. But I'm choosing this dream over another. One I never let myself have before.

"That's big news, Elle. Congratulations." He smiles.

"Well, I don't have it yet, but at least I still have a shot. I have to get back on before my handle time goes from high to atrocious. I'll walk out with you after shift." I give him a small wave and return to work, continuing my great mood throughout my shift.

***

Liv meets up with us at a bar around the corner from the call center. She floats in, wearing a dark purple sweater dress with black tights and knee-high boots that make her look taller than she is with the large chunky heel. She smiles at us and runs into me for a hug before giving one to Keith and sliding into our booth next to him.

"Guys, it has been WAY too long since we got together. I hate how busy we all have been!" She complains, grabbing a menu and looking through the cocktails.

"I think we need a celebratory shot to start the night." Her eyes flip back to Keith and me. Hers hold a mischievous glint to them as she waves over our waitress.

"Three Kamikazes, please, and a screwdriver. Make it a double." She smiles sweetly at the older woman before turning her attention to me.

"So tell us about the job. This is all so exciting!"

"I'm not sure it's that big of a deal. I don't have the job yet. I just made it to the next step in the hiring process. But, I fly out the night of the 26th and return late the afternoon of the 29th. It seems pretty routine for their hiring process." I explain.

"So you won't be here for most of your birthday?" Keith asks, a little surprised by this news.

"Well, I'll be home that night, but most of the day, I'll be in meetings and at the airport," I respond, not wanting to sound too upset about it. My birthday has never been a massive deal to me except when Sam was around. Now it reminds me of how alone I am, despite having Liv and Keith.

Someday I will have roots somewhere and start my own family.

My brain immediately brings up an image of Cain. Chasing after a toddler. Fixing a tile on the roof. Holding me in front of a fire with a Christmas tree decorated with handmade ornaments drinking hot chocolate. Sitting on the porch, watching the lightning bugs dance in the open fields under the moonlight. It is all so easy to picture. So easy to drop him right into my world and build a future.

If only life was that easy.

Liv pulls me out of my revere with birthday plans.

"I think we should still do something fun. You only turn twenty-two once," Liv pipes in as our waitress returns to us with the drinks. Liv hands her a credit card without another thought and begins a toast to me getting the new job. I can't think of any occasion Liv can't find time to celebrate.

The moment is bittersweet. I love these two people more than anything, but I know that leaving them is what I need to do for myself. I try to hold onto the joy I have been carrying all day and push back the feeling of loneliness that begins to claw at me. My phone vibrates in my pocket, and I pull it out to see a text from Cain.

> **You get home, ok?**

> **Out at a bar with Liv and Keith, should be another hour**

> **You going to be ok to drive?**

I look at the text for a long moment before answering. I probably will be perfectly fine to drive, I have only had one shot and have been nursing the White Claw I ordered when Keith and I first arrived, but I also want to see him tonight.

> **I may need to be rescued.... Do you know of anyone who could save me?**

He responds faster than I expect.

> **I mean, I could call Hudson for you if just ANYONE would do...**

My jaw drops, and I giggle a little, pulling the attention of both Liv and Keith.

"Sorry, I'll only be a second," I say, but I see Liv putting together who I'm on the phone with, and I'm desperately trying to stay away from this subject around Keith since he has such a strong opinion when it comes to Cain.

> I never did get to finish my night with him. Maybe that would be the prudent choice

I know riling him up will be easy, but I'm not sure how easy until I see the three bubbles jump to life immediately.

> You are playing with fire, little Firefly .... I'll be there in an hour, and I'll remind you who you belong to

> Looking forward to it

And I was. The thought of having another night like last night has me wet for him. I look back at the table. Two sets of eyes are waiting for an explanation.

"What?" I ask, wondering why they are so intently staring at me.

"You slept with him?" Her question is innocent, but I can tell from the posture of Keith next to her this isn't going to go over well.

Not to mention I had signed an NDA, so I literally couldn't talk about it.

"Liv, you know me. When have I ever jumped into bed with anyone?" It isn't a lie, but it isn't the truth. It is all I can say to avoid hurting my friends while keeping this new relationship in its safety bubble.

Relationship? We slept together. That was it, and I told him we couldn't be more, so why was I thinking this way?

Keith relaxes his shoulders, and Liv goes back to talking about Jeffrey.

At least I learned the guy's name!

The remaining time at the bar flies by with us reminiscing about our trip after high school, the girls Keith takes home but never keeps, and plans they were already making to visit me in Boston. It settles my heart to have them both here with me, supporting me through what will be the most significant transition of my life. At least the biggest one I get to choose for myself.

We finish our drinks and head outside. Liv left a few minutes before. Her boyfriend,

yes, officially

Picked her up, and she won't be home tonight. Keith is catching an Uber and offers to share it with me, but since he lives in the opposite direction, that won't make sense, even if I didn't have a tall, dark, and handsome man on his way to me.

Please let the timing work out on this. Let him leave before Cain arrives.

However, my wishful thinking doesn't work because when I look out into the parking lot, there he is, leaning against a motorcycle.

I'm not sure being that sexy is legal. I'll have to look into it.

Thankfully before Keith can fully grasp the situation, his Uber pulls up in front of us. I turn and hug Keith for a long moment, smelling the whiskey he has been drinking. He pulls back and speaks to me seriously.

"I'm proud of you, Elle. I have always known you are special and will do great things. I'm just glad you are finally getting to see that too. Be careful in Boston, and let us know how it goes." He ends with a lighter tone to his words before he turns and locks eyes with Cain. I can't see Cain's expression from this far away, but the tension rolling off Keith doesn't bode well. To his credit, Keith just gets into the car and waves out the window as he pulls away.

I saunter over to Cain, feeling the draw to be near him immediately. His steel gray eyes sweep up my body as I approach, and I feel a blush heat my skin. I just saw him this morning, yet I miss him and have felt his absence today.

"Now, Mr. Mingan, who comes to rescue an inebriated woman with a motorcycle? With my luck, I may fall right off the back." I ask him, my hands landing on my hips. He stands up to his full height and slides his hands around my waist, pulling me into a hug before responding.

"Well, I guess you'll have to hold on really tight." The glint in his eyes tells me that this is precisely what he was hoping for. He drops his face into my neck, breathing me in. "You smell like him," he says, a rumble forming in his chest.

"What? Who?" I respond, confused because I've been at work all day and then in a smokey bar.

"Your friend, Keith, I believe it is." He replies and pulls back some to look at my face.

"What is it with you two? He is always weird about you. You seem oddly protective of me with him, despite the fact that he has been my friend for a decade, and nothing has ever happened between us. I totally peg you for the alpha male response to a male friend, but I don't understand his." I rattle on the alcohol, removing any filter between my brain and mouth. I lean my forehead into his. "Boys are complicated." He laughs, full and loud. It certainly isn't the reaction I'm expecting.

"Maybe he worries I will take his spot as your best friend, and then you won't need him anymore. Or maybe he is right, and I'm trouble, and getting involved with me might just change your world." His voice is deep and playful.

"Oh, you certainly are trouble, " I reply, biting my lip a little before continuing, "but maybe you are right, and spending so much time with you makes him feel like he is losing me as a friend. I should be more understanding of that." I make a note to call him more often so he doesn't continue to think that way.

"You truly are too good of a person, Firefly. It isn't your fault he's feeling that way. People grow apart through different times in their lives. You'll be moving across the country in a few months. I'm sure he would have felt the same thing then." His words make logical sense to me, but he doesn't understand the bond that Keith and I have fostered over the last eleven years or all of the things Keith has done to prove his friendship to me when I was in no place to be a good friend. I owe him more than just pulling away; I'll rectify that as soon as possible.

I nod, not letting on to my internal argument. I take the helmet he extends to me. "Let's go to your place tonight," I state rather boldly and hope he agrees. I have been looking for an opportunity to see more into his world. I even looked up his security company earlier this week to see if I could get a better handle on what he does to make all the money he is spending.

"Not sure that's a great idea," he replies before helping me fasten my chin strap and placing me on the seat.

"Why not? You have seen my place, and my friends, and my classmates. I barely know anything about you." I finish with a pout because I genuinely want to understand more about this man. His eyes swirl as I see him contemplating.

"Ok, Firefly. But let's grab food on the way there. I haven't eaten, and you will need your strength." He winks at me before starting his motorcycle and pushing away from the ground. I squeal loudly and grip him tighter, and I feel him laugh as we turn into the night.

Let's get to know the real you, Cain Mingan. What makes you tick?

Chapter 21

Cain

The feel of Bri's arms around me as we ride through town has me wanting to take the longest route possible to get back to my apartment. I can't believe I'm even considering bringing her there with everything going on, but when she looked at me like I was a stranger, something inside me bent. I want her to know me. All of me, and that's going to mean opening a few doors. It's also going to mean that I'll have to hope no one's around or up this late.

I drive us to a 24-hour, drive-thru taco joint near my place and order enough food to feed us both with extras in case we need food in the morning since my kitchen's rarely stocked, unlike Bri. Once we have everything, I drive my motorcycle up to the back side of the building, avoiding the parking lot so that she doesn't see the line of work SUVs, most of which have been tailing her and are parked on the bottom floor of our garage.

VP Securities owns the entire apartment building, and every occupant inside's one of ours. We keep rooms open to accommodate traveling pack members from neighboring packs and those that come here for retreats.

As I think about who may be inside, I realize we are coming up on another retreat we are hosting at the beginning of December.

No need to attend that now. I have my Mate.

The pack retreats allow unmated wolves to meet for training, updated species law classes, and to strengthen pack alliances through bondings. So far, none of the unmated in my pack have found their Mates, so we have broadened our reach to central and east coast packs for the upcoming retreat.

With everything else going on over the last couple of weeks, I had forgotten. I'll need to talk with Presley about security arrangements with our looming controversy with Reno. They haven't been invited to any retreats during Dante's reign and not for a few years prior due to the shaky alliance between our packs, but I won't put it past them to strike while we are distracted with politics.

I pull my bike onto the side street by our rear exit and climb off, reaching back to help Bri off. I can smell the alcohol on her, just like I had been able to smell her friend's cologne.

That guy's time was coming.

We know Keith met up with someone earlier this week, but we can't figure out who. He shook the tail we placed on him, and he has been radio silent on his devices that we have access to since then.

I turn my attention to Bri as she stumbles a little, climbing up the back steps while holding the bags of food. I reach out to grab the food with one hand and place the other on the small of her back, partly because I want to touch her and partly to ensure she doesn't injure herself.

We enter the back hallway and walk down to the elevator, pressing the button and waiting for it to arrive. Bri's mumbling something about the perfection of Mexican food as the doors open, revealing Dante in his gym clothes on his way out.

He steps off the elevator, his face assessing the situation he just walked into.

"Hey Cain," he says, his voice giving little away as his eyes scan from Bri to me.

"Dante. You headed out?" I ask as Bri interrupts me at the sound of his name.

"DANTE!" she shouts louder than necessary due to the alcohol she has consumed. "I had a dream about a Dante, well, sort of. You must be the one with the orange corvette. Man, that was an amazing car to drive." She smiles at him sweetly as his eyes slide back over to mine.

Dante: She drove the Vette?

Cain: I can explain

Dante: No one drives the Vette.… I barely let you drive it.

Dante's face is beginning to give away our mind-link conversation, so I speak out loud to ensure Bri doesn't catch on to anything.

"It certainly is. Well, we are going to head up. I'll see you for our meeting at ten." I finish, letting him know this isn't the time or the place.

"Cain's just being rude. Hi, I'm Brielle, his....tutor?" she says, looking at me to answer the unasked question of what we were now. "You must be his best friend who allows him to drive outrageously ostentatious vehicles to try and woo the ladies, am I right?" Dante laughs out loud like he can't contain himself. His eyes dance with humor as he responds to my Mate playfully.

"That's me, always trying to help the poor guy out. His attitude does nothing for him regarding females, so we try to do what we can for him." Dante's smile grows, and I know he'll never let this go.

Great.

"How's your girlfriend doing these days, Dante?" I shoot back at him. "Oh wait, still can't get anyone to take on that particular role." I raise my eyebrow in challenge knowing this could turn to blows and possibly an unwanted shift if we kept up this back and forth.

"Oh man, two sexy men fighting is kinda hot," Bri blurts out, her face turning back and forth between us. Dante's face lights up like he's about to comment on that when he sees my eyes shift, a panicked look replacing the humor that was once there.

Dante: Calm down, Cain. I want no claim to your Mate.

*Cain: **Leave. Now.***

"On that note, I'm going to head out. It was nice to meet you, Brielle," Dante says, laughter forced into his tone, and he turns to exit the building.

"See you later," she replies with an awkward wave that has her rocking slightly as if she might fall.

"In your dreams," Dante shoots back over his shoulder with a wink before picking up the pace of his exit. I take a few deep, calming breaths with my face turned, watching Dante's retreating back. My wolf's begging to come out and fight for our Mate. I finally fight back for control as Bri turns back toward the elevator.

"He's nice," Bri says, utterly unaware of the turmoil between Dante and me, and she reaches over to push the lift button again, causing the doors to open immediately.

"So, you have dreams about my best friend?" I ask, raising an eyebrow to appear less irritated by the whole encounter.

We step inside while she giggles a little, my heart rate calming as I wrap my arm around her waist. "Not exactly, more like crazy dreams that I'm a wolf and thinking I needed to tell someone named Dante something." She shrugs as if her statement holds little interest when in reality, I have stopped breathing.

How could she have dreams of being Awakened? How strong is her wolf if it's already trying to push her toward the pack? Toward our Alpha.

I press the button for the eleventh floor, and the elevator begins its ascent while I shake off the ever-increasing alarm I have felt since she got off my bike. She leans into me to help keep her balance, and I realize that whatever she drank tonight had to be more than I have ever seen her consume. She sways to the music playing as we ride up, mumbling random words to the instrumental. I have to smile at how adorable she is at this moment. How pure and utterly innocent of the world around her.

What would she think if she knew you brought her into a den of wolves?

The thought jars me. It makes me wonder where I fit in her human world. Even if I follow her to Boston, how can I keep that part of myself from her?

Maybe I won't have to...

As we reach my floor, the doors open with a ding. My apartment's one of only two on this floor. Dante lives in the penthouse, which takes up the entire top floor. Pres and I share half of this floor; each large suite had access from this one hallway, her door to the right, mine to the left. The floor beneath us holds only four apartments for the rest of the council members Jake, Erik, James, and Elijah. Beneath that, twelve units were placed on each floor until you hit the lobby, which houses our commercial-sized MMA-style gym, sauna, pool, billiards room, and lounge area with big screens for football, hockey, or movies. The setup's perfect for our lifestyle and has everything we need in-house if we need a place to bunker down.

Like when Marlo decides to make his move.

I steer Bri to the door and enter my code number in the panel beside it, allowing us entry inside.

"Wow, high-tech." Bri hiccups while watching the camera perched above the door and making faces at it. I chuckle. I can't help myself. Everything about my Mate is perfect, even the drunk and delirious version.

"Actually, it's pretty normal these days, and besides, I like my privacy." I counter, flipping the light switch on as I guide her inside. Her jaw drops as she enters, her eyes scanning the enormity of the room.

Maybe my mom was right, and I should have more furniture. I place the food on the small dining table outside my kitchen.

My apartment is an open concept, with most of the space blending into the next. I have a state-of-the-art kitchen that hardly ever gets used. An island countertop big enough to play ping pong. A corner bar fully stocked with alcohol. An area that's supposed to be a formal dining room but instead houses my pool table. Then there's the living room area which could easily hold fifty people with three oversized sofa sets placed around for seating and, of course, my 96-inch TV.

"This? This is where you live?" she shakes her head, her fiery brown eyes large and taking everything in, "I could fit ten of my apartments in here and probably still have room."

"Actually, it's only about six. If we are being technical." I shrug, feeling more self-conscious and exposed than I ever have with her.

"Oh, well, in that case, never mind. I'm not sure how you manage to live here with barely any space, you poor thing," she deadpans, her words dripping with sarcasm.

"It's a struggle," I smirk back, trying to read her. "What are you thinking right now?" I ask, sliding my arms around her waist and placing my chin on the top of her head. She leans back into me, relaxing against my body.

"That I should have asked for more money," she laughs, turning in my arms to plant a kiss on my chin.

"I'm open to negotiations, but I may be amending some of the stipulations to include you being mine all the time, off the clock, of course." I smile, taunting her to counter me while bringing my lips to her ear.

"I want you to stop paying me, and I want to return the money you have already paid me. It doesn't feel right taking it from you," she says, changing the mood so quickly that I pull back to examine her eyes. She could lie to me, but her eyes always give her away. They no longer had the glassy alcohol-induced sheen she has been carrying all night. They are clear and focused and, if I were to guess, uncertain.

"What, why? I'm sorry if I have come on too strong with you. We can slow down," I respond quickly before adding in a voice that carries all of my vulnerability.

"I can't lose you now." My heart's beating out of my chest, my teeth grinding together as I await her response.

I knew coming here was a mistake. Why did I bring up the contract?

"Cain, that's not what I mean." She grabs my chin in her hand, so I look at her, searching for answers in her beautiful eyes. "I just don't feel right taking your money now that we're..." She lets the sentence trail off, and her eyes jump around as if searching for the word in the air.

"Well, I don't know what we are, but I don't want you to feel like the only reason I'm sticking around is that you are paying me."

The relief I feel at that moment causes my muscles to relax and my eyes to slide closed while I breathe out all the tension I have just pulled into my body.

"I know you only agreed to tutor me because of the money, but I haven't felt that's why we became this." I pull her into a hug, "The two have nothing to do with each other, except that the time I got to spend with you every day made me want you more than I did when I saw you at

Livinia's birthday party." She gasps, her shoulders tensing slightly in my arms.

"You remember seeing me at Liv's party?" she whispers as she pulls back, her head shaking back and forth like she's arguing with herself about that comment, unable to wrap her head around the idea.

"You are the only thing I remember about Liv's party." My eyes lock on hers, and I lean down to kiss her, indulging in the soft pillows of her lips. She wraps her arms around my neck as she sinks into me. The kiss isn't rushed or demanding. It's a serenade that intensifies as it continues to build. She tastes like vodka with a hint of citrus, but she still smells like the apple-vanilla combination I have come to love.

Her hands grip my neck, pulling her deeper into me, with a moan tumbling out of her. In one smooth motion, my arms slide down from her waist to her perfect ass, massaging it lightly before I pull her up to me, forcing her to wrap her long legs around my waist. My feet are moving before I even realize I'm walking. I carry her down the hall toward my master bedroom.

This time I'm not in a rush. This time I plan on taking my time, learning every sound she makes and every touch that causes them. I set her down next to the bed, my lips only leaving hers as I tug her oversized hoodie off in a single pull. She adjusts her focus to begin grasping at the hem of my shirt, and I reach behind my head, grab a handful of material, and yank it off over my head. Then my lips are back on hers. My hands fumble behind her, trying to remove her bra while her fingers play with my jeans button. I pull away from her lips.

"Out of your clothes. Now." I demand and give her the room to begin pulling off her remaining items while I remove mine. I stand there for a moment taking in the curves of her body, the shimmer of her porcelain skin, splattered with freckles, and the blush of red I have come to love, which begins creeping up once she realizes I'm watching her.

So innocent. So pure. Mine. Mate.

I take a deep breath, trying to cull the urges that my wolf is sending me.

No. It'll be her choice. I won't force her hand by losing control.

When we first slept together, I barely held onto my humanity as she came on my cock.

"Get on the bed," she orders me, and I tense, raising an eyebrow in question.

"Making demands now, are we, Firefly?" But I follow her commands. An action that has never happened with any other female. I crawl onto the bed and turn over to sit with my back on the headboard. She looks a little unsure as she crawls onto the bed after me, her breasts bouncing beautifully before her, making me want to capture them in my mouth. Before I can move to grab her, her hands land on my thighs, and a sparkle plays in her eyes which freezes me in place.

"I want to taste you," she offers, a small playful smile on her face as she makes herself comfortable. My cock twitches at her words, precum leaking from my head.

Fuck.

"Take what you want from me," I say, grinning at her as she leans down and flicks her tongue, lapping the glistening drops. Her eyes stay locked on mine as she licks her lips before returning her focus to my fully erect cock. My entire body's tense, holding onto my restraint while feeling like a teenager about to blow my load well before we even got started. She begins slowly, her tongue circling my head, teasing as she lightly sucks just the tip for a moment stretching her lips to slide around my thickness. My hips begin to rise, urging her to take me deeper.

I grip my hands into the blanket, straining, so I don't grab her head and start fucking her delicious mouth. Her hand begins twisting and moving up and down my shaft in a solid rhythm that has me closing my eyes and dropping my head onto the pillow as I feel her. My chest rumbles as she hits the vein on the underside of my cock with her tongue, and then she claims me, sliding my cock into her throat, fighting to handle all of me.

Holy. Fucking. Shit.

I almost lose it right there at the feel of myself completely inserted in her warm mouth, sliding in and out in a building rhythm. She chokes a little but maintains her pace as her eyes glisten from her gag reflex.

Instinctively, I grab her hair, fisting it to pull her off me and up to my lips. A strangled growl escapes her as I capture her mouth, tasting myself on her tongue. She pulls back from me in an attempt to head back down toward my throbbing cock.

"Unless you want this to be over before it has begun, you need to slow down, Firefly." I kiss her nose playfully before sliding my lips toward the breasts I had been admiring. She sits on top of me, straddled above my hips, her hands threaded through my hair as she pulls me closer. The feel of her soft skin responding beneath my calloused fingers makes me want to spend hours bringing goosebumps to her flesh. Her body's a livewire of electricity with every graze. Sliding my free hand down to the center of her slit, I tease her until I feel her already pulsing clit beneath my fingers. I strum it slowly, circling, pulling, and playing as I indulge in the perfection of her tits.

Perfect. Mate. Mine.

Her body tenses as she falls over the edge of her orgasm, her dilated eyes catching mine before rolling back in ecstasy. I let her ride it out, enjoying the sounds my hands are able to pull from her before moving for a condom, tearing it open in one try and rolling it onto me.

Grabbing her hips, I lift her with ease as I line her up with my cock. Her eyes flash to me, and every fire-filled fleck is alight in her post-orgasmic state. She adjusts her legs to hold herself better and slides slowly down my shaft, allowing her body to adjust to my size until I'm fully seated.

So tight. So perfect.

Pausing a minute, I feel her tension release as her body allows all of me, before I begin rocking my hips underneath her. She feels my rhythm and matches my pace. Sliding up and down, her hands holding her weight on my chest. My hands are on her hips, helping her keep pace. I squeeze, pushing my thumbs right above her bones, and she gasps, her eyes widening with desire. The way her body responds to mine pushes me closer to the edge, and I see the telltale blush creeping up her body which tells me she's almost there.

My hand moves back to her clit, and use my thumb to circle it, increasing pressure until her head falls back and her body clenches. She stops breathing as she reaches her peak, and her cunt tightens on my cock, gripping and massaging until I can no longer hold out. I ride her through her orgasm, sending myself into mine with a feral growl.

Mine. Mate. Awaken her.

She falls to my chest, her breathing ragged, her hair looking sexed. I stare at the ceiling for a long moment fighting to regain my hold on my wolf. I can tell my eyes have already shifted as if he's clawing his way out of me. Having her body on mine increases my struggle. Her scent, the softness of her skin, and even the pounding of her heart are testing my resolve.

Mine.

My arms lock around her, both holding her to me while also keeping her from seeing my face. I wouldn't be able to explain my shifted eyes, and if she looks at me right now I might do the one thing I vowed I wouldn't. Take away her choice. My instinct to bite her, to Awaken her wolf and seal our mate bond's all-consuming. I can taste the change in my saliva as I take deep, calming breaths, the Alpha venom leaking through.

Claim her. Mate.

I never truly understood the fascination with finding a mate. I never even considered what mine would be like, but now that she's in my arms, I understand why mates go crazy when one of them dies. The thought of a world without her has my wolf howling, and we aren't even bonded yet.

Yet? I like the sound of yet...

My wolf relents, allowing me to refocus. I kiss the top of her head as I fully regain my control and slide out from under her to clean us up before grabbing some waters and the Mexican food from the kitchen. When I return, she's curled under my blanket, cuddling a pillow to her chest, still fully naked. My cock twitches in response, and I take a breath to stop myself from being ready for round two.

Her eyes open, and a smile lights her face.

"Food! It's like you are a mind reader," she cheers, pulling herself up and using the pillow as an impromptu table.

Not yet.

I think to myself, knowing I'll be able to hear her once we are mated. We will be able to mind-speak as I do with Dante, and he does with the pack. Some of the stronger mating pairs can even see through each other's eyes.

We eat in relative silence, except for her moaning almost every bite. I can't tell what pleases her more, me or this food, which makes me smile. Seeing her happy brings peace to both my wolf and me.

I send her off to shower in my bathroom, knowing if I go with her, we will end up tangled up again, and I know she needs sleep. I grab her some Ibuprofen to take before going to sleep, so she doesn't wake up with a massive headache after all her drinking tonight. When she walks out twenty minutes later, wrapped in only a towel, pink skin from the shower's heat, it's pure torture on my cock.

After finding her one of my t-shirts and a pair of boxers to wear, I tuck her into what we established is her side of the bed, and I go off to shower, promising her I will be quick, but knowing that it won't matter, she will be asleep in a matter of minutes.

As I shower, I think about the mess I'm making for myself. Seeing her in my bed, in my shirt, smelling of my soap made me yearn for more. It made me want to give her all of me and tell her all my secrets. It's those secrets that I fear the most.

What if she became afraid of me? What if she couldn't accept that I'm something else? What if it means I lose her? I hate that whenever I think about it, I only conclude that she can't find out. But then, how would that work if we did make it forever? Our kids would be shifters. I wouldn't deny them their birth rite, and then I would risk losing her all over again.

My mood drops some as I finish my shower, steam filling the bathroom as my carousel of thoughts keeps me in there for longer than I intend. I wipe off the mirror with my towel and brush my teeth. In the reflection, I can see the nail marks Bri left on my chest and shoulder as she clung to me when she came. What a beautiful sight it is to see her completely fall apart on my cock. Three more weeks will never be enough, forever doesn't even feel like enough time. I'm losing myself to her, and I don't know if I will ever be ok with a result that means we aren't together.

Before returning to the room, I shut off the light, trying not to wake her, only to find that she's no longer in bed. On instinct, I sharpen my hearing and search for sounds of her in the apartment, but come up empty. My heart rate increases as I begin to panic, rushing into the main area and the guest rooms finding them also vacant. I return to the bedroom, looking for my phone. It's then I see my t-shirt and boxers on the bed. My head whips across the room, only to realize that her clothes are no longer on the floor.

Rushing out the door, I throw on a pair of shorts as I head for the elevator, but before I get there I think better of it and take the stairs two at a time until I reach the bottom. The main lobby's empty, probably due to the late hour, so I check every adjoining room, but nothing.

I run out the back doors and around to the front. Nothing. I shift into my wolf, tearing the shorts completely from my form with no regard to who may have been outside or could have seen. I can't hold him back any longer, and I know he has a better shot at finding her than I do. He searches for her scent trail, running to both exits before circling the area.

He catches her path for a moment as the scent of my soap lingers in the air outside the back entrance, but he loses it just as quickly. He howls. The sound vocalizes our hearts breaking as we realize Bri is gone.

Chapter 22
Bri

*S*tupid.

That's how I feel as I sit in the back of the Uber.

Fucking stupid.

Before letting myself fall into any of this, I knew he was trouble. I knew he was out of my league and that falling for him would be a huge mistake.

A monumental mistake.

I shake off the tear falling from my cheek, reminding myself I'm crying because I'm mad, not because I'm heartbroken.

How could I be so stupid?

This man has had "player" written all over him from the moment I saw him at that party.

At the party he SAYS he only remembers seeing me. Asshole.

I told myself to keep my distance. I told myself to keep it professional. I told myself not to let him in. And still, my stupid needy heart didn't listen. I close my eyes and replay the entire scene tonight, wondering where it all went wrong.

He leaves to shower, and I snuggle into the bed, enjoying how it smells so much of him. I pull my phone out and text Liv that I'm not coming home tonight, only to see that she has also told me she won't be home. I smile, thinking how nice it is that we are both so happy—what a way to end college. I'm scrolling through Liv's social media and see the pictures of us celebrating tonight.

That is when I hear the knocking. Gentle at first, but then more insistent. Cain is still in the shower, and I wonder if maybe Dante is back and needs a key, so I get up and walk out to the main living area. The knocking continues; only now, a voice is coming through the other side. A female voice.

"Come on, Cain, I know you're in there. I don't think I need to remind you what happened the last time I was here. Come on, open up. I need you."

I pause, shell-shocked for a moment as I put together that there is a woman at his door at two in the morning telling him she needs him. I see red. I feel pure fury and hate, and I feel like a fool. I swing open the door to see a beautiful redhead about my age in a barely-there green spaghetti-strap camisole and some tiny running shorts. Her freckled face drops in surprise as she looks at me, which tells me she isn't expecting anyone to be here either. She looks over my shoulder, hoping to see Cain materialize behind me.

"Oh... hello," I say, not attempting to sound pleasant.

"Ummm, hi... I'm so sorry to interrupt. I didn't know you were here." *She puts on a smile that seems about as fake as it can be before she takes a step back.* *"I will come back later."* *She turns and hurries down the hall as I close the door. My heart is racing. She will come back later? Are you fucking kidding me?*

It had only taken me five minutes to get dressed and call for an Uber before I was out the door without looking back. I feel the splinters of my heart spreading as it breaks into a million pieces. Another tear falls, and I don't even attempt to catch it. I glance at my Uber driver and thank whoever is looking out for me tonight. She is an older woman who has not tried to force conversation or ask about my crying. She just turned on the radio and headed toward my address.

My phone starts buzzing, and I look down to see Cain's name flash across the screen. I close my eyes, allowing more tears to spill as I power it off. The last thing I need right now is to talk to him. I would chuck it out the window, but this isn't some movie. I need my phone, and I can't exactly be having a temper tantrum every time a boy hurts my feelings.

The ache in my heart steadily worsens the farther I get from him. My body knows the tie to him is being broken, and its trying to hang on for dear life. I think back to every time he reassured me, every time he told me that I was it for him, every time he looked at me as if I hung the moon.

Fucking Stupid.

As the driver pulls into my complex, I take a second to compose myself. I'm distracted as I get out and mumble a quick goodbye. My eyes are on the ground as I head up the stairs, only to find someone already standing on them.

"Hudson? What are you doing here?" I ask before realizing it. "Did Cain send you over here? Unbelievable. You can tell that mother-fucker that I never want to see him again." I have lost all the composure I thought I regained in the car, and the fuming anger has risen within me again.

"Bri, are you ok? What happened?" He looks at me, his face set in concern.

Nice try, buddy, but you aren't covering for your friend there.

"Don't play dumb with me. You know Cain is a player and has been seeing that redheaded bitch while telling me he was only seeing me. Well, I'm just not that kind of girl. He wants her. Fine. I'm out." I'm shouting by the end of my rant, and recognition flashes on his face.

"You mean Presley?" He asks, taking a step toward me. "I think there has been a misunderstanding here."

"Bull shit. Bull fucking shit, Hudson. I know you boys will cover for each other, so I don't have anything else to say. You can return to Cain and tell him I'm done. DONE. I've had a long night and want to get some sleep." I walk past him, not bothering to move entirely out of his way before I pass. He grabs my shoulders and turns me toward him before wrapping me in a hug. I'm so startled by the act that I don't immediately pull away. It is then that I hear him whisper near my ear.

"I'm so sorry, Bri, I'm sorry, but I don't have a choice." Then, I feel it. One small puncture at the base of my neck.

What the fuck?

My world starts to grow fuzzy as I look back into Hudson's eyes. He looks terrified. My weight slumps onto him as he pulls out his phone and makes a call. My limbs feel fuzzy, and my brain is fighting to put the pieces together as it starts to fog. My last thought is that I will die having never seen lightning bugs, having never left this city, having never fulfilled any of the promises I made to my brother in his last moments on this earth.

I'm so sorry, Sam. I failed you.

The last thing I hear before I lose consciousness is the beginning of Hudson's phone call as he drags me back into the parking lot.

"Tell Marlo I have something I think will interest him. I'm ready to buy my freedom." A pause, "No, I have someone he needs to meet," and the world goes black.

Chapter 23

Cain

I t takes everything in me to push back against my wolf. I spend nearly fifteen minutes trying to force myself back before he finally relents. I race back to my room completely naked and not giving a fuck.

She's gone.

I grab my phone and call hers, waiting for a lifetime before it goes to her voicemail.

Shit.

I call again. This time it goes straight there without ringing.

Fuck, it's off.

I go to find the shadow phone, hoping to see if she has contacted anyone.

Nothing.

I nearly throw it into a wall. I grab my phone and call Pres while throwing on another pair of shorts and walking out of my apartment. I'm at her door pounding before she even answers the call.

"Hey, what's up?" Pres asks as she opens her door, and I rush through it. "You ok?"

"No. She's gone." I respond, trying to form words as I panic about what it may mean.

"What do you mean she's gone? She was just in your apartment. I just saw her," Pres looks confused.

"You have to find her. Pull up her surveillance, her GPS tracker, anything. I need to know where she is."

"Slow down. You aren't making any sense. I thought Brielle was with you. I came by a little bit ago to update you on some news, and she answered the door." She is looking at me as if I have grown another head.

"What did you say to her?" I grind out through clenched teeth.

Presley's eyes bulge for a second. "Oh shit."

"What does that mean?" my impatience is showing, and my hands keep trying to shift into claws.

"She opened the door. I was surprised because I didn't know she was with you tonight. So I told her I was sorry to bother her and would come back later." She pauses. " I didn't think much of it at the time, but she seemed mad that I was there."

"You show up this early in the morning looking for me, and you don't even think to mention that you work with me, that you are Dante's kid sister, or that I don't know, we aren't fucking?! Damnit Pres! No wonder she up and left." I'm fuming by the end of my rant. Presley's face falls.

"I am so sorry, Cain. I'll find her. I will make this right." She turns and heads into her home office, which is basically a miniature version of her regular office. Six screens, its own server, and tech piles everywhere. While she gets everything running, she continues her apology. "I sometimes forget that just because I know everything about a person, they don't necessarily know anything about me. Take the hacker, for example, I know more about his aunt Rita's golden doodle than anyone should, and I've never spoken to him." She rambles when she's nervous, and I can tell by her posture that she is upset with what happened.

"Just find her." It's all I can say. I'm too busy coming up with an apology for Bri, so she knows how fucking sorry I am.

I should've just taken her into the shower with me.

Hindsight is what it is.

"Ok, here are the camera feeds," she says as she flips through them. "It doesn't look like our girl is at home. No activity other than the cat in the last several hours. Let me pull her phone and car GPS to see if I can get a location." I pace as she begins pulling up tabs and typing in commands faster than I can keep up with.

"Her phone is off. I don't know if that matters." I say, rubbing my hands down my face.

"It does. I can't power it up remotely. It will give me the last location it pinged before it was powered off, and if she got home and took her car, that GPS will be active. Shit. The car is still at her work with no movement since it arrived for her shift. So she's not at home, and she's not driving around somewhere. Let's see what we can get from her phone before it went off." I find myself unraveling slowly. Barely able to hang on to this form as my wolf riots inside me.

If I had claimed her, I could mind-speak with her. I could sense where she was. I could keep her safe.

"Hmmm, that doesn't make any sense." She says as I bring my focus back to the room.

"What? What doesn't make sense." I crowd behind her, trying to understand the screens.

"She took an Uber through the app. It left here at 2:17 am and said it dropped her off at the indicated address at 2:33 am. It doesn't make sense because it's 2:49 am now. She isn't at home, but that's where it says they dropped her off, and she hasn't left in her car or messaged any of her friends to come to get her, so where did she go?" Pres turns to me, confusion marring her face as she tries to solve this puzzle before her but finds it has too many missing pieces.

"Do we have anyone in the area? Anyone who could get over there before I can?" I ask, already heading back toward the front of the house.

"Let me pull up personnel GPS trackers." after another pause, "Cain." The strain in her voice as she turns toward me is evident, as is the fear now showing on her face.

"What?"

"Earlier, when I came to your place, it was because I think I found our mole, I couldn't believe it at first, but the evidence seems pretty damning."

"Why the fuck are you telling me this now? Can it wait until we find her?"

"Because we believe that Hudson is the mole, and his phone tracker is showing up at her apartment."

She barely gets the words out before I run. I'm racing as fast as possible to get to my bike and Bri.

No, No, No, This can't be happening.

Cain: I need help. Talk to Pres. I need everyone. Everyone but Hudson.

Dante: Hold on, what's going on?

He sounds half asleep in his response, and I can tell I have woken him up, but I don't care.

Cain: Bri is in trouble. Hudson has her. Hudson is the mole. Hudson knows she's important to me if he takes her to Marlo….

I let my thoughts end there because I can't even begin to fathom the pain I will unleash on their pack if anything happens to her. I jump onto my bike and take off, hoping to get there in time.

This is all my fault.

I should have stayed away. I should have protected her. Now she is in the middle of this and has no idea about our world. Another fucking stupid mistake. My breath catches as I realize Marlo can smell her wolf. My heart thunders and my wolf goes insane at the thought of anyone turning her. Dante sends another message.

Dante: I'm sending Jake and Erik to meet you at her place. We will figure this out.

I accelerate, leaning down on my bike to increase my speed and get there faster. I make it to her complex in record time. I throw my bike to the ground as I race up to her door, but I only make it halfway. Halfway up the steps, her purse lays scattered haphazardly on the floor. Her cell phone is sitting on the top platform, cracked next to another phone I immediately recognized as one of ours.

Fuck!

I hear footsteps behind me, but no one speaks. I stand, filling every void within myself with fury. I turn, eyes shifting and howl, pulling Jake and Jay in with me.

When I finish, I look at two of my closest friends, fear and agony rolling off them as they unflinchingly await my command.

"Find him."

Want to know what happens next in Bri and Cain's story?

Fate Awakened: Vegas Wolf Pack Series Book 2 is out now!

Fate Awakened: Vegas Wolf Pack Series Book 2

Before you go... here is a sneak peek!

Fate Awakened
Prologue
Bri

*I*t's the cold that breaks you down first. The kind of piercing frost that burrows deep into the core of you and latches on with no intention of release. It covers me like a blanket, hell-bent on numbing every feeling until I turn to stone. My teeth chatter in the darkness, their cadence echoing off the barren, empty floor on which I lay upon a tattered, dust-filled sheet that does little to pad my body from the firmness of the floor.

It's a small room, hardly more spacious than a closet, with barely enough capacity to lay out flat. It consists of a single light bulb overhead which I imagine once contained a long chain used as a switch for illuminating the space. Now, however, its only control lies beyond the bolt-locked door. The faintest sliver of light sneaks through the gaping at the bottom of that solitary exit.

I have to get out of here. I let out a shaky breath, my body trembling, and I adjust my position, tucking in my legs and wrapping myself in my arms to maintain some body heat. I avoid breathing through my nose as the black spots, barely visible along the corners and the crack in the ceiling, scream of mold and smell of wet mildew.

Outside the door, a television drones on with the latest news propaganda warning citizens to protect their money, their houses, their rights. Occasionally, I hear him. Moving to the bathroom or opening another cheap beer can before settling back into his oversized, deteriorating recliner. Every time he gets up, my pulse accelerates in anticipation that he's coming for me.

And I wait.

Time drags on as I struggle to formulate a plan, my brain foggy from the lack of food and biting cold. By now, I assume his wife's passed out, a needle in her arm drifting her away to another world. So, unfortunately, she won't be any help.

Part of me holds onto the hope that he, too, will overindulge and end up drunk and asleep the rest of the night. The other part of me worries that he won't. My fear races through my body, forcing my hands to grip tighter and push away the cold. To keep me alert and ready, counting the minutes until the sun comes out again.

It's then I hear the footsteps, slowly plodding closer. The floor creaks involuntarily as he nears, and I freeze, temper my breathing, and close my eyes. My heartbeat pounds so loudly against my ribs that I'm sure he can hear it. The sharp creak from the top step announces his arrival as the hinges groan with the opening of the door.

I haven't been here long, but I already know this is the most dangerous predicament I have been in yet. Nothing before could have prepared me for the darkness that exists here.

Reader's Note

Dear Readers,

I know you are probably upset with me for the cliffhanger I have left you with but fear not! The second book in the Vegas Wolf Pack Series is already available in eBook, paperback, and audiobook with a full multicast. Thank you for taking a chance on a brand-new writer and allowing me to share Cain and Brielle's story with you all.

Additionally, I would be so grateful if you would leave a review for this book. Reviews help other readers find their way to my books, so please spare a few minutes to tell us what you think! Please don't spoil the ending for others, as I hope they will be able to feel all of the same emotions you did as you came to the climax of this story. Once you complete that, please sign up for my email list to stay current on all of the happenings within this series and any to come. I will be sending out announcements about release dates, author signings, and character merchandise.

Thank you so much!!!!

Amanda

XX

Acknowledgments

There are so many people I want to thank for this book.

First off, I want to thank you, the readers, for taking the time to read my book! You're the reason we authors throw our words onto pages in hopes our characters' stories come to life in the minds and hearts of others. The characters in this book certainly went off script and made this stand-alone, happily-ever-after book morph quickly into a duet, and, subsequently, a series. Thank you for your patience as I get the rest of our characters connected with their future partners. I hope you enjoyed meeting some of them in this book. The fate of the rest of the Vegas pack and Bri's inner circle will shake out over the next several books. I hope that you enjoyed the character back and forth, and felt every heartbreaking, laughable, tension-building moment.

Next, I want to thank my husband, for the hours of watching the kids, so I could stow away and write. The hundreds of questions I would ask about software, male orgasms, and bro relationships to make the story more real. Without you, none of this would be possible. I love you Rabbit.

I want to send a huge hug to my Beta readers, who held my hand through making this story what it is today. Ann, Ashley, Jessica, Laneie, Mary, Megan, Sonia, & Yelena. You helped me bring this book to a place where I can be so proud of it. You made me a better author.

Your incredible feedback and unending support gave me the confidence to push through and show the world what I have, so THANK YOU!

To my students, who pushed me to dream bigger than I ever thought I could. Thank you. You are brave and wonderful humans, and I cannot wait to see what beautiful change you bring to this world with your drive, passion, and always expanding exemplary vocabulary.

To my friends, family, and coworkers who have shared their lives and stories over the years, which provided me the pieces to create well-rounded believable characters to pull this story through. While none of the characters in this book are real, many of the small details come from my real life and the lives of those close to me :) I hope some of you saw pieces of yourselves within the characters.

About Author

Amanda writes urban fantasy with a little spice. She believes her characters guide her stories and let them run amok busting outlines, timelines, and even causing series headaches. While writing was a passion she came to find later in life, her love for reading has always been a huge part of her. She spends her days teaching English Language Arts to 8th graders, and her nights and weekends chasing around her three wild children and husband, often on the slopes with a snowboard. In stolen moments in between, she sneaks in a chapter or two to satisfy the need to tell her characters' stories. Amanda lives her life trying to soak in every possible moment, and because of this, drinks an exorbitant amount of caffeine to fuel her busy schedule. Most of all, Amanda hates talking about herself in the third person and is terrible at tooting her own horn.

See more from Amanda at her website authoramandanichole.com or follow her on social media platforms (TikTok, Instagram, Facebook, and X using @AuthorAmandaNichole)

Also by

- Unawakened Fate: Vegas Wolf Pack Series Book 1 – January 2023

- Fate Awakened: Vegas Wolf Pack Series Book 2 – September 2023

- Villainous Fate: Vegas Wolf Pack Series Villain Origin Story Book 2.5 – May 2024

- Understanding Fate: Vegas Wolf Pack Series Book 3 – November 2024

- Fate Encoded: Vegas Wolf Pack Series Book 4 – Coming 2025

This book is part of the Vegas Wolf Pack Series. For the latest information about this series see the author's website
AuthorAmandaNichole.com
All caught up on Amanda's books? Check out Juliet Thomas who writes Contemporary Romance with all the feelings.

- Uncaged

- Uncharted

- The Christmas Cracker Novella

- Uncertain

Made in the USA
Monee, IL
19 October 2024

67675382R00173